'THOUGHTS'

'THOUGHTS'

Shola Babatunde

AuthorHouse™ UK Ltd.
1663 Liberty Drive
Bloomington, IN 47403 USA
www.authorhouse.co.uk
Phone: 0800.197.4150

© *2013 by Shola Babatunde. All rights reserved.*

No part of this book may be reproduced, stored in a retrieval system, or transmitted by any means without the written permission of the author.

Published by AuthorHouse   06/18/2013

ISBN: 978-1-4817-9729-0 (sc)
ISBN: 978-1-4817-9730-6 (e)

Any people depicted in stock imagery provided by Thinkstock are models, and such images are being used for illustrative purposes only.
Certain stock imagery © Thinkstock.

This book is printed on acid-free paper.

Because of the dynamic nature of the Internet, any web addresses or links contained in this book may have changed since publication and may no longer be valid. The views expressed in this work are solely those of the author and do not necessarily reflect the views of the publisher, and the publisher hereby disclaims any responsibility for them.

CONTENTS

PREFACE 1
INTRODUCTION 3
POEMS 7
ACKNOWLEDGMENT 17
APARTHEID 19
    Apartheid 21
    Land And Freedom 23
    Free At Last 25
    Pleadings That Turned Sour 27
REFLECTIONS 29
    F.G.C. Ido-Ani 31
    Ivcu History 33
    Education 35
    Beauty 36
    Happy Birthday 37
    Truth 38
    Decision Making 39
    Life 40
    Promise 42

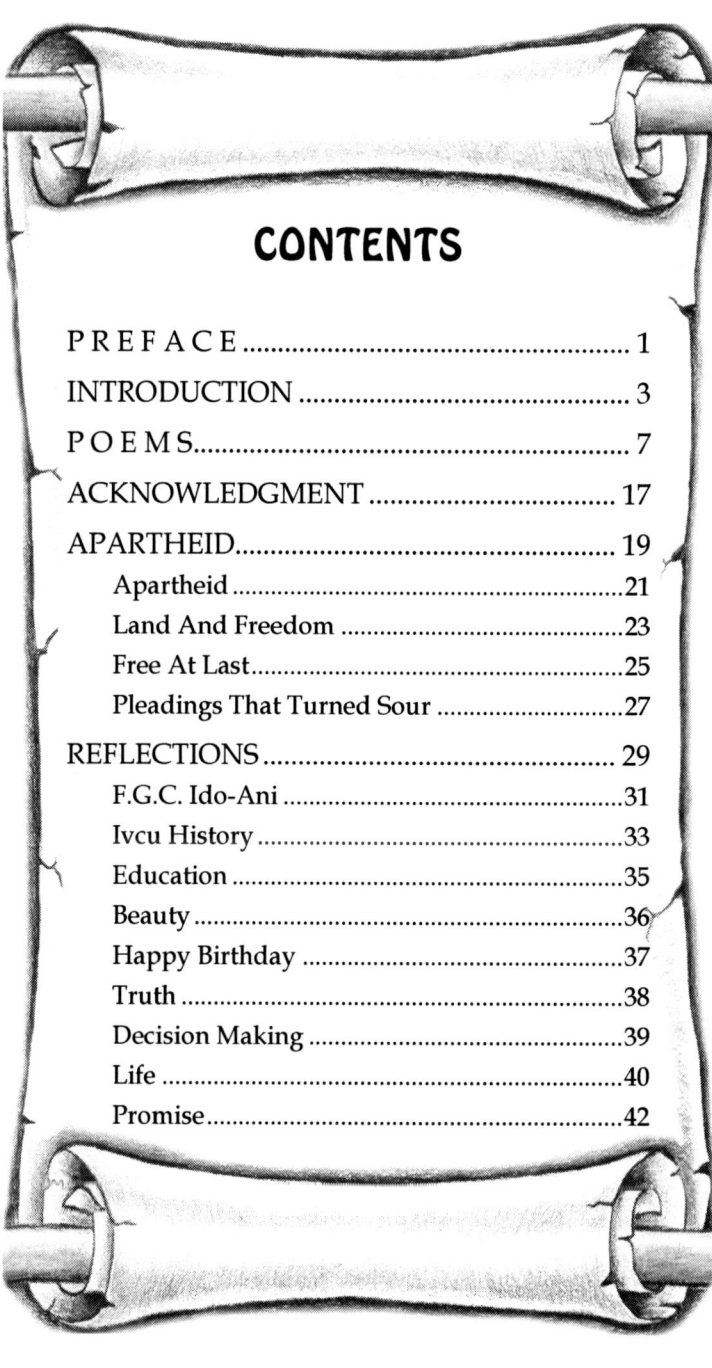

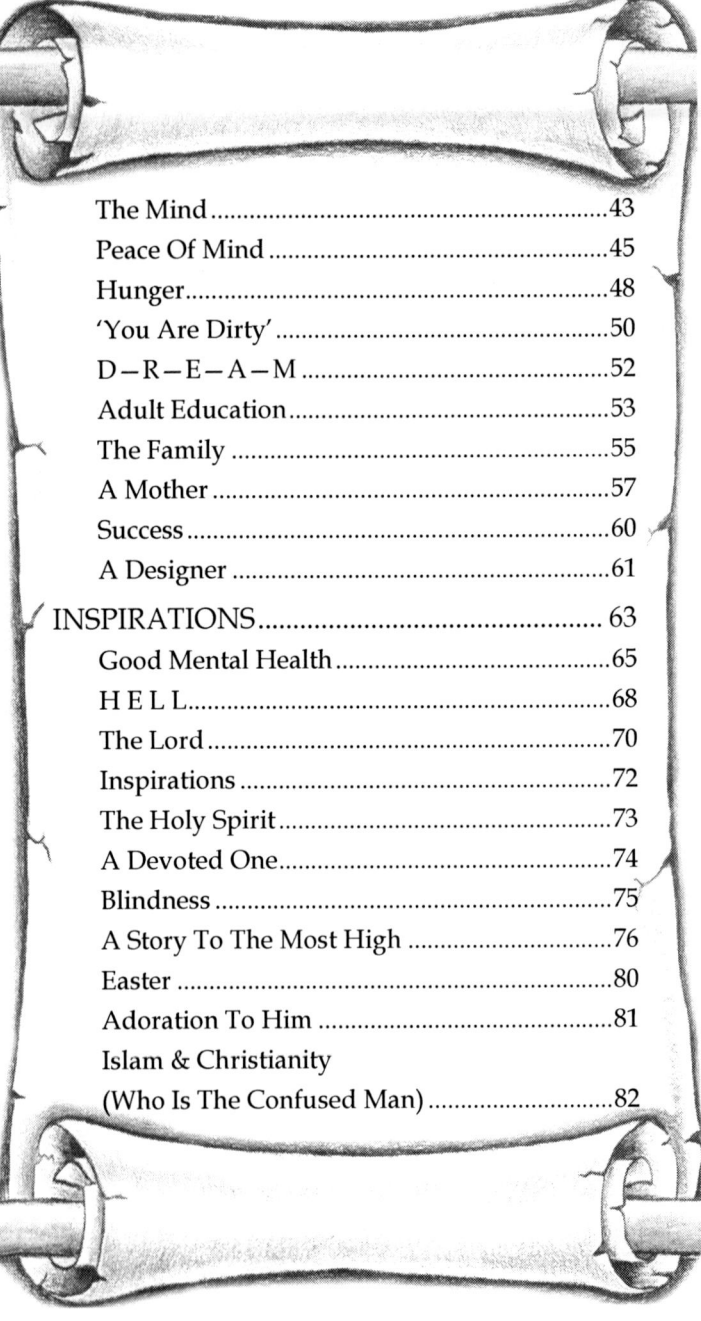

The Mind	43
Peace Of Mind	45
Hunger	48
'You Are Dirty'	50
D – R – E – A – M	52
Adult Education	53
The Family	55
A Mother	57
Success	60
A Designer	61
INSPIRATIONS	**63**
Good Mental Health	65
H E L L	68
The Lord	70
Inspirations	72
The Holy Spirit	73
A Devoted One	74
Blindness	75
A Story To The Most High	76
Easter	80
Adoration To Him	81
Islam & Christianity (Who Is The Confused Man)	82

The Rock Of My Refuge 85
Indescribable God 86
The Devil 88
He Abides Forever 91
Perfunctory Prayer 92
Believe In Yourself 94
The Mercy Of God 96
Beautiful 98
The Holy Spirit 101
Thank God For Rccg Tottenham Branch 103
Zoe: Life Of God 105
Open Your Eyes 107

EMOTIONS 109
L O V E! 111
Love – A Touch 112
Hatred 113
Fear 115
A Naughty Girl 117
A Night To Grow 119
I Love Him 121
Patience 123
L-O-V-E 124
I Want A Man 126

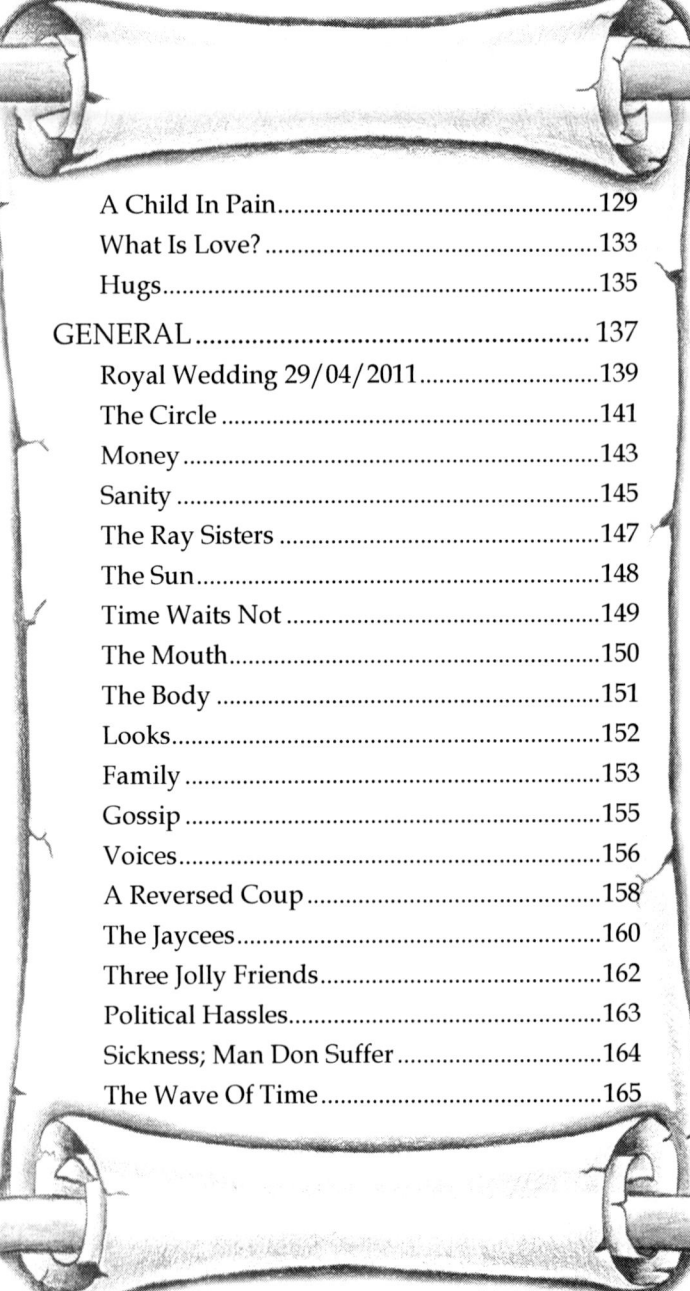

A Child In Pain 129
What Is Love? 133
Hugs 135

GENERAL 137
Royal Wedding 29/04/2011 139
The Circle 141
Money 143
Sanity 145
The Ray Sisters 147
The Sun 148
Time Waits Not 149
The Mouth 150
The Body 151
Looks 152
Family 153
Gossip 155
Voices 156
A Reversed Coup 158
The Jaycees 160
Three Jolly Friends 162
Political Hassles 163
Sickness; Man Don Suffer 164
The Wave Of Time 165

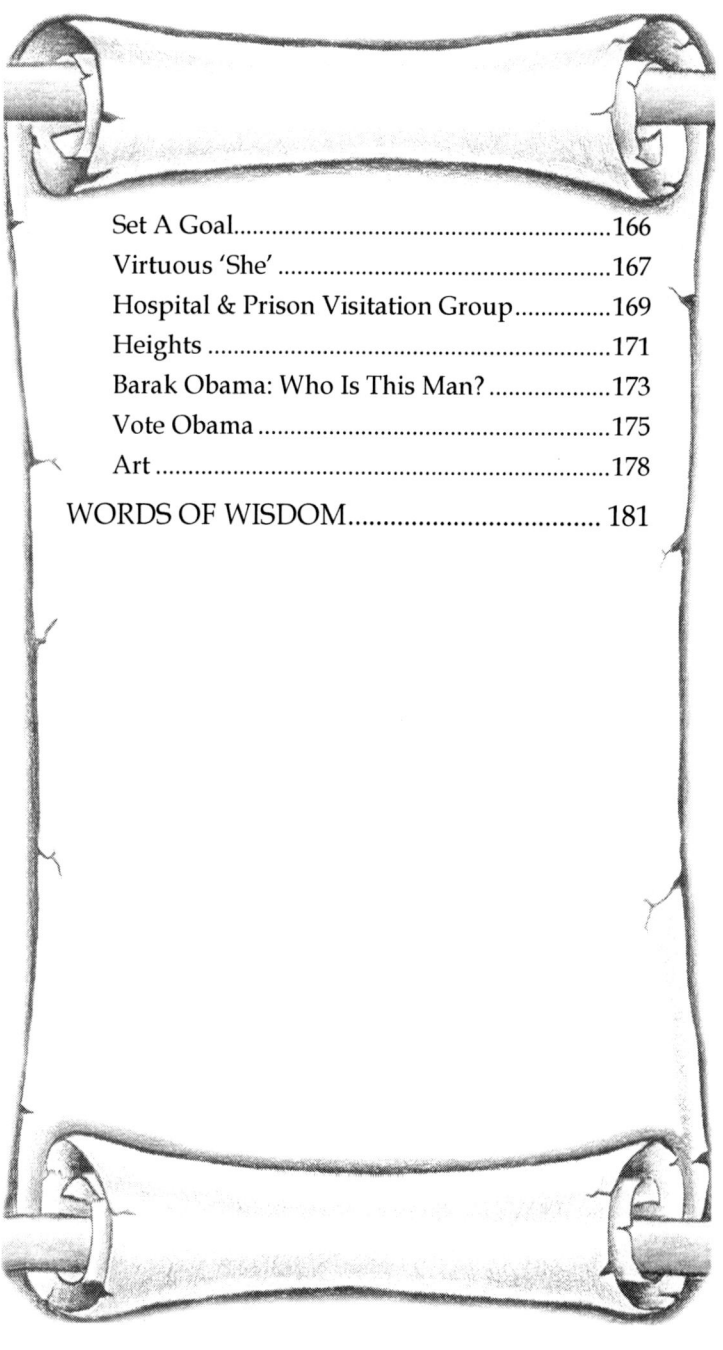

Set A Goal	166
Virtuous 'She'	167
Hospital & Prison Visitation Group	169
Heights	171
Barak Obama: Who Is This Man?	173
Vote Obama	175
Art	178

WORDS OF WISDOM 181

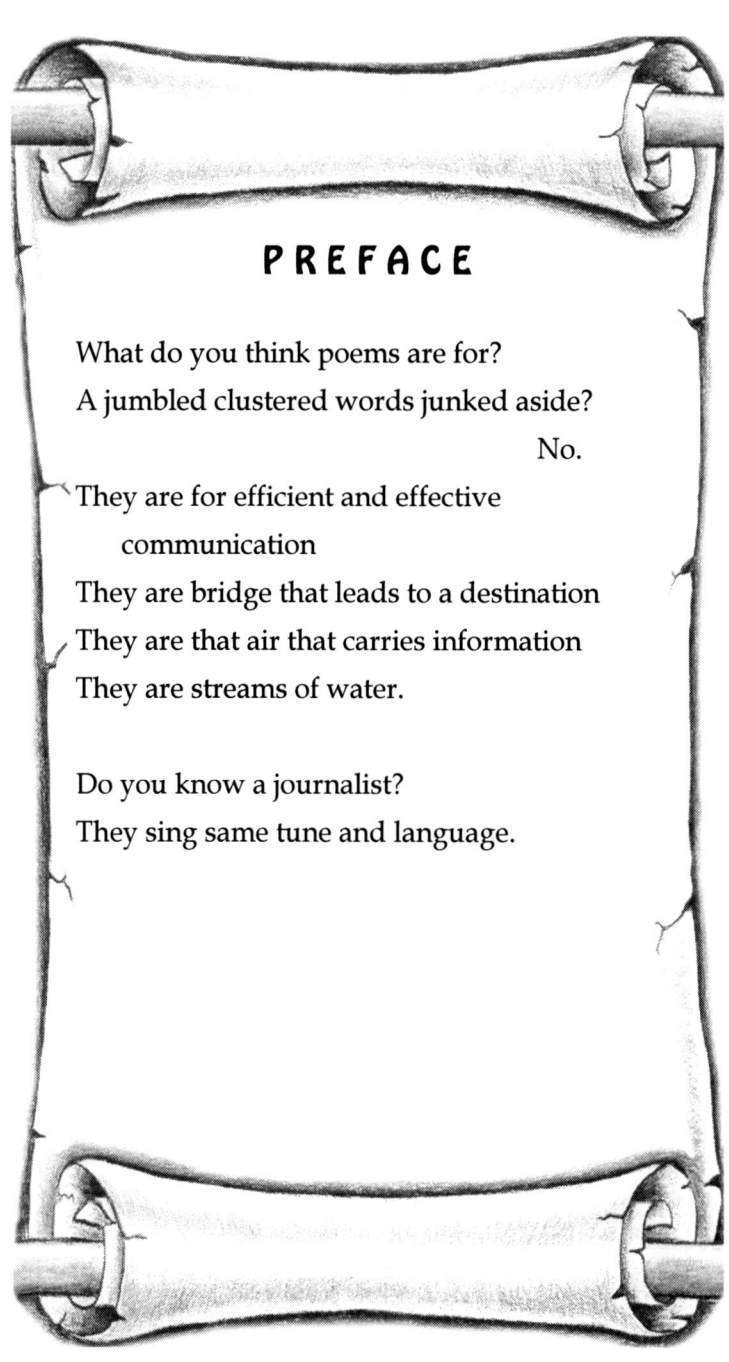

PREFACE

What do you think poems are for?
A jumbled clustered words junked aside?
                               No.
They are for efficient and effective
    communication
They are bridge that leads to a destination
They are that air that carries information
They are streams of water.

Do you know a journalist?
They sing same tune and language.

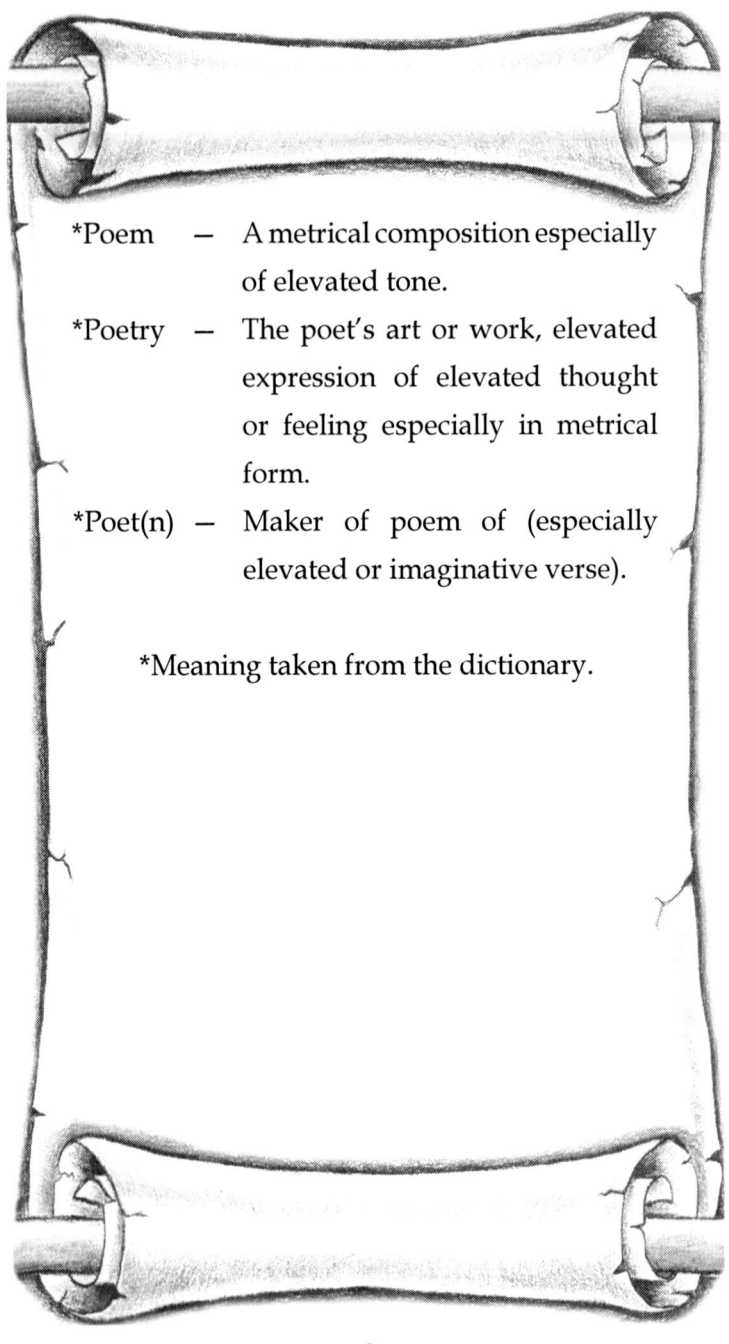

*Poem — A metrical composition especially of elevated tone.

*Poetry — The poet's art or work, elevated expression of elevated thought or feeling especially in metrical form.

*Poet(n) — Maker of poem of (especially elevated or imaginative verse).

*Meaning taken from the dictionary.

INTRODUCTION

This poem book is a compilation of different hearing, tuning and seeing of a side or the other. They are feelings, emotions and thoughts of the writer which have been put down in a thoughtful, systematic poetic way and form to help readers to visualise, think into the past, present and future. A poet should be able to break down words, phrases, sentences, verses, stanzas, even poems into its simplest utmost letters to know the meaning, act on it and bring the best out of it.

This book is divided into five different parts, namely: Apartheid, Reflections, Inspirations, Emotions and the General aspect of the book. This book is meant for all with the purpose to educate, change individual life positively and challenge your thinking process and your mind.

Note that there is high possibility for this book to change individual or groups life spiritually, physically and emotionally for the glory of God.

No age discrimination
No racial discrimination
No religion discrimination
No type of discrimination.

'Thoughts' have been written with the help of the Almighty God over the years to help 'a person' realise something he/she never knew, remove ignorance, and see reality and essence of a vital life. The book is planned to help students in the primary, secondary and tertiary

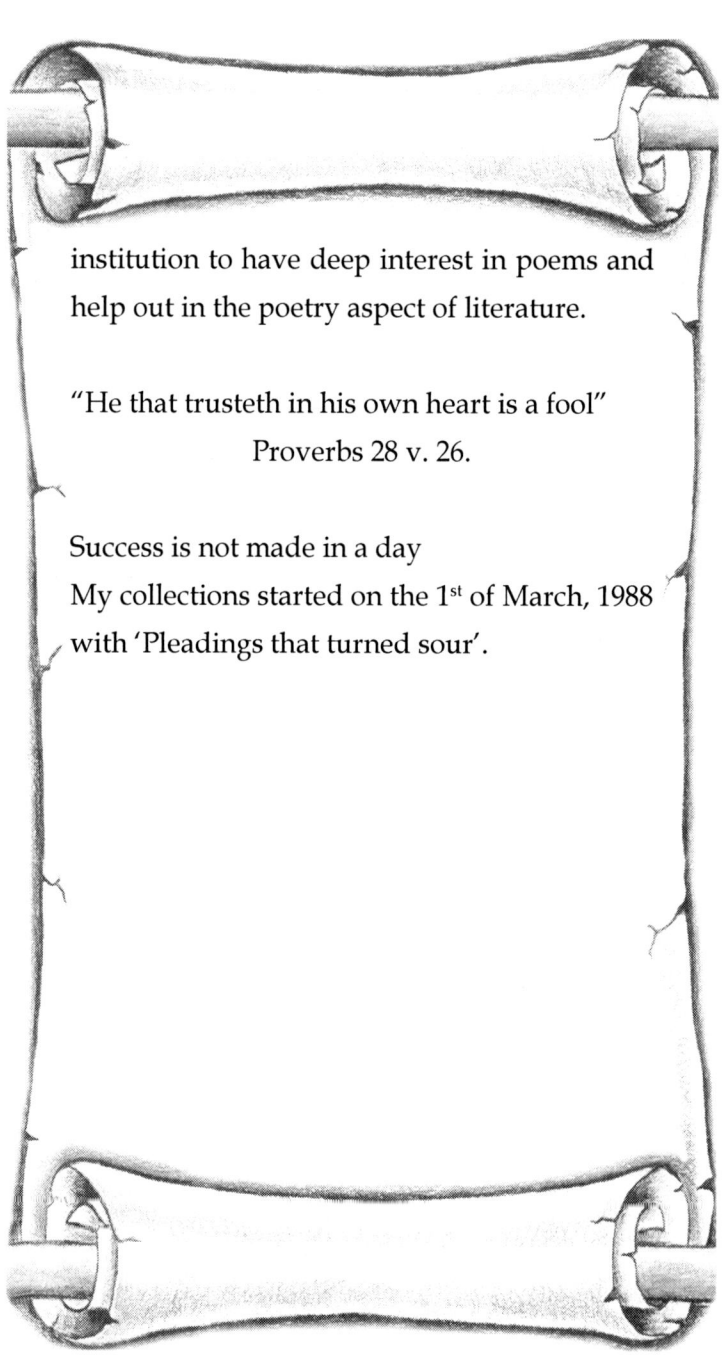

institution to have deep interest in poems and help out in the poetry aspect of literature.

"He that trusteth in his own heart is a fool"
Proverbs 28 v. 26.

Success is not made in a day
My collections started on the 1st of March, 1988 with 'Pleadings that turned sour'.

POEMS

P — Poetry
O — Oral
E — Eminent
M — Mission
S — Stage

POEMS

    A poet stages what he wants
    He puts down his feelings
    He writes down his mission
    He frees and fights with his sword
    — 'The pen'.

Apartheid
Reflections
Inspirations
Emotions
General

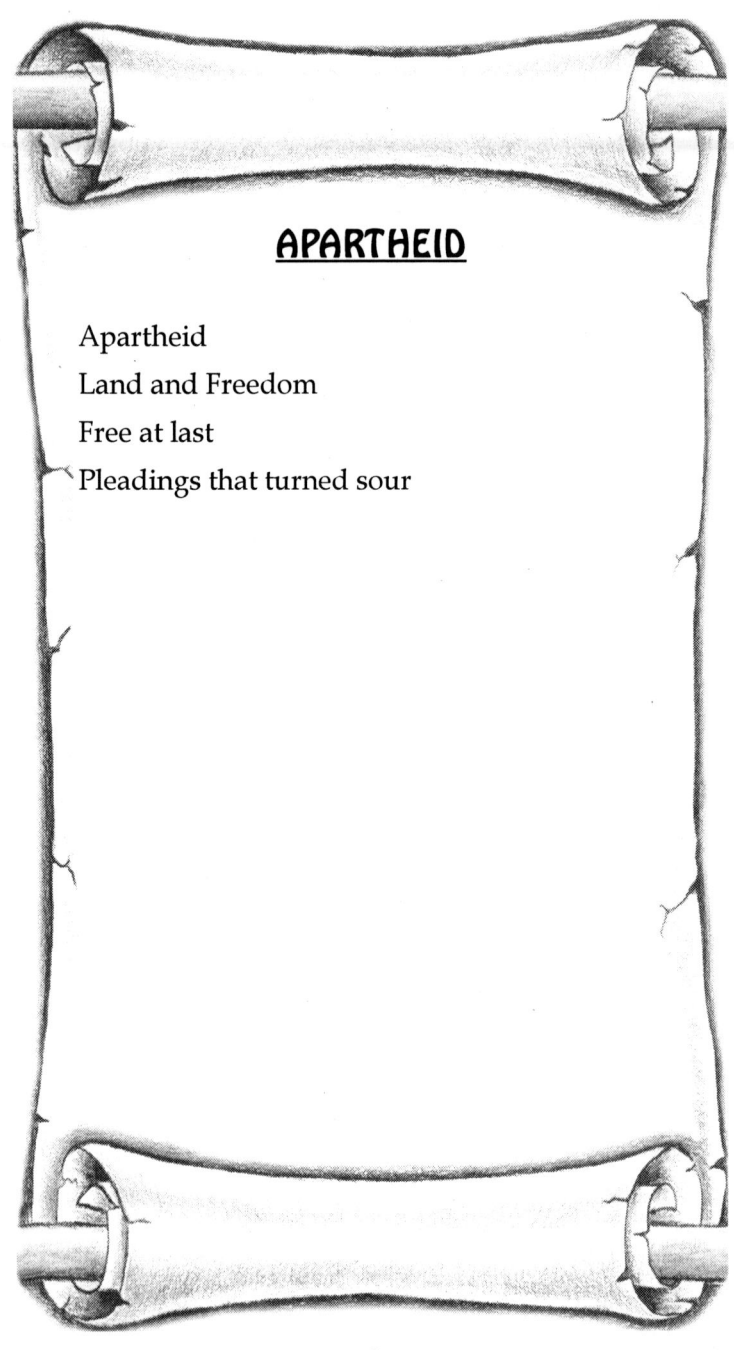

APARTHEID

Apartheid
Land and Freedom
Free at last
Pleadings that turned sour

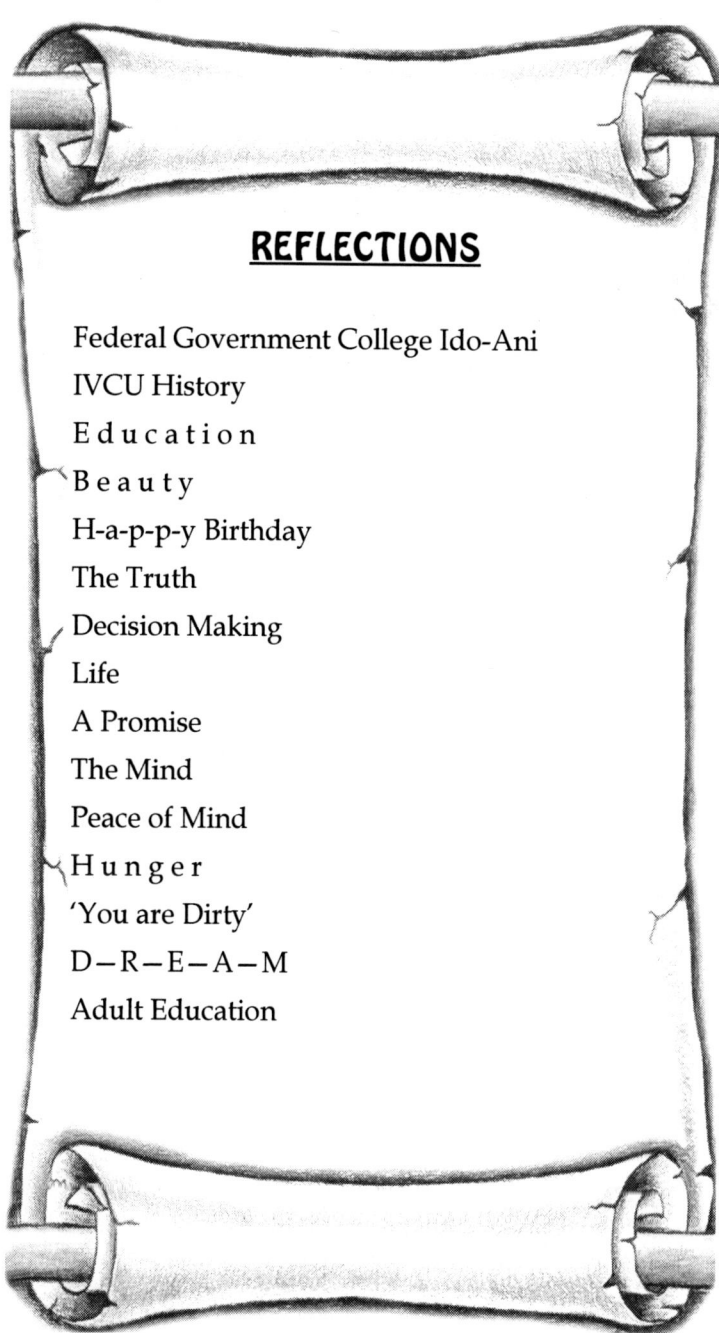

REFLECTIONS

Federal Government College Ido-Ani

IVCU History

E d u c a t i o n

B e a u t y

H-a-p-p-y Birthday

The Truth

Decision Making

Life

A Promise

The Mind

Peace of Mind

H u n g e r

'You are Dirty'

D – R – E – A – M

Adult Education

The Family
A Mother
Success
A Designer

INSPIRATIONS

Good Mental Health
Hell
The Lord
Inspirations
The Holy Spirit
A Devoted One
Blindness
A Story to the Most High
Easter
Adoration to Him
Islam & Christianity
The Rock of My Refuge
The Devil
He Abides Forever
Perfunctory Prayer
Believe in Yourself
Indescribable God

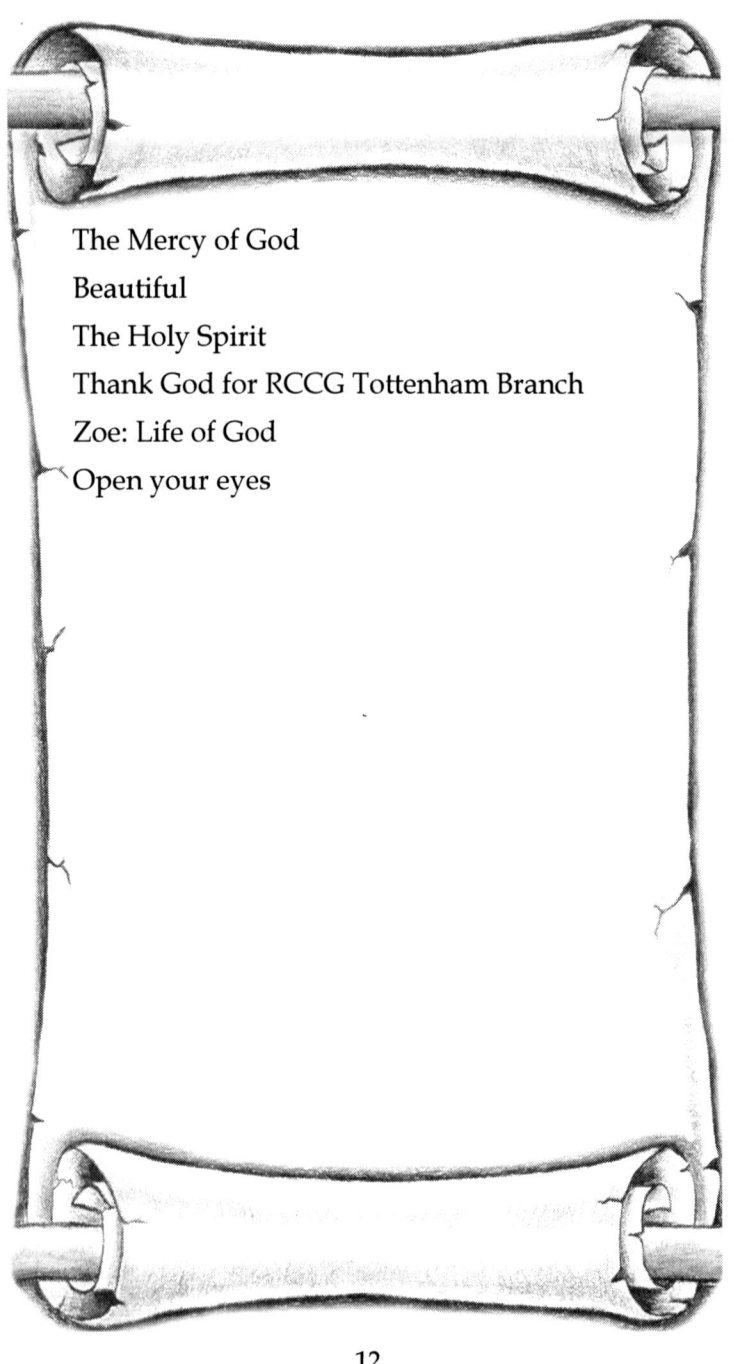

The Mercy of God
Beautiful
The Holy Spirit
Thank God for RCCG Tottenham Branch
Zoe: Life of God
Open your eyes

EMOTIONS

L-o-v-e!

Love — A Touch

H-a-t-r-e-d

A Naughty Girl

A Night to Grow

I Love Him

D-e-a-t-h

Patience

Love

I want a Man

A Child in Pain

What is Love?

Hugs

Fear

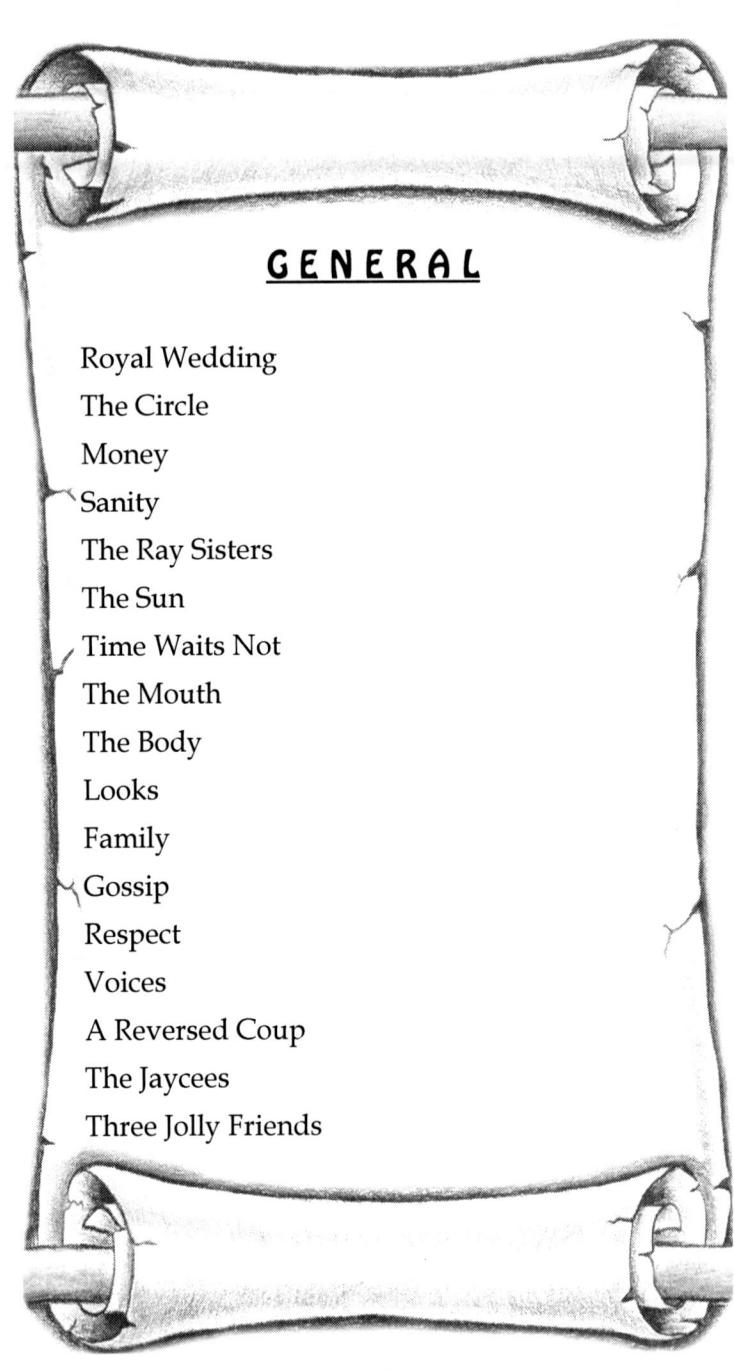

GENERAL

Royal Wedding
The Circle
Money
Sanity
The Ray Sisters
The Sun
Time Waits Not
The Mouth
The Body
Looks
Family
Gossip
Respect
Voices
A Reversed Coup
The Jaycees
Three Jolly Friends

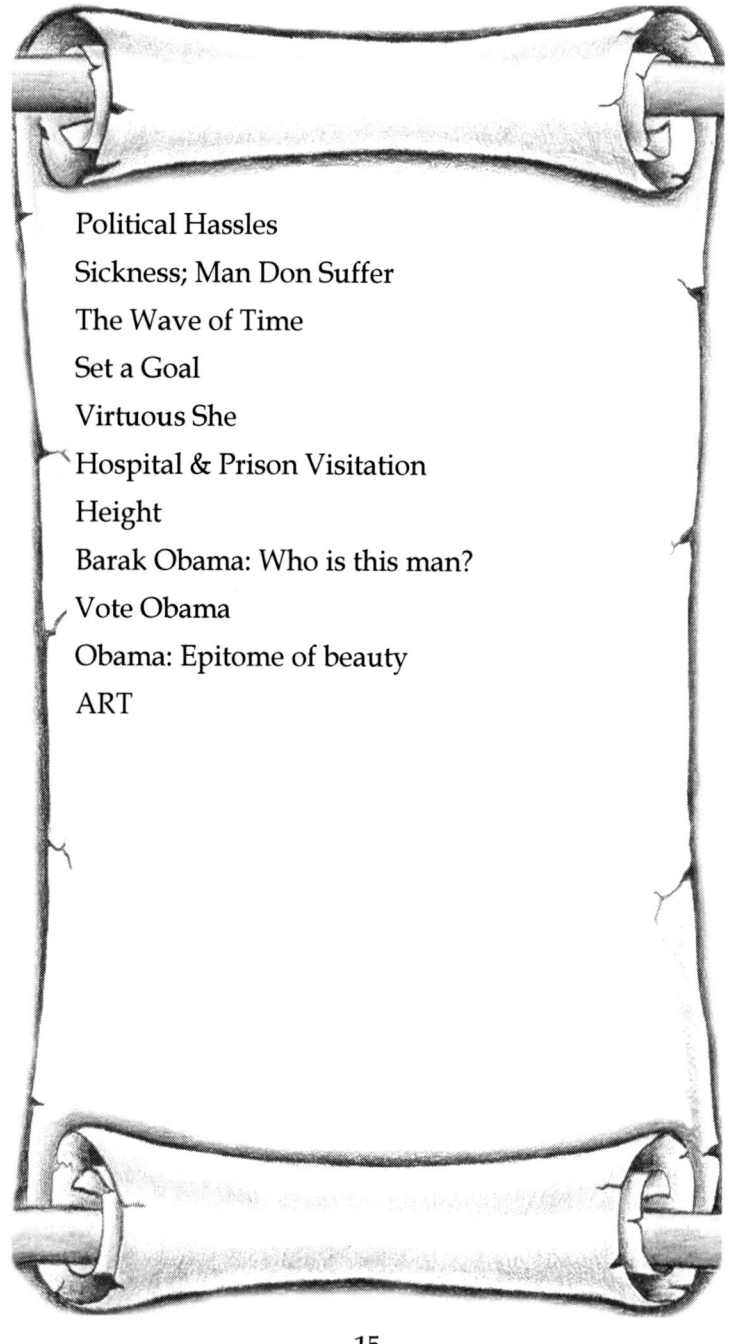

Political Hassles

Sickness; Man Don Suffer

The Wave of Time

Set a Goal

Virtuous She

Hospital & Prison Visitation

Height

Barak Obama: Who is this man?

Vote Obama

Obama: Epitome of beauty

ART

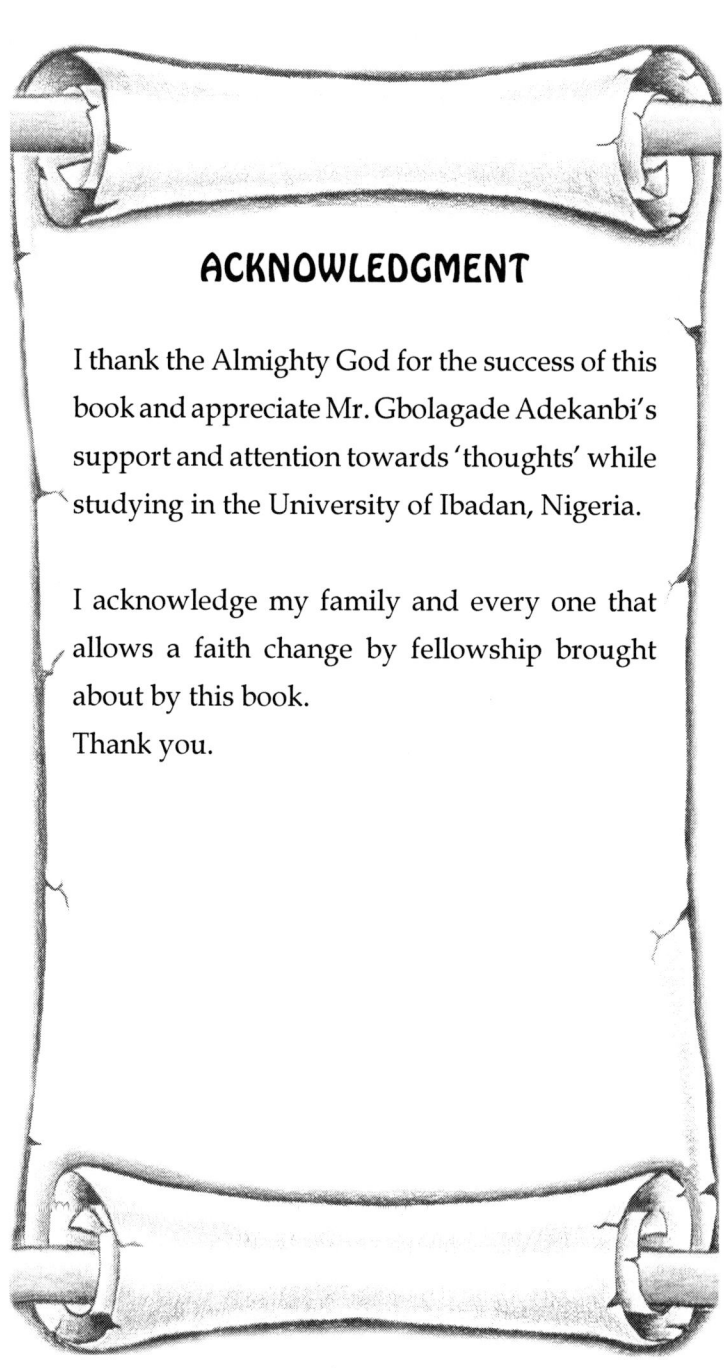

ACKNOWLEDGMENT

I thank the Almighty God for the success of this book and appreciate Mr. Gbolagade Adekanbi's support and attention towards 'thoughts' while studying in the University of Ibadan, Nigeria.

I acknowledge my family and every one that allows a faith change by fellowship brought about by this book.
Thank you.

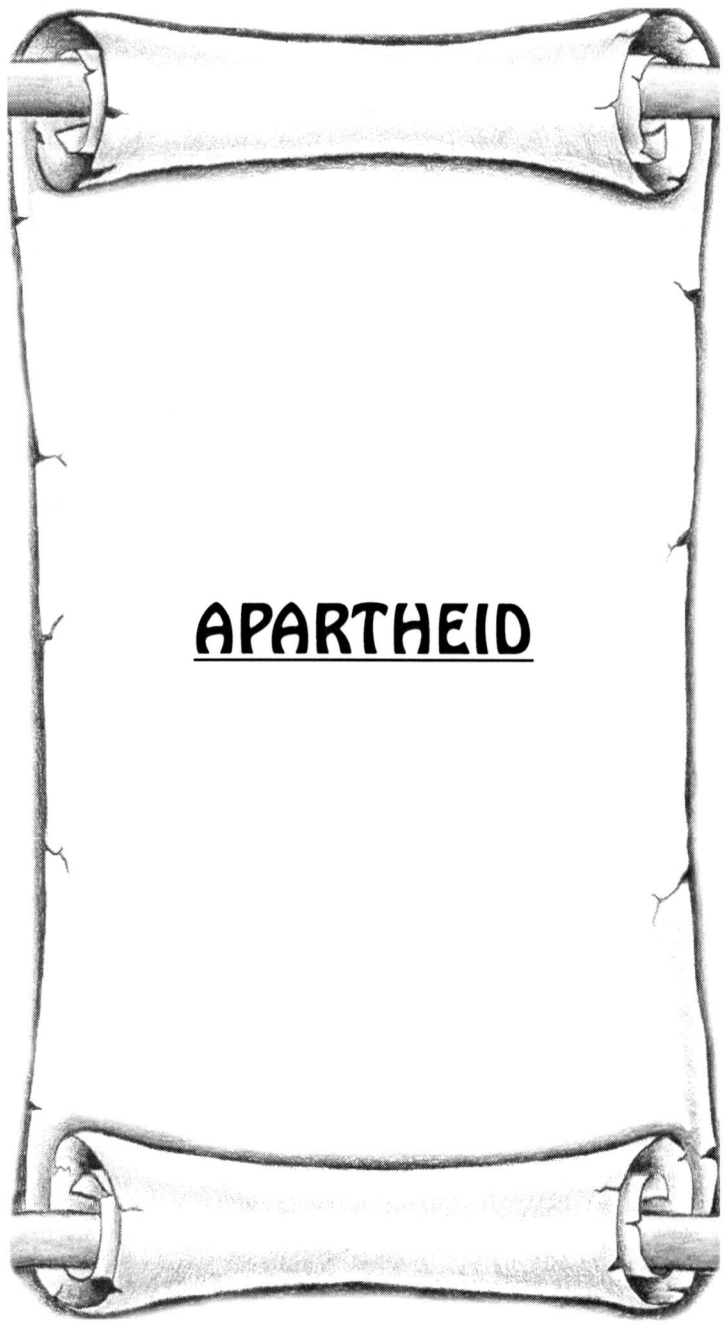

APARTHEID

You say Apartheid
You feel Apartheid
Ain't you Apartheid
You are Apartheid.

Who is this Apartheid?
Apartheid is segregation, preference
Apartheid is individual complex
Complex of heart, mind, spirit.

Feeling of a son to a daughter
Feeling of a worker to a worker
Feeling of an individual to individual
What is this?

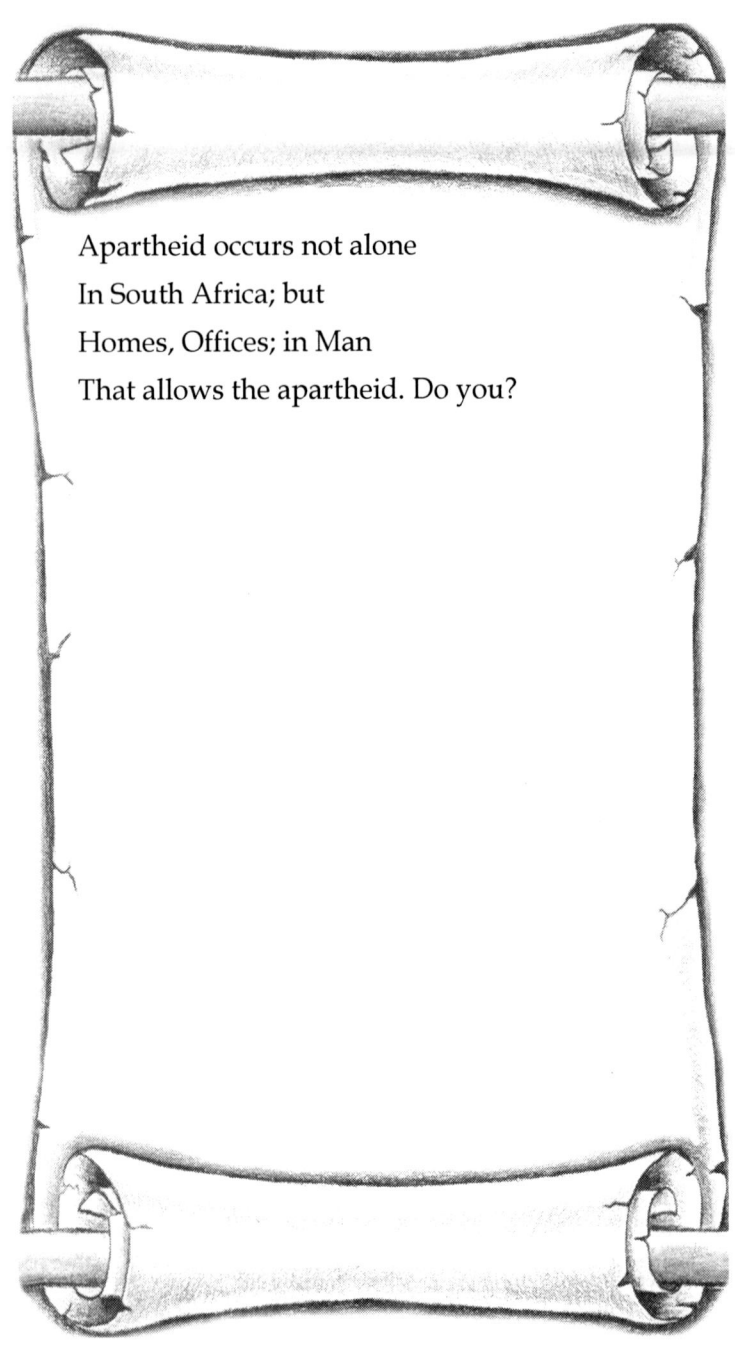

Apartheid occurs not alone
In South Africa; but
Homes, Offices; in Man
That allows the apartheid. Do you?

LAND AND FREEDOM

Oh! Nelson Nelson
The strong minded communist
He came like a new spring to a big family
Bringing rays of hope light to his generation

But the sea Lord masters so Inhuman
So Inhuman gave they gave hand
And sentenced the black's leadership
To untold suffering suffering untold

Sufferings which were not meant
Came from the supposed people from the seas
Seas which we never went to came blinding
But they came and here they are in them a devouring lion.

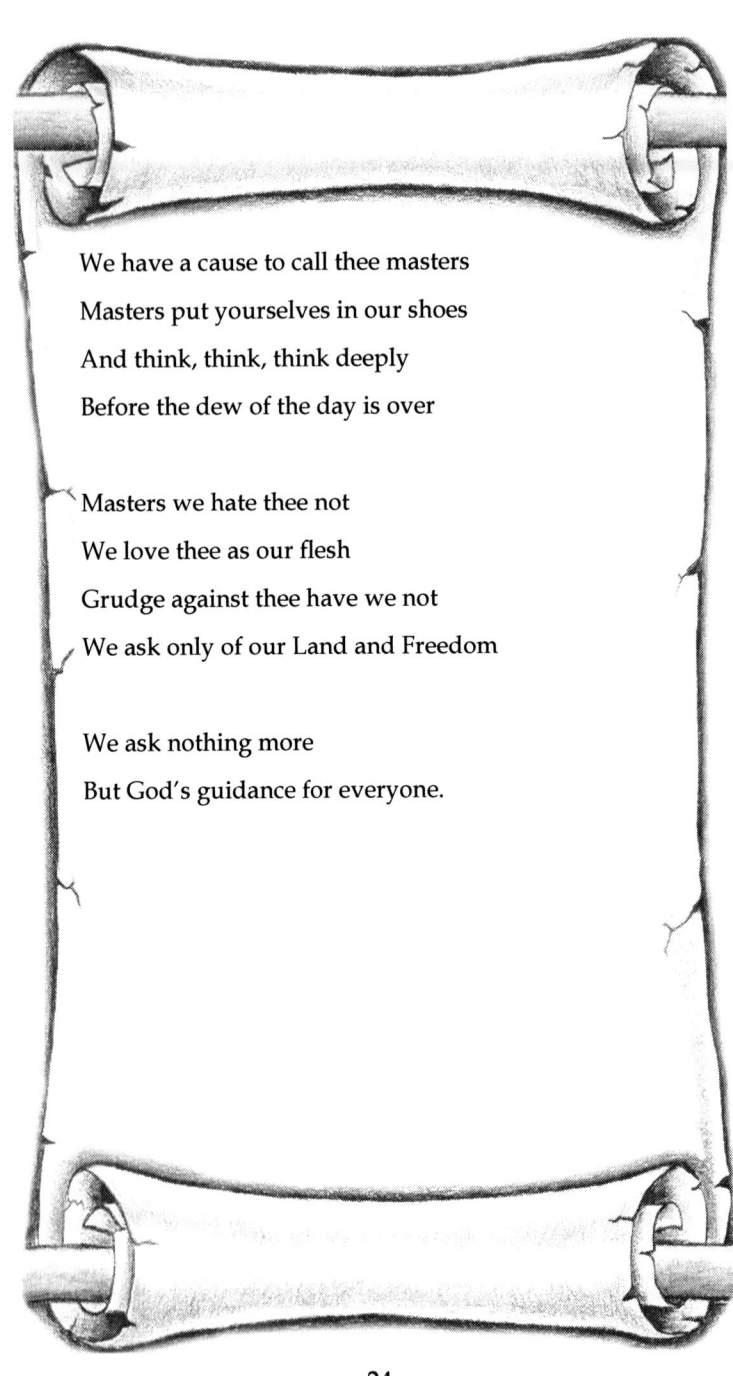

We have a cause to call thee masters
Masters put yourselves in our shoes
And think, think, think deeply
Before the dew of the day is over

Masters we hate thee not
We love thee as our flesh
Grudge against thee have we not
We ask only of our Land and Freedom

We ask nothing more
But God's guidance for everyone.

FREE AT LAST

A free bird turned caged
Why?
He spoke, sang, whistled
To break the barricade wall.

Hurrah —
He did it his doing it, his doing it
After twenty seven years of wired out
Twenty seven years of agony, pain and writhe.

Last but not the least
Liberty, but yet no freedom
A free bird turned caged
A lad but yet a hero.

11th of February, 1990
Turned the sage into news.

Dedicated to:
Nelson Mandela.

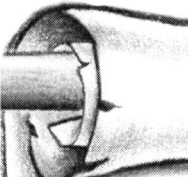

PLEADINGS THAT TURNED SOUR

Hmm!

The white skinned spirited dogs came

They came they came to Africa

Pretending pretending with their ever soft eyes

Ready for pleadings that turned sour

Our warm hearted father took them

With both hands made them their friends

But what have the ungrateful spirited dogs done?

They sprang like watered flowers

And bit the fingers who took them.

Oh! What a pity a pity truly it is

South Africa, our stolen motherland

Our motherland flowing with milk and honey

Inherited by the fruits the ancestors lay down

Inherited sale of black on black for a piece of mirror

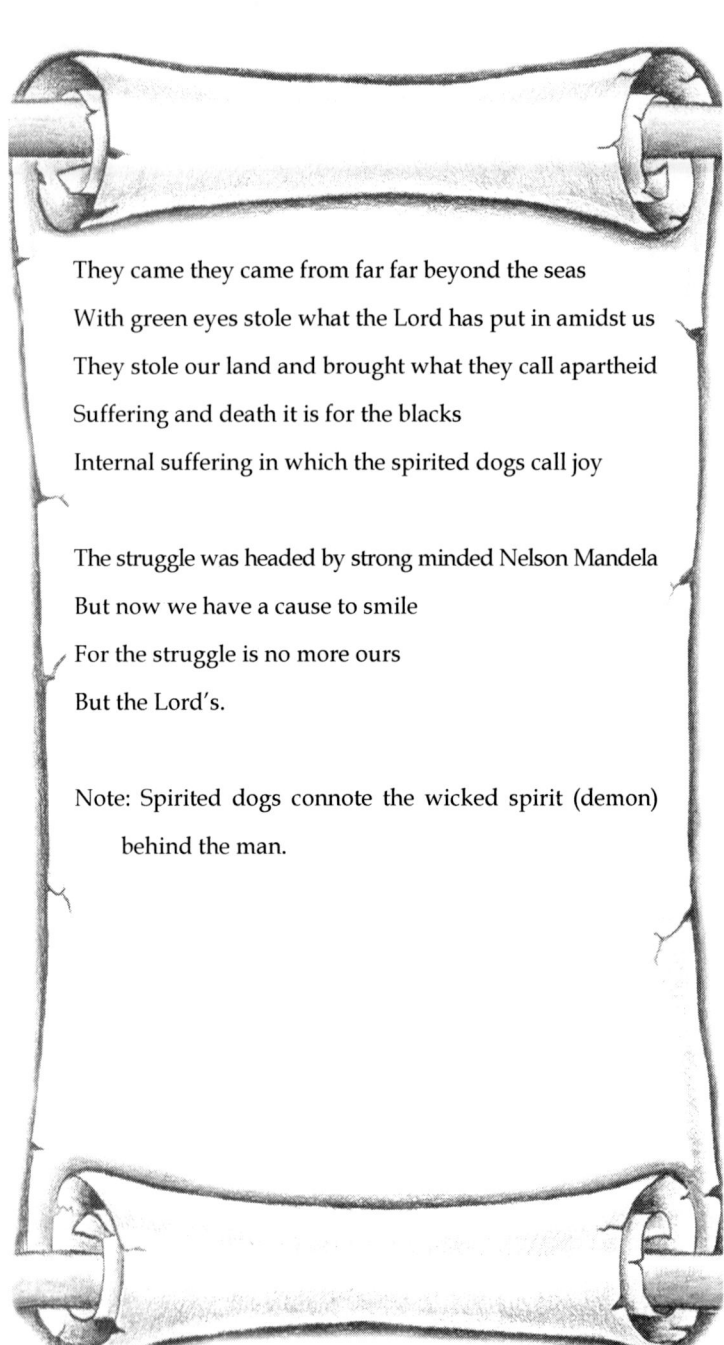

They came they came from far far beyond the seas
With green eyes stole what the Lord has put in amidst us
They stole our land and brought what they call apartheid
Suffering and death it is for the blacks
Internal suffering in which the spirited dogs call joy

The struggle was headed by strong minded Nelson Mandela
But now we have a cause to smile
For the struggle is no more ours
But the Lord's.

Note: Spirited dogs connote the wicked spirit (demon) behind the man.

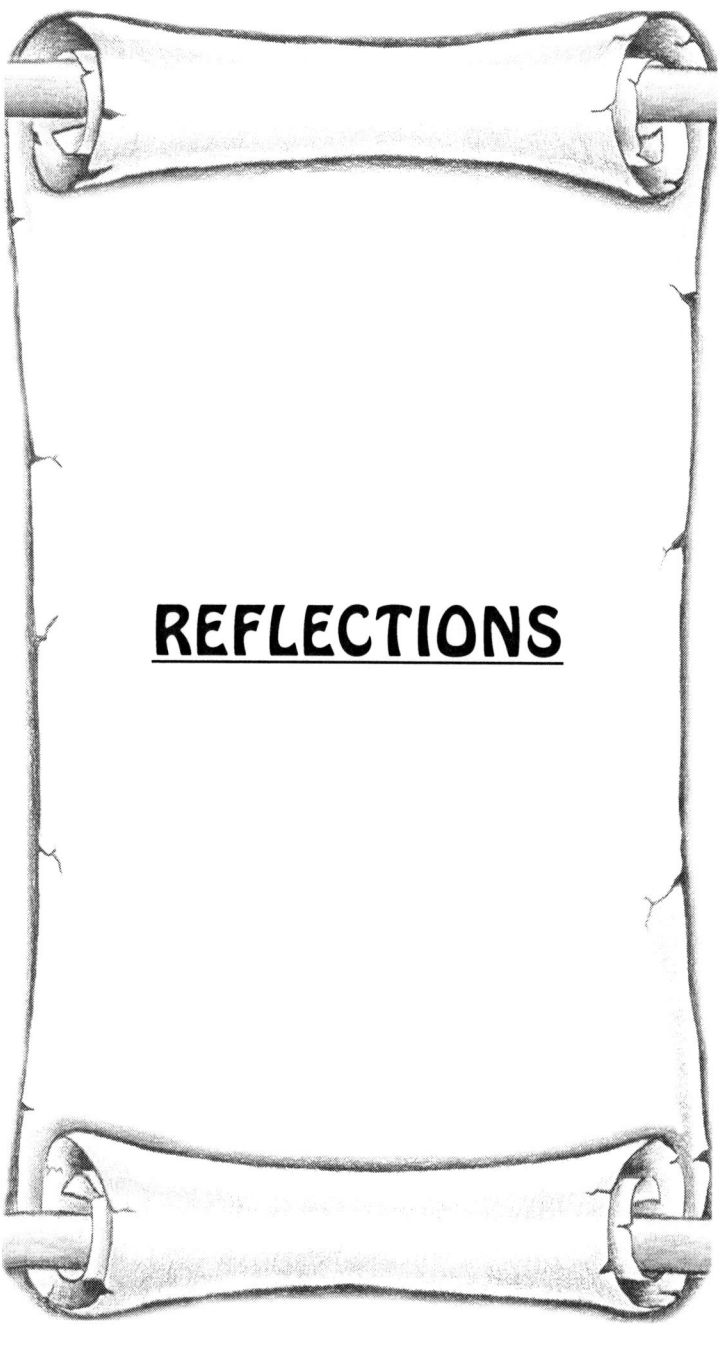

REFLECTIONS

F.G.C. IDO-ANI

Ages ago
There lived a village
A village named Ido-Ani
Where noble men live

In the living village
Came F.G.C. Ido-Ani
A great Image
Of all times

F.G.C., a great name to reckon with
A school of mixed bread
A school of brains, morals and morale
Oh! What a great name to reckon with

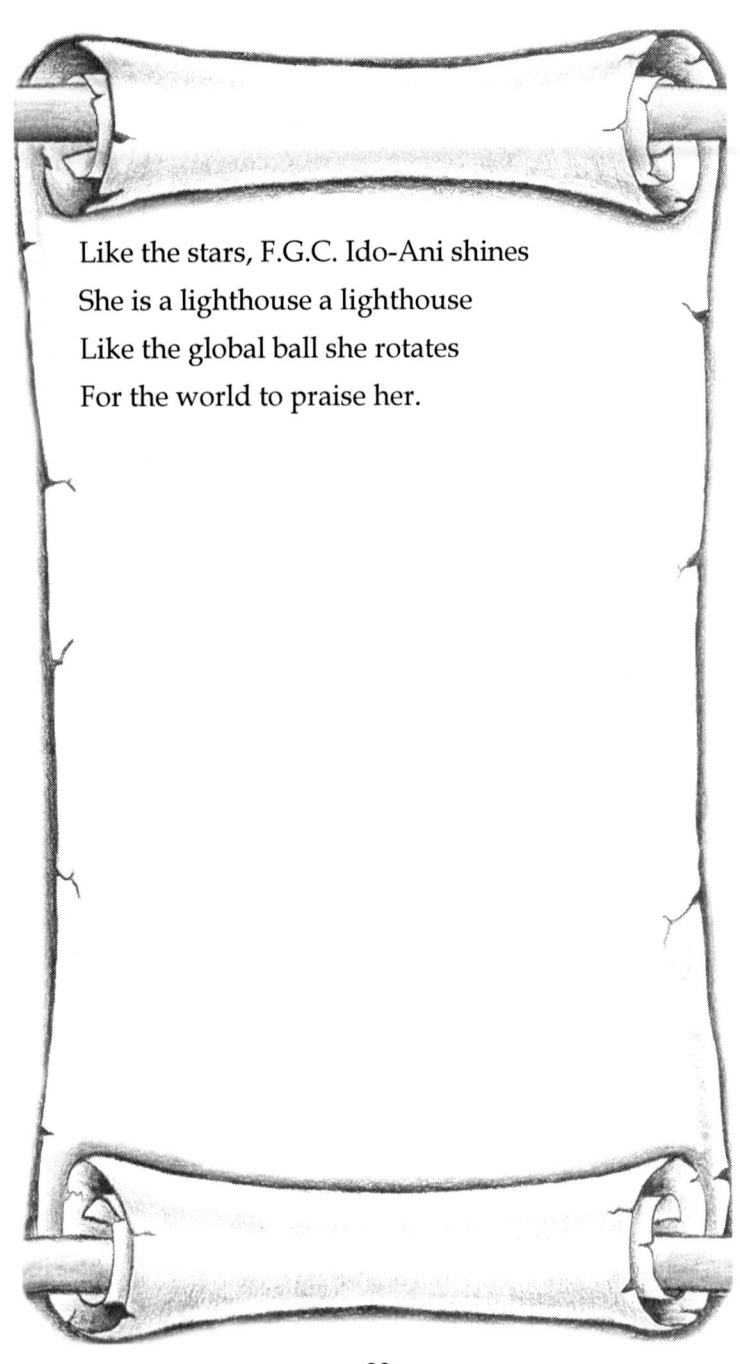

Like the stars, F.G.C. Ido-Ani shines
She is a lighthouse a lighthouse
Like the global ball she rotates
For the world to praise her.

IVCU HISTORY

IVCU

Is like a seed growing into a Mighty Tree

A Mighty Tree full of flourished vine: leaf, fruit

The Mighty Tree is our Lord Jesus Christ

IVCU is a family

A family that cares for body, soul and spirit

A family with smiles, hope, pains, challenges and faith

A family above all gaining the victory together

Singing, Praising, fellowshipping together

Smiling, laughing, shouting together

To blast open the walls of Jericho

Y—e a—h! The victory is ours

Hey! You there
Don't you dare give up?
'Cause the victory is ours
Yes! The victory is ours.

EDUCATION

Hmm!
    Ancient of days
    Ancient days of Colonisation
    Colonization came Education
    Education came Wisdom
    Oh! What a tete a tete

    What a great thing to reckon with
    Education
    The word of all times
    Education
    The move of generations

    Learning that knows no age
    The den in which the lion lies
    Is the pride of all to learning
    To knowledge bringing employee employer relationship.

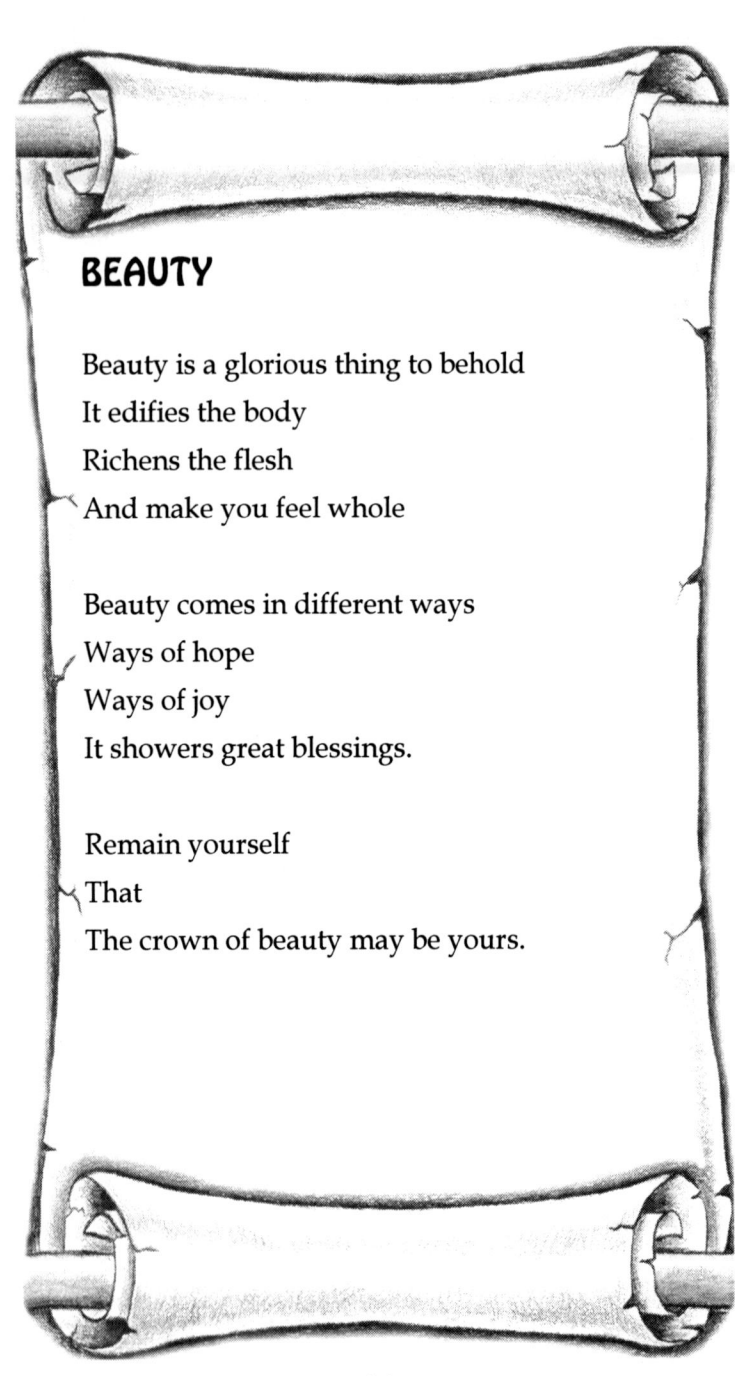

BEAUTY

Beauty is a glorious thing to behold
It edifies the body
Richens the flesh
And make you feel whole

Beauty comes in different ways
Ways of hope
Ways of joy
It showers great blessings.

Remain yourself
That
The crown of beauty may be yours.

HAPPY BIRTHDAY

Year after Year
Day after Day
Minute after Minute
Life springs In and Out

Thank God
The day passed by
Silently - - - - - - - - - -
Silently giving another chance.

Hurrah!
What a day to remember
I am a year older
What a splendid thing to know.

By and by the days roll on
Not definite on another but by grace.

TRUTH

The truth may be bitter
The truth may cause tears and fears
But the truth, the truth
Sets me and you free.

The truth may be hidden today
But with time the truth surfaces
Never be deceived
The truth is always the truth.

It never dies it never withers
But it hangs around you
Makes you as white as snow
Makes you an angel of all.

Swear not to make yourself justified
The truth knows when his spoken.

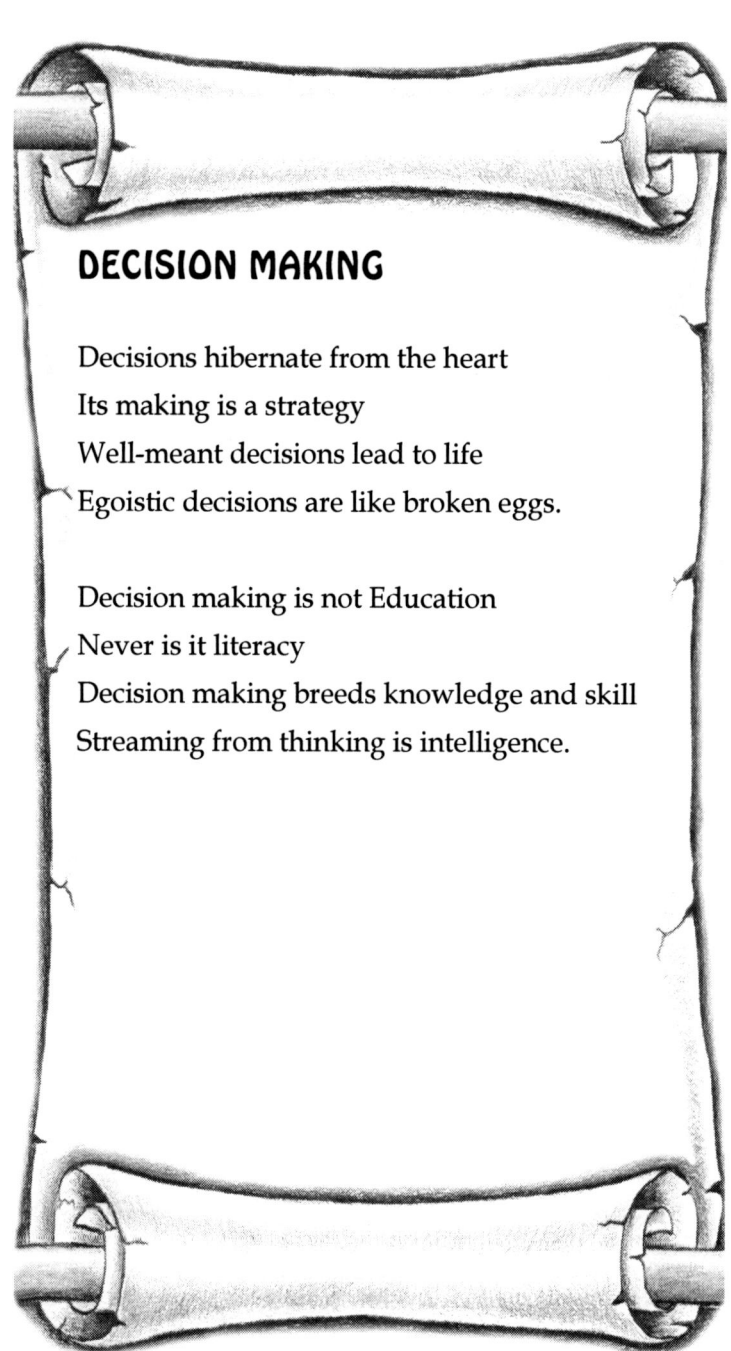

DECISION MAKING

Decisions hibernate from the heart
Its making is a strategy
Well-meant decisions lead to life
Egoistic decisions are like broken eggs.

Decision making is not Education
Never is it literacy
Decision making breeds knowledge and skill
Streaming from thinking is intelligence.

LIFE

Life is an era of time you spend on earth
The era may be giving the era may be taking
There is none that has not a reward
You can't drive this lane without His glory.

Life is but a trifle, which has to be spent
In the trickest positive way
To achieve First, the Way of the Cross
Then, the other possibilities of life in truth
Some spend theirs in their wallow and weakness.

A weakness which bends its person
Like a bent leaf unfed for ages
Hmm! What a calamity
A habit consciously unknown; needing stopping
To attain dignity and a height of never return.

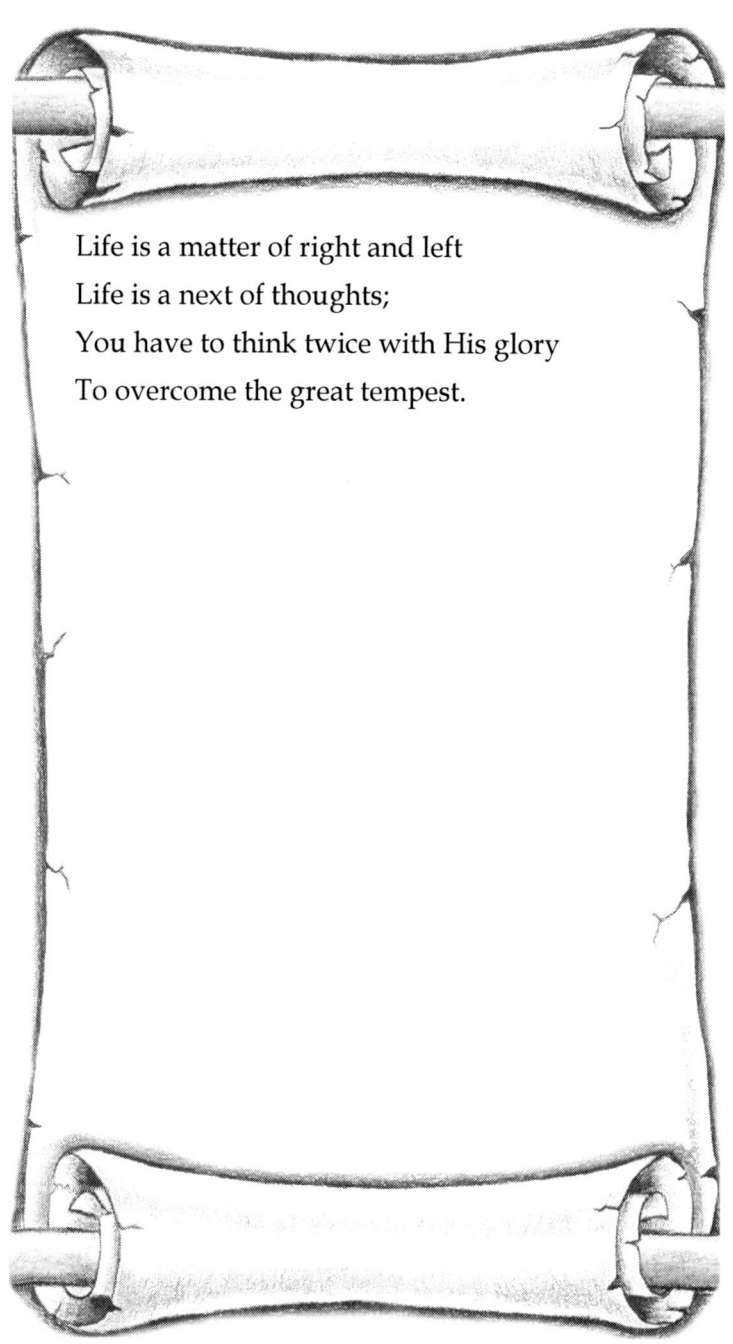

Life is a matter of right and left
Life is a next of thoughts;
You have to think twice with His glory
To overcome the great tempest.

PROMISE

The heart brings forth waves of promise
To those who runneth the race
To those who walketh the race
To those who standeth the promise.

Blessing is a standing word
It clings his person forever
Death is a standing word
It spots his man mor'ever.

A stone unturned in times
A corner that corners not
A debt thou oweth him
A mystery becometh whole.

Man in promise is like a filthy rag
God in promise is holy.

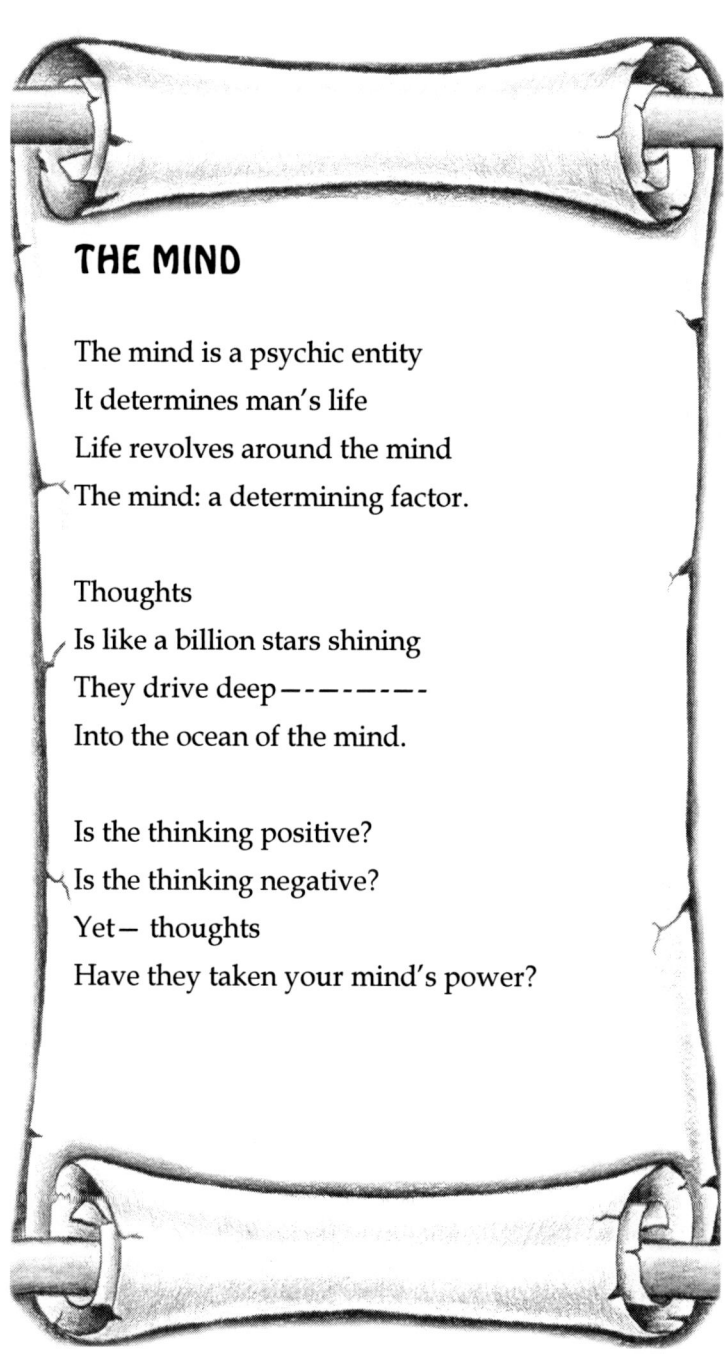

THE MIND

The mind is a psychic entity
It determines man's life
Life revolves around the mind
The mind: a determining factor.

Thoughts
Is like a billion stars shining
They drive deep————-
Into the ocean of the mind.

Is the thinking positive?
Is the thinking negative?
Yet— thoughts
Have they taken your mind's power?

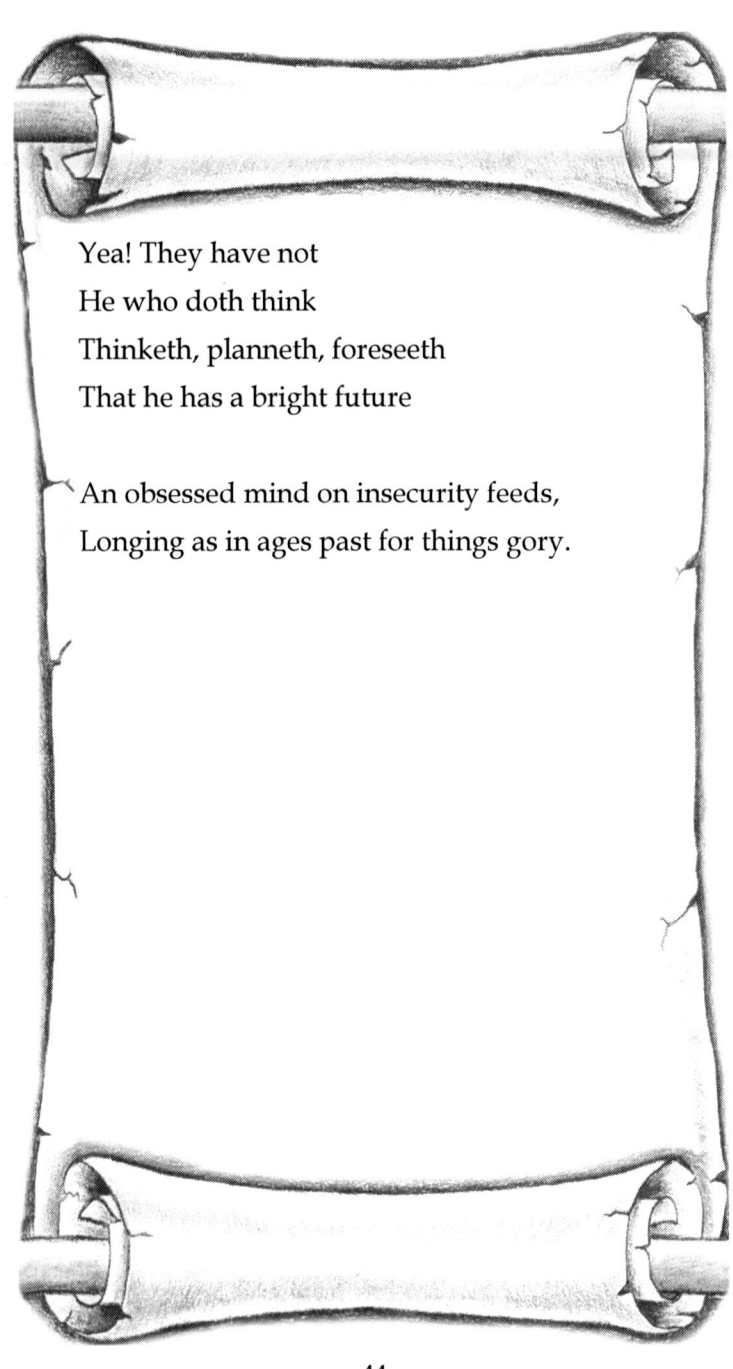

Yea! They have not
He who doth think
Thinketh, planneth, foreseeth
That he has a bright future

An obsessed mind on insecurity feeds,
Longing as in ages past for things gory.

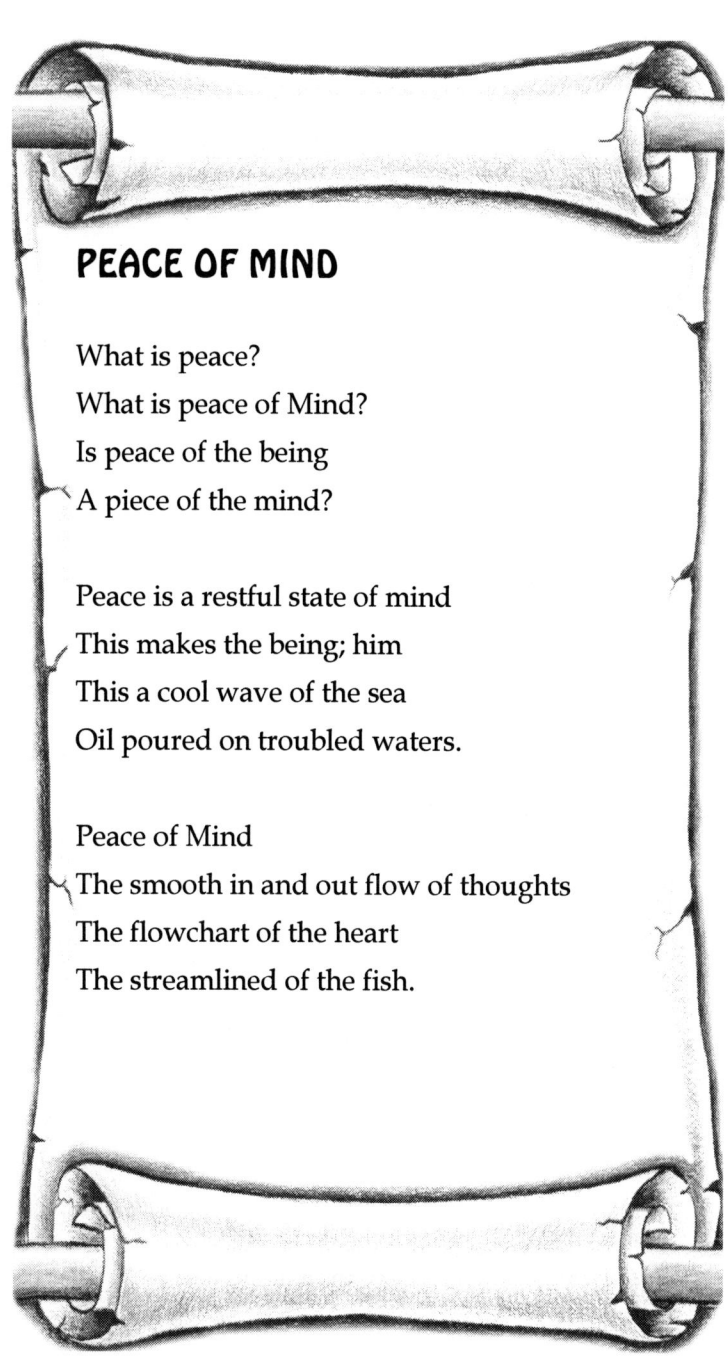

PEACE OF MIND

What is peace?
What is peace of Mind?
Is peace of the being
A piece of the mind?

Peace is a restful state of mind
This makes the being; him
This a cool wave of the sea
Oil poured on troubled waters.

Peace of Mind
The smooth in and out flow of thoughts
The flowchart of the heart
The streamlined of the fish.

Peace is of him who thinketh peace
Wouldst thou thinketh trouble
And think peace would flow ? No
Think tranquillity, serenity, peace

Thoughts create ideas
Words — vehicles of ideas
Thoughts affect words create attitudes
Affect attitudes affect actions

Thinking starts with talking
The tongue the smallest organ
Yet
Death and life in the organ lay.

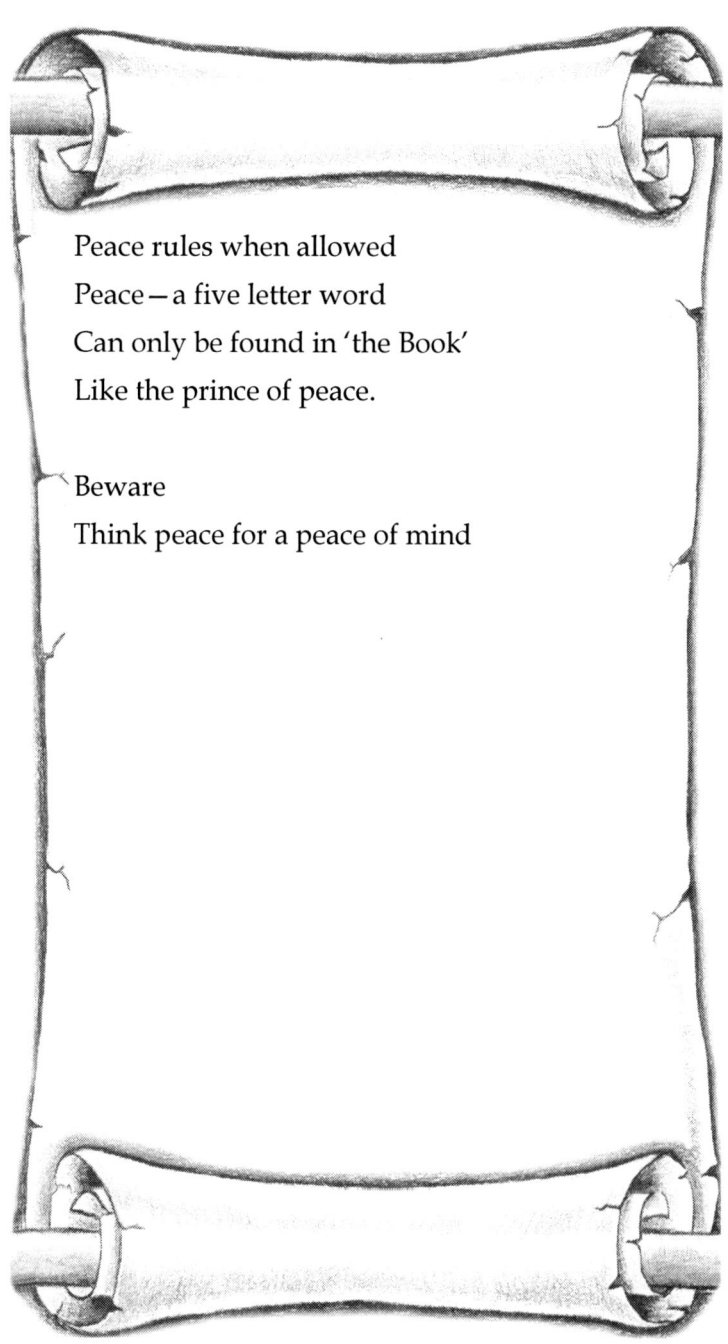

Peace rules when allowed
Peace — a five letter word
Can only be found in 'the Book'
Like the prince of peace.

Beware
Think peace for a peace of mind

HUNGER

Hunger is an act of men
Hunger is a malicious acumen
A fighter of the innermost
A defeater of the outermost parts.

A times! It gives a gear
Most times! It goes tump tump tump
Like a piece of yam suffering under mortals
Like the depth of the ocean

A hungry man is an angry man
When allowed an angry man
Prigs slowly the intestinal organs
Prigs slowly to death.

Hunger and anger are brothers
They come hand in hand like brothers
Hunger! What he leads a man to
Reduces a king to a slave.

'YOU ARE DIRTY'

You are dirty
An eleven letter word
You are dirty
An eleven letter word.

Have you seen pigs
Have you seen how they wallow in the mud?
Have you seen pigs
Have you seen how they prove in the mud ?

In dirts
Piglets follow their image for food, shelter, etc.
In dirts! Am I dirty?
Let me prove my image, status and follow the image.

Oh! You are dirty

Am I dirty?

Prove,

The eleven letter word.

D—R—E—A—M

Looking into the horizons
Then, Now and beyond
Dreaming in the physical realm
What is your dream?

Sleep a harmless death
Dream origin of physical and spiritual
Sleep well, Sweet dreams
D – R – E – A – M.

ADULT EDUCATION

An adult is he who thinks likewise
An adult thinks the development
Of 'I', 'You', 'Him' and 'Her'
She builds her to step up never to step down.

Education brings forth knowledge
Knowledge the eye for Education
Allows a voice to be heard, eyes to see, nose to smell
Modification, rejection and creation.

You call her 'eko agba'
I note her as literacy for adults
Literacy and learning for young adults
It's of the then, now and future to grow.

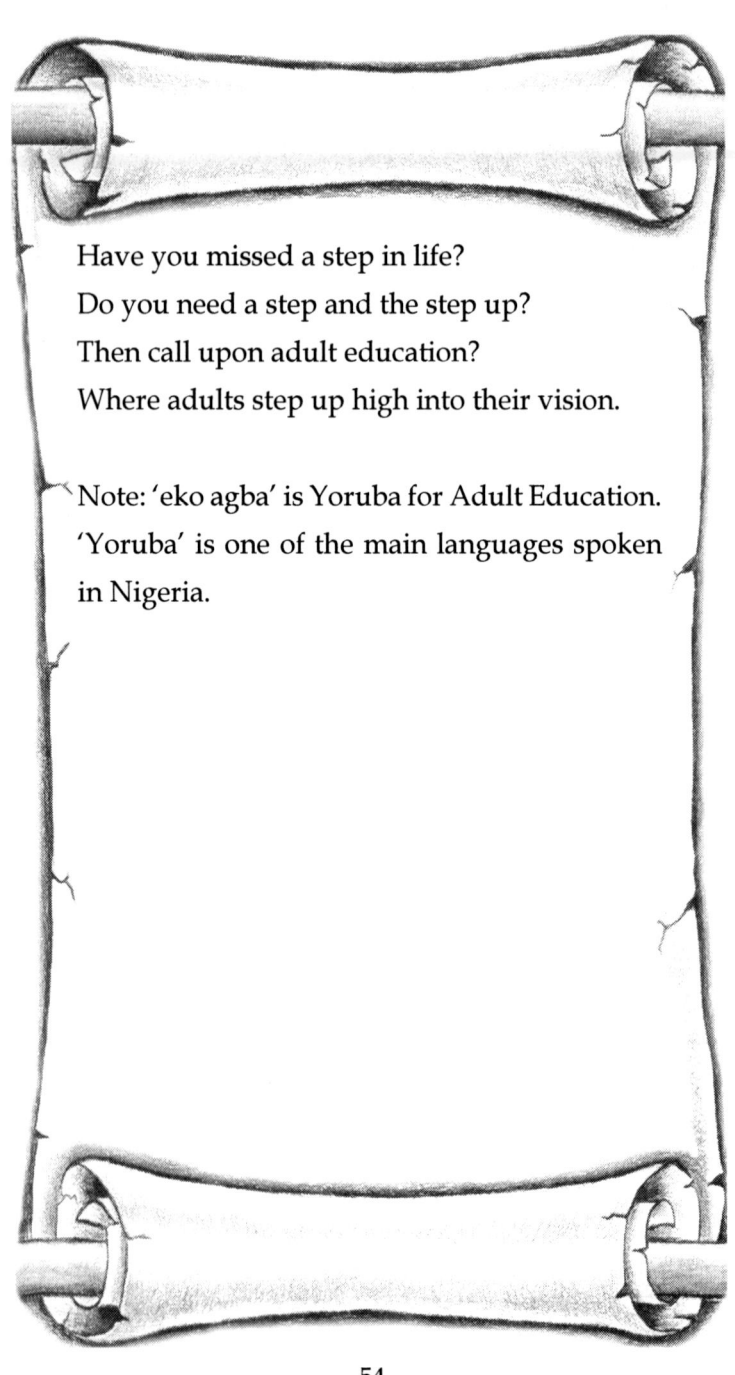

Have you missed a step in life?
Do you need a step and the step up?
Then call upon adult education?
Where adults step up high into their vision.

Note: 'eko agba' is Yoruba for Adult Education. 'Yoruba' is one of the main languages spoken in Nigeria.

THE FAMILY

The Family is the centre of my heart
My heart desire a family based on love
Love through the eyes of the family: the family of old
Love through making a child a child

A child living through to his/her destiny
A child in the family not as an adult
An adult in the family as an adult
Not a child, just a friend or a figure.

Hum! What is this figure?
For any child, a child that is looked after
Who does this figure represent?
How does the child understand this figure?

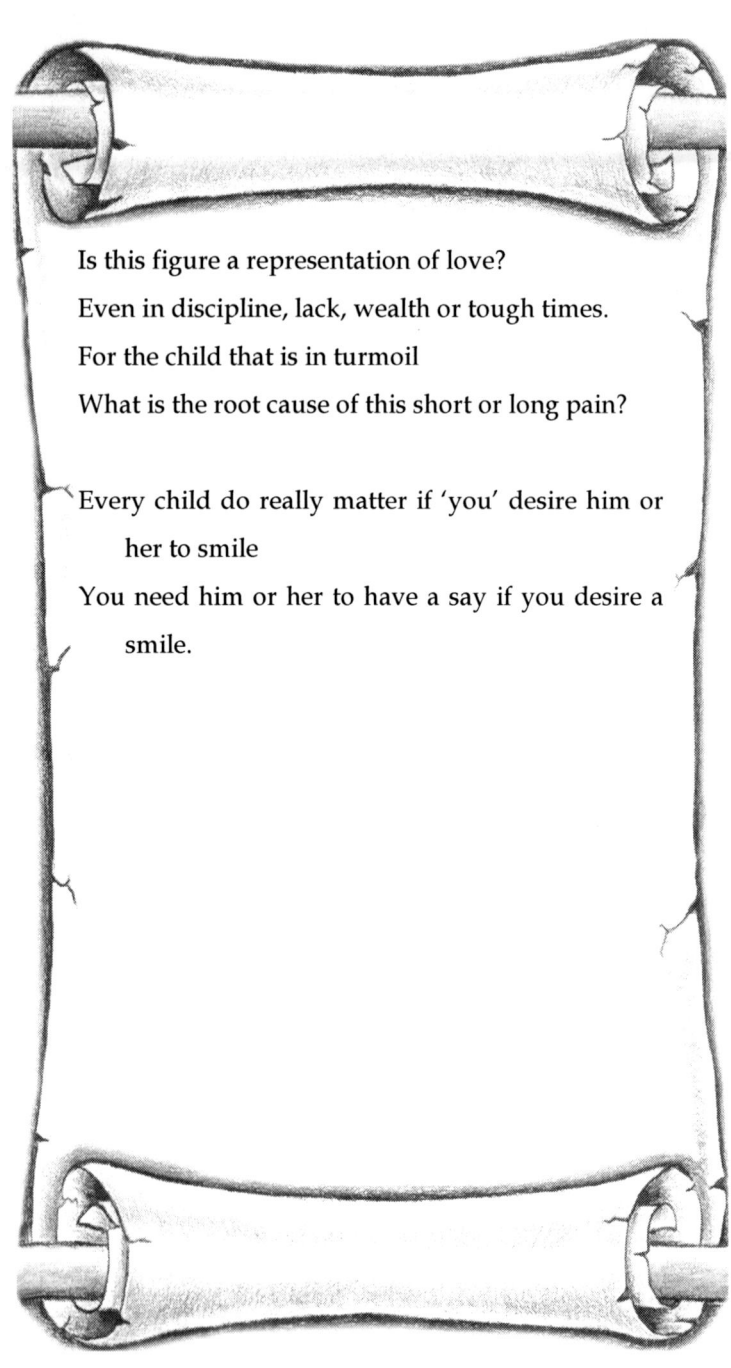

Is this figure a representation of love?
Even in discipline, lack, wealth or tough times.
For the child that is in turmoil
What is the root cause of this short or long pain?

Every child do really matter if 'you' desire him or her to smile
You need him or her to have a say if you desire a smile.

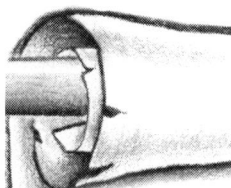

A MOTHER

A mother is the heart of her family
The family:
'The heart' pumps life into the body
'The Heart' perfects the body
Thou she may not be perfect
Her warmth, smiles, wisdom
Faith, faithfulness, hugs, endurance
Tenderness, fights, thanksgiving, praise
Soaks to build her family up

He elevates her to become perfect
To become perfect is not only by her works
But in His faith: in His faith
They build straw together to build a house

She is now a beauty: isn't it by the Father's glory?

Her husband lifts her up
He loves and appreciates her to continue to build her.
He covers her to glory
Her husband and her perfects the family
Thou she remains the heart
The function of the family remains all.

A mother prepares the dance floor for her family and dances the dance
To success, victory, and glory
For it is never over until it is over
With any battle any war
Any war is won, won and won in Christ

A mother smiles
Even in her face of hunger
A mother hugs
Even in the face of fury

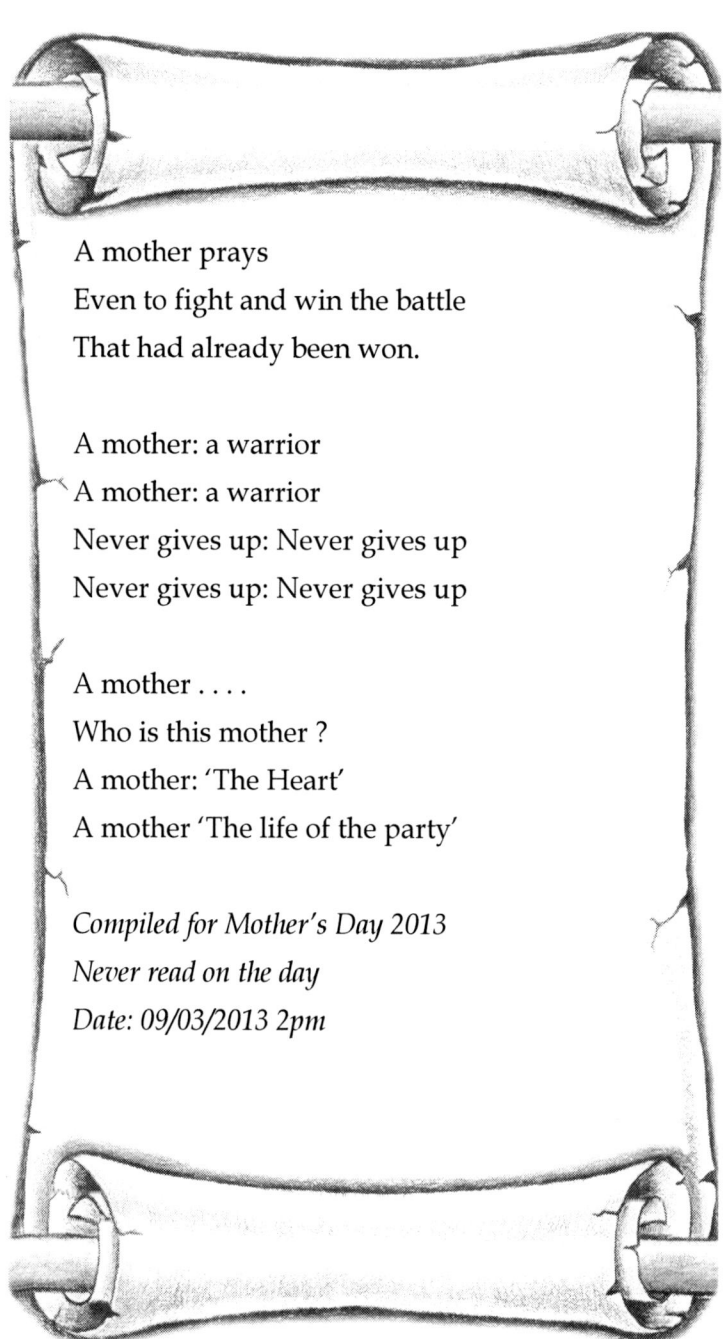

A mother prays
Even to fight and win the battle
That had already been won.

A mother: a warrior
A mother: a warrior
Never gives up: Never gives up
Never gives up: Never gives up

A mother . . . .
Who is this mother ?
A mother: 'The Heart'
A mother 'The life of the party'

Compiled for Mother's Day 2013
Never read on the day
Date: 09/03/2013 2pm

SUCCESS

A man that waits is patient to gain his success
He never gives up
He lays awake watching his prey
To grip 'his neck' cause he never gives up

To succeed in itself is a battle
A battle of the body
A battle of the soul
A battle of the mind

A battle of the mind: I must win
To win that of the body and soul for success
Thou success is not made in a day
It must be done first in the mind.

Compiled 26/04/2013

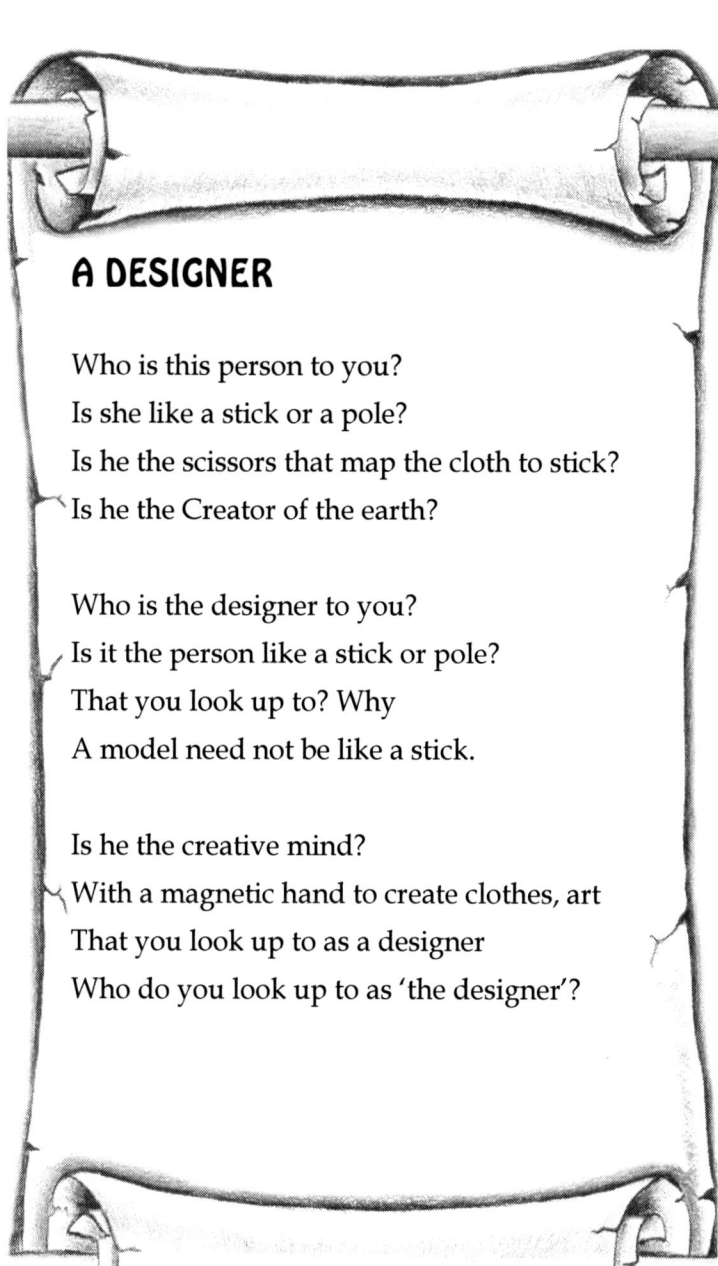

A DESIGNER

Who is this person to you?
Is she like a stick or a pole?
Is he the scissors that map the cloth to stick?
Is he the Creator of the earth?

Who is the designer to you?
Is it the person like a stick or pole?
That you look up to? Why
A model need not be like a stick.

Is he the creative mind?
With a magnetic hand to create clothes, art
That you look up to as a designer
Who do you look up to as 'the designer'?

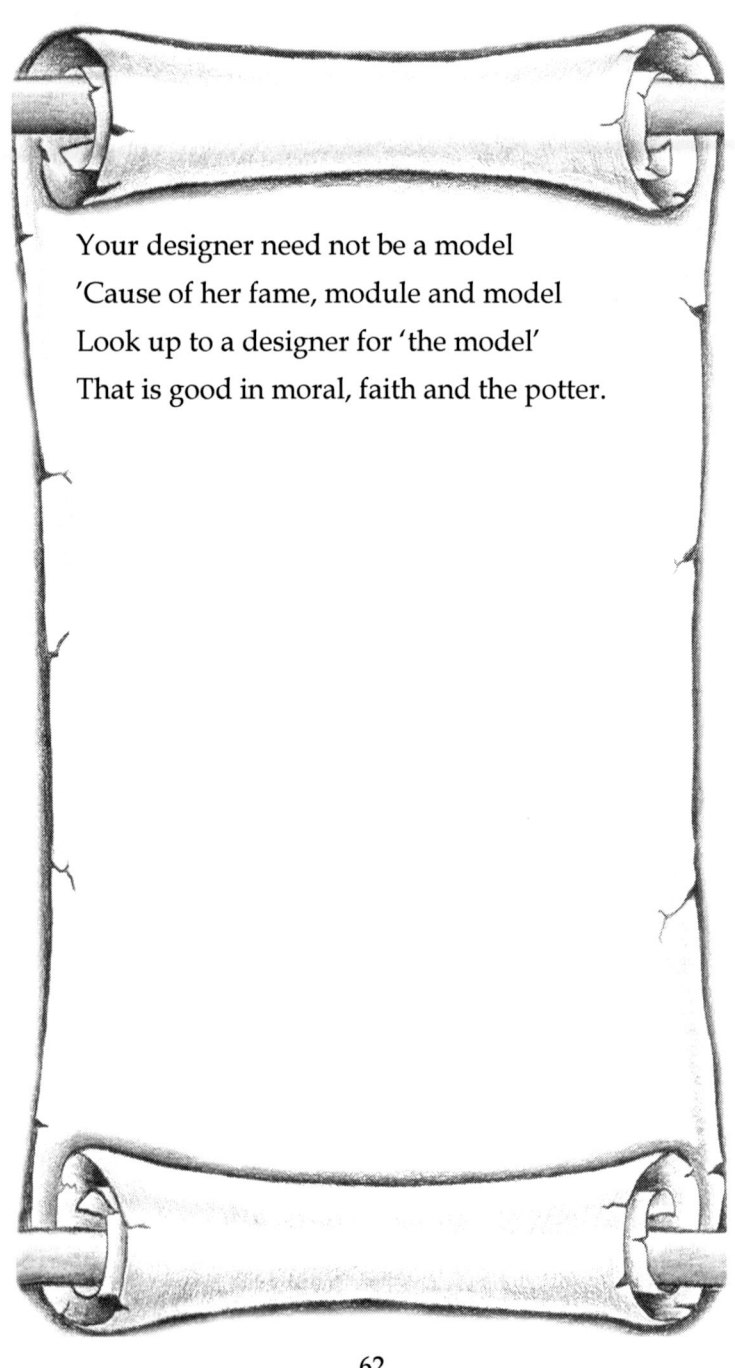

Your designer need not be a model
'Cause of her fame, module and model
Look up to a designer for 'the model'
That is good in moral, faith and the potter.

INSPIRATIONS

Good Mental Health

Mental Health is mind's stability
Or is it not?

A man that is able to smile, laugh
Like beauty in her nature has good mental health
A man that is able to talk and discuss
Like the talk 'He' called in Isaiah 1v 18 has good mental health

Oh yes the first hope is salvation
Relationship with 'Him' deliverance through 'Him'
Or a living Holy Ghost filled Son of God of 'His' repute
Other second best includes professionals not medium/s

Therapy, Medication or both seek
Family and friends could listen, love and listen
Appreciate the person not the strange voice
Listen to the person talk not demean

Give hope like a seed grown by a farmer
Knowing that the harvest is nigh
Never give up to that third voice
Kill the demon/s with the word of God

Know that the power of the gun
Shout, cries, anger, suicide cannot
Touch or kill this spirit from hell
'cause it's a spirit so you need the 'Spirit'

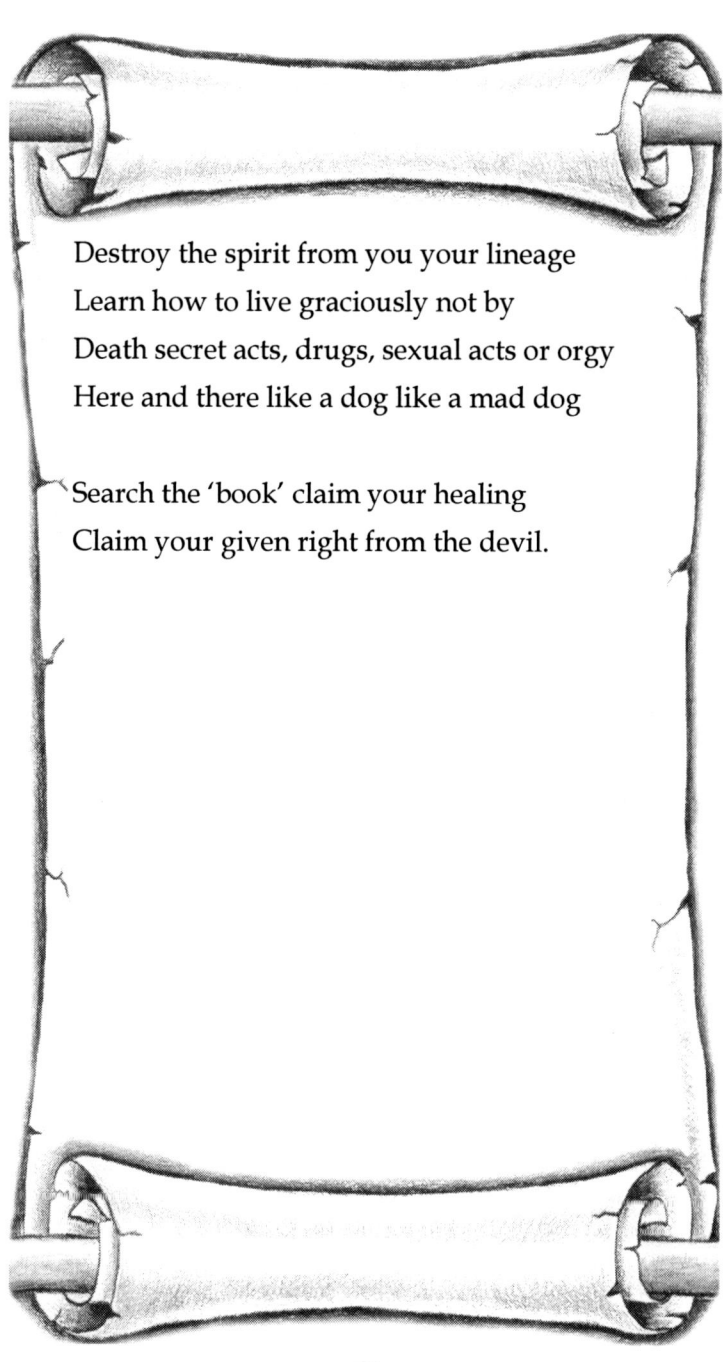

Destroy the spirit from you your lineage
Learn how to live graciously not by
Death secret acts, drugs, sexual acts or orgy
Here and there like a dog like a mad dog

Search the 'book' claim your healing
Claim your given right from the devil.

HELL

Hell is a doomsday
A place full of lake of fire
Where you know no one
Hmm

The fool says in his heart
"There is no God."
They are corrupt, doing abominable iniquity;
There is none that does good
This class belongs to hell if they do not repent.

Death warns not
Death comes like a thief
The pangs of death are painful
It stops a cherished life
To take to where we know not.

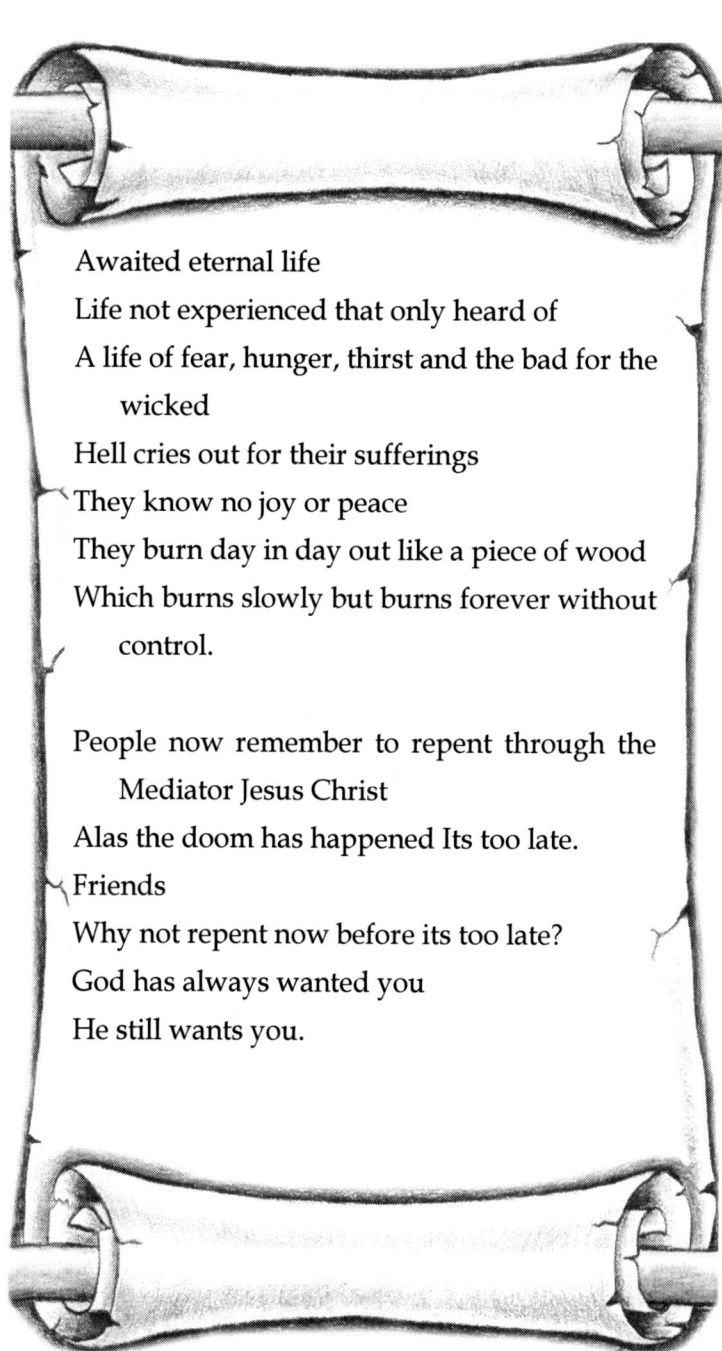

Awaited eternal life
Life not experienced that only heard of
A life of fear, hunger, thirst and the bad for the wicked
Hell cries out for their sufferings
They know no joy or peace
They burn day in day out like a piece of wood
Which burns slowly but burns forever without control.

People now remember to repent through the Mediator Jesus Christ
Alas the doom has happened Its too late.
Friends
Why not repent now before its too late?
God has always wanted you
He still wants you.

THE LORD

The Lord is a proverbial Spirit
Who liveth from the beginning
Ever shall he live
Above, Beneath, Everywhere.

He is the Lord of Lords
King of kings
Father of Fathers
Head of all.

He is Alpha and Omega
Omnipotent and Omniscience
Meek, kind and gentle
Slow to anger firm in his words

To worship Him takes not much
Put on His armour the sword
In your hand shining as ever
Walking in his path.

You lose in the least not
Gaining ever is yours
Deceive ye not by satan
Who takes, taketh him in, out to leave but none.

Only if allowed. WARNING!
Do not allow him, allow Him
'Him' The God of Abraham, Isaac and Jacob
The God of Elijah.

Dedicated to the Living God.

INSPIRATIONS

Inspirations are deep
They are deep-seated
Inspirations are colossal
They pronounce and beautify the world
They come in different fields
Of nature; of thoughts
Of inspirations.

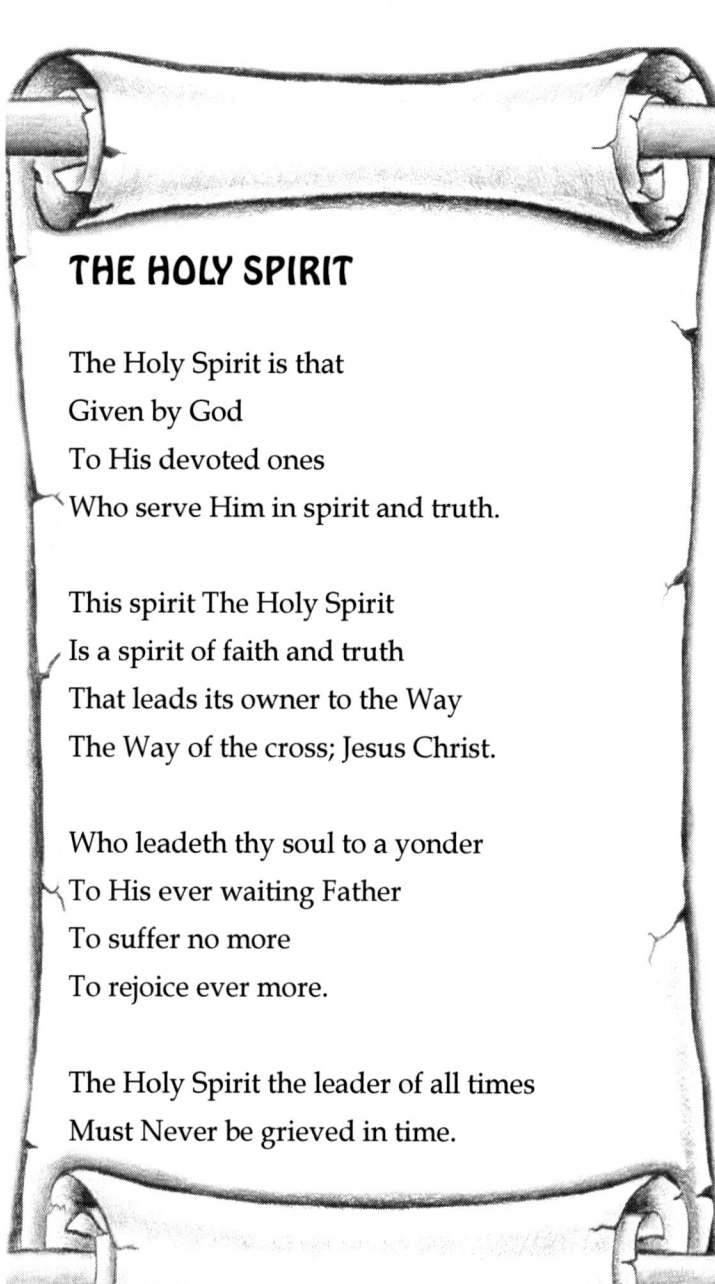

THE HOLY SPIRIT

The Holy Spirit is that
Given by God
To His devoted ones
Who serve Him in spirit and truth.

This spirit The Holy Spirit
Is a spirit of faith and truth
That leads its owner to the Way
The Way of the cross; Jesus Christ.

Who leadeth thy soul to a yonder
To His ever waiting Father
To suffer no more
To rejoice ever more.

The Holy Spirit the leader of all times
Must Never be grieved in time.

A DEVOTED ONE

A devoted One
Likes of Christ little Christ
Christians at Antioch were named,
A devoted One

A devoted One
Walks in the light of the Holy Trinity
The Father, Son and the Holy Spirit
He tends on good path
He heads for salvation
Love and truth is written over him
A devoted One.

By his deeds it is known
A devoted One.

BLINDNESS

Being blind is a disease
A disease that brings death
Without actually being dead
Hmm! What an omen the body craves not?

If the body craves not this ailment
Why do you the owner crave it?
You crave this because of the disease in you
Ignorance! Logics! Moralist behaviour.

Ignorance is no plea to justice
If you can't escape blindness of the eyes
You can escape that of the mind
Don't give the deceiver an iota of space.

Note: A man is blind only if his inner eyes are not open as stated above.

A STORY TO THE MOST HIGH

Ages ago,
> Lived the Most High God, He lives; ever shall He reign
> With Him lived Angels, lives, ever shall they reign
> In Thy glory. Of these lived Lucifer
> The guardian 'cherub' protecting the intimacy of God's presence
> The most powerful of all spirits
> Created originally without sin by God
> A creation of extraordinary beauty and intelligence
> He wanted to be the Most High
> Because of his beauty
> He was content not with his position.

Of proud in pride in delusion
He became satan enemy of the living God
Devil, slanderer, the accuser who attacks from behind
A liar of all times.

From that moment he was driven out
And lost fellowship with God
He is no Lord but god of this world
His power but a non-entity
I give thanks to 'Him'
For a Mightier power subdues him forever

That power is in and of Christ the blood of Jesus
Jesus Christ is the Saviour
Satan's chief objective is not necessarily to tempt people to sin
But to turn them from the truth of Christ

For in Christ alone can we gain a true idea of God
Satan wants to wrap the 'image' of God in men's thinking
So that he may pass himself as God
He never has changed his objective
He wants to be the Most High

Ye worshippers of the devil; the occult — - — -
See forth your master's doom
He has been judged by the Most High
His going to burn in hell forever.

The Most High didn't say
All will ever burn in hell
He loves you and I
No matter your obscure ways; sins
Repent! Repent! Repent

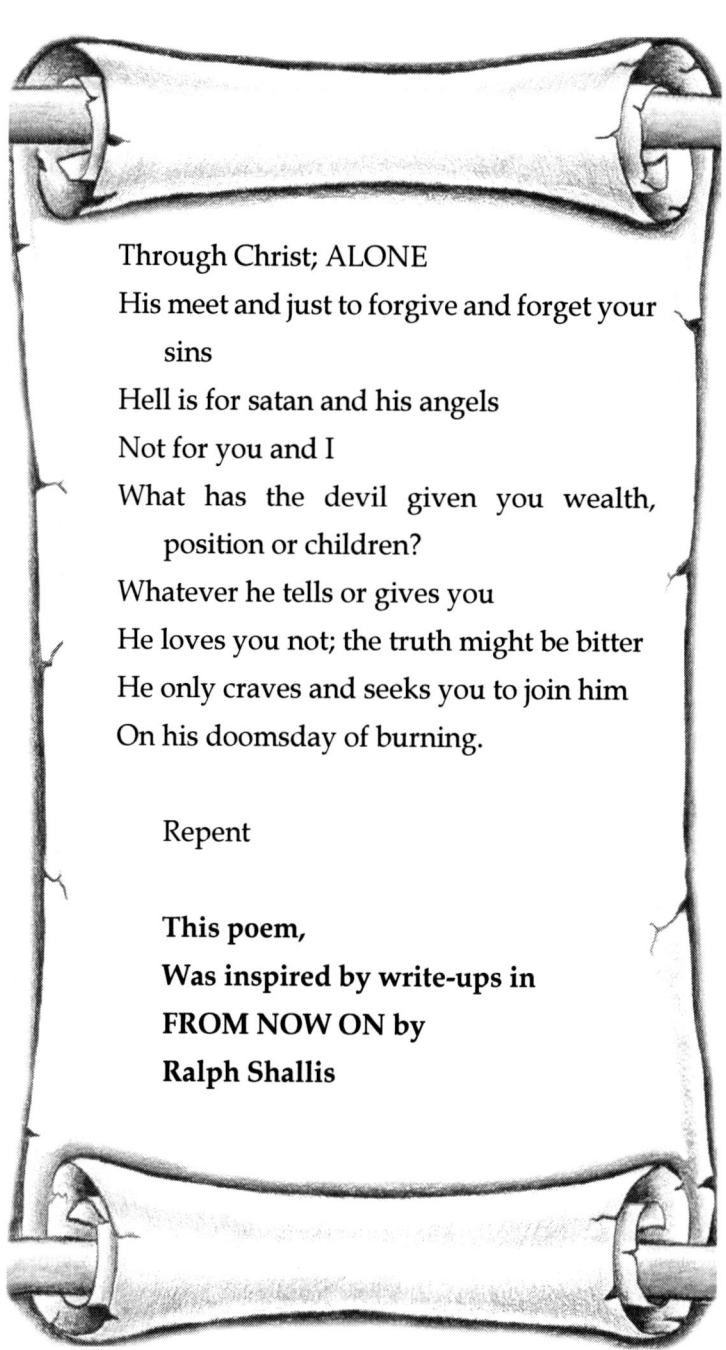

Through Christ; ALONE
His meet and just to forgive and forget your sins
Hell is for satan and his angels
Not for you and I
What has the devil given you wealth, position or children?
Whatever he tells or gives you
He loves you not; the truth might be bitter
He only craves and seeks you to join him
On his doomsday of burning.

Repent

This poem,
Was inspired by write-ups in
FROM NOW ON by
Ralph Shallis

EASTER

Easter,
    A day of love, joy, peace
    A day filled with the morning star
    A day of death in one
    A day of life to live evermore.

There is a holy Thursday
A good Friday
The day he was crucified
An Easter Sunday
The day he rose and is risen
Ever Ever to live
Never Never to die.

In Him,
We stay, hope and find peace.

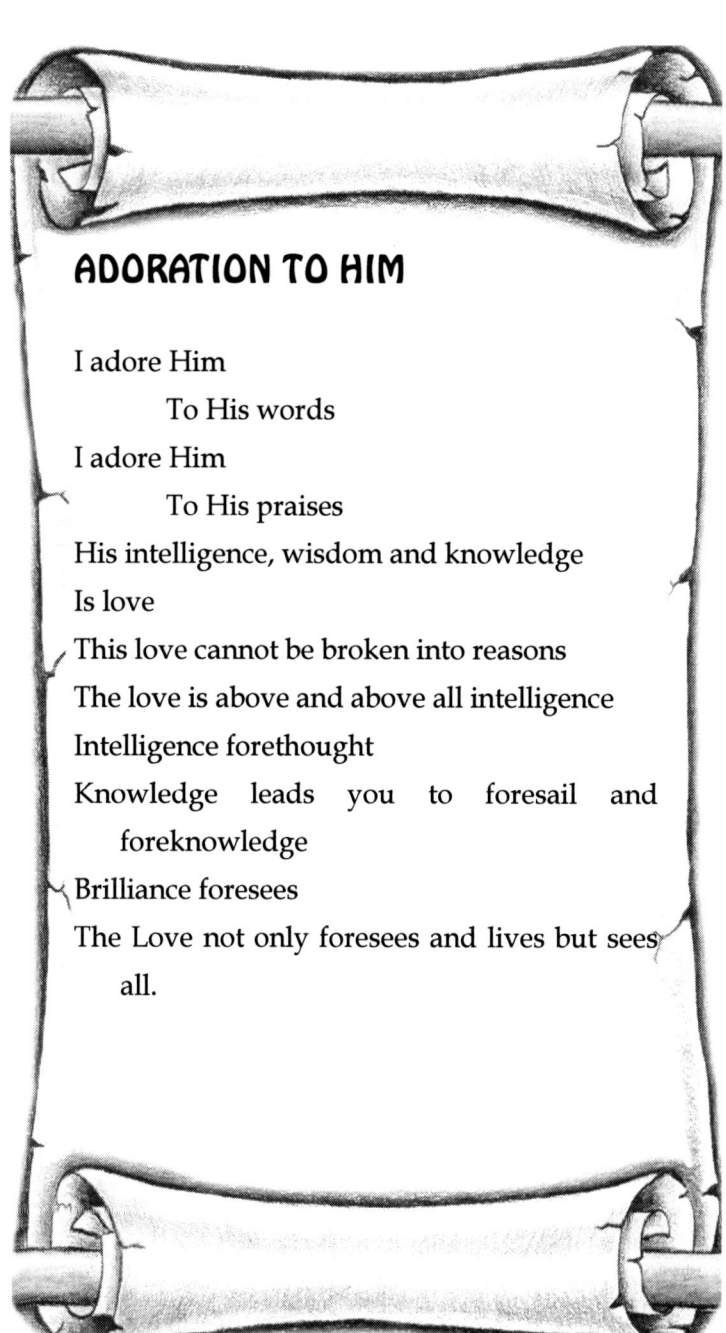

ADORATION TO HIM

I adore Him
> To His words

I adore Him
> To His praises

His intelligence, wisdom and knowledge
Is love
This love cannot be broken into reasons
The love is above and above all intelligence
Intelligence forethought
Knowledge leads you to foresail and foreknowledge
Brilliance foresees
The Love not only foresees and lives but sees all.

ISLAM & CHRISTIANITY
(WHO IS THE CONFUSED MAN)

Religion; word of the mind
A word that gives, takes and brings
Religion — A mesmerising spirit
A spirit that mesmerises to death

A philosopher like the mesmerising spirit
Think think and searches and searches
Religion like a philosopher's journey
Hardly smiles to 'Yes', the Faith

Christians preach Way of Christ; Trust it
Muhammed preach Islam (submission); Read it
Look, think and reason out the Way?
Can you really reason or think it?

I may be tagged 'confusion'
To a man in a confused state in doubt
Which is the Way?
Today it is right tomorrow it is left

In time the Jews knew God
To wave His people from gods
In time came worship of Islam
Idols the worship of diaBonos.

Ha; never did problems solve
Men still sinned problems remained
Though sacrifices did them day in day out
Their gods hands remained folded eyes shut

With time,
He sent forth Jesus Christ
For an everlasting sacrificial lamb
That in 'Him' He will commune with His.

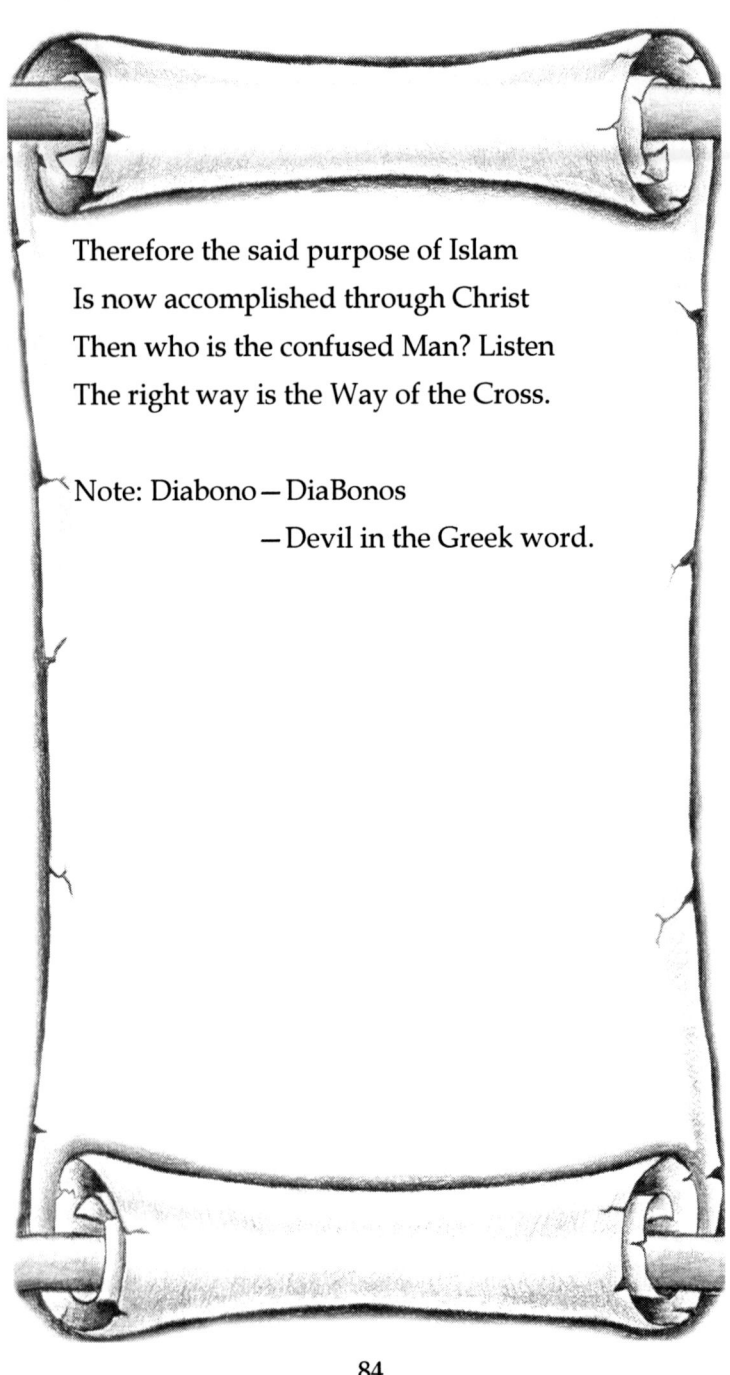

Therefore the said purpose of Islam
Is now accomplished through Christ
Then who is the confused Man? Listen
The right way is the Way of the Cross.

Note: Diabono — DiaBonos
— Devil in the Greek word.

THE ROCK OF MY REFUGE

The Lord is the Rock of My Refuge
The Rock in which I am shield
The Rock of ages
Here I come.

The Lord is the Rock of My Refuge
The rock of my domain
The Rock of rocks
Here I come.

Thou who givest life
Thou who takest life
The owner and giver of life
Here I come.

Rock of My Refuge
Here I come.

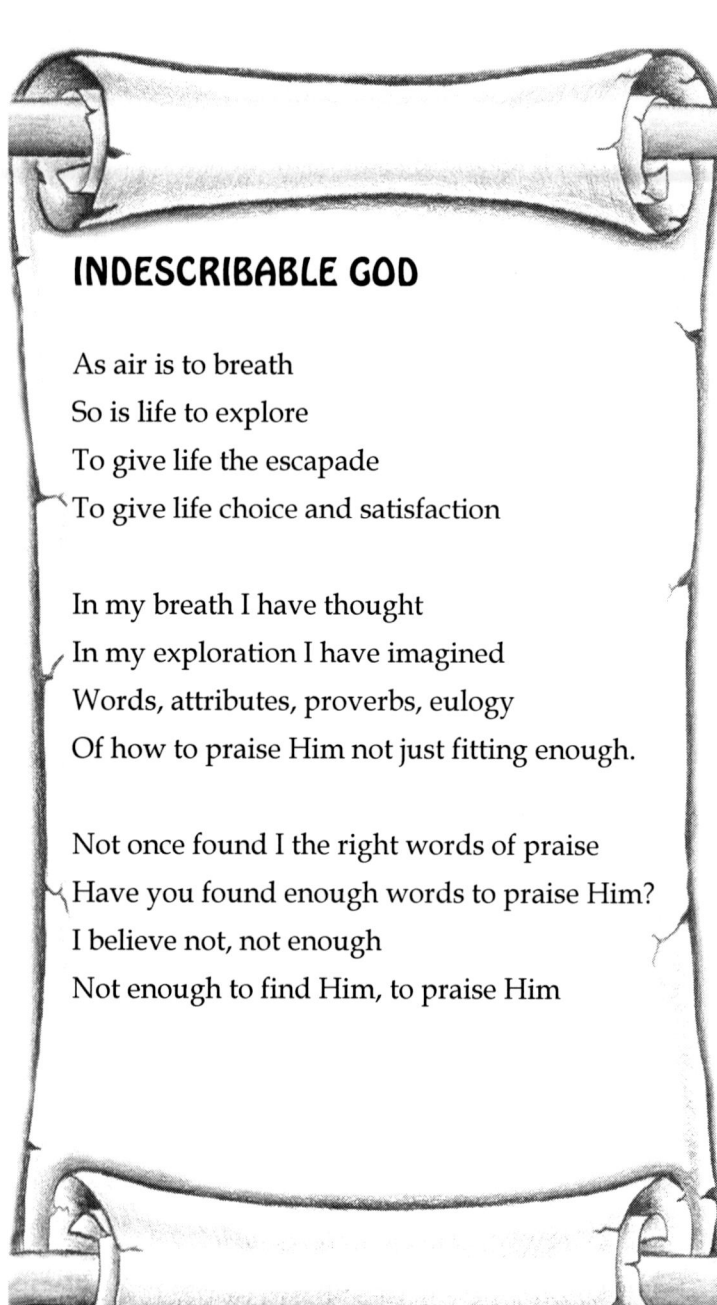

INDESCRIBABLE GOD

As air is to breath
So is life to explore
To give life the escapade
To give life choice and satisfaction

In my breath I have thought
In my exploration I have imagined
Words, attributes, proverbs, eulogy
Of how to praise Him not just fitting enough.

Not once found I the right words of praise
Have you found enough words to praise Him?
I believe not, not enough
Not enough to find Him, to praise Him

We all lack enough utensils to really find Him
Praise Him His Majesty His Glory
We cannot find Him enough
Because His beauty is indescribable

Unless revealed and communicated by 'Him'
Yet nothing created is fitted enough
Fitted enough to body to describe
His mystical robe: Mystical Majesty.

Why reason God out
When you cannot even reason 'you' out
To accept Him reason Him in hope, in love
Thank Him accept His saving grace

His mercy is uncomprehensive
His effects like Him cannot be fully known

Compiled 17/09/08

THE DEVIL

Who is this being or spirit?
What does he want?
Where does he come from?
How did he come and is he real?

Hmm! What an amazing answer
Yet 'A man' say his superstitious
Yet he has been since the Ancient One created him
What ignorance of depth beyond that of the oceans.

The devil, Lucifer, the enemy of the saints, A liar,
Was the guardian 'cherub' protecting the intimacy of God
Then why did he leave such a high post?

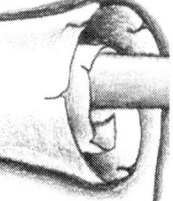

Because of greed he wanted to be like the 'Most High'

Of course his first plan opted from pride in heaven failed
In the plan angels in heaven followed out of his deceit
Angels that followed him are now his demons
Harken! Harken! Follow not his demons or him

The liar since has hooked up with his first plan
That 'I will disguise myself in every possible way
To make the living worship me'; Ha! Ha! Ha!
For he still wants to be the Most High God

Know this he knows he can never be the Most High God
So he forces man to steal, kill and destroy

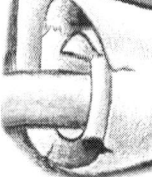

He co-opt man to think he gives him power,
   wealth, fame
When he takes his most priced possession, his
   life, his soul

In ignorance 'a being' worship him
Through idols; a great source of demons
Through cults, mediums, love of money as a
   medium
Through man for he has the image of 'Him'

Isn't he achieving his first aim?
Is he achieving it through you, hope not?
Is he achieving it through you, hope not?
Be determined; he must not win through you.

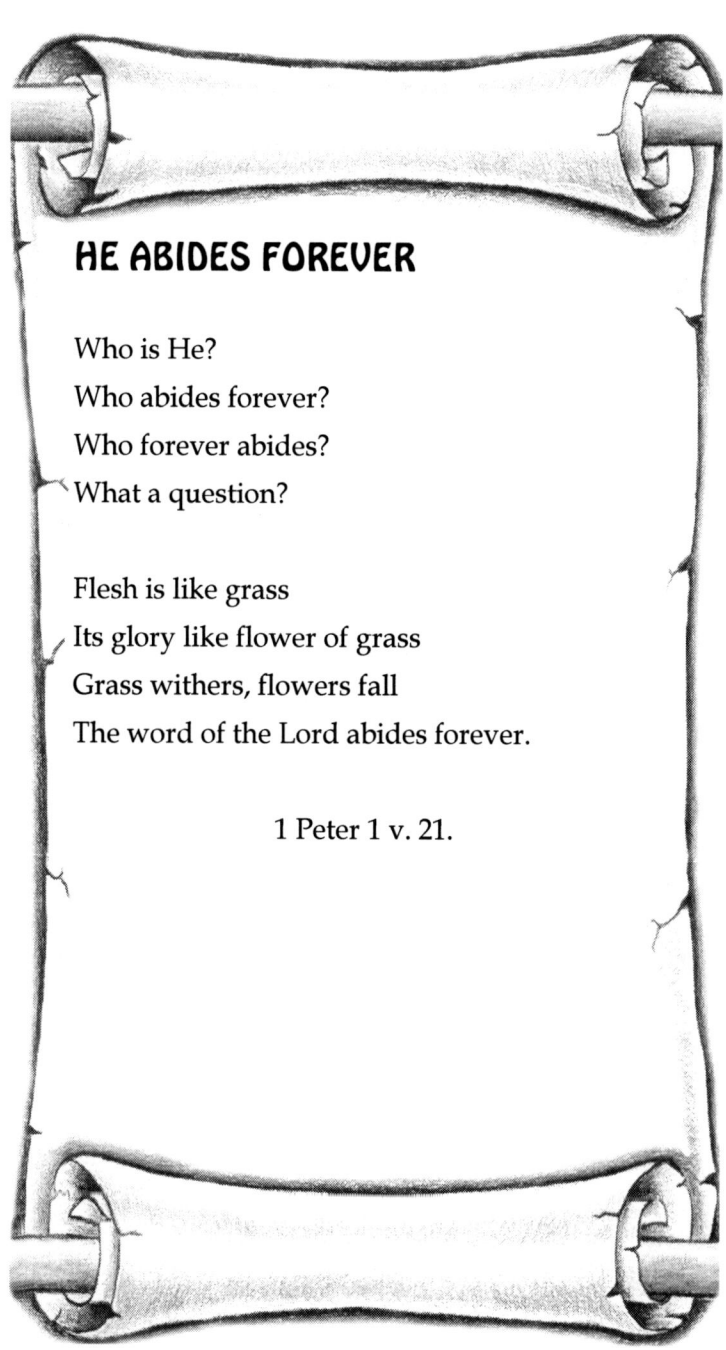

HE ABIDES FOREVER

Who is He?
Who abides forever?
Who forever abides?
What a question?

Flesh is like grass
Its glory like flower of grass
Grass withers, flowers fall
The word of the Lord abides forever.

1 Peter 1 v. 21.

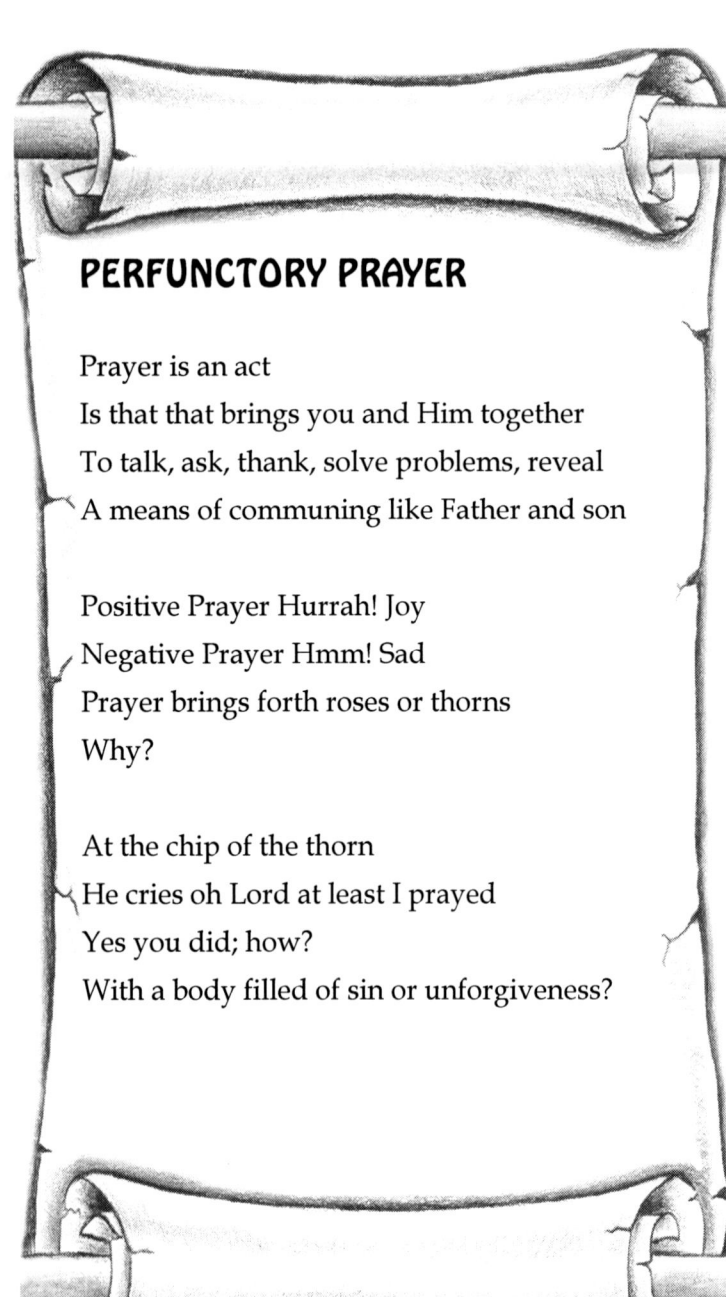

PERFUNCTORY PRAYER

Prayer is an act
Is that that brings you and Him together
To talk, ask, thank, solve problems, reveal
A means of communing like Father and son

Positive Prayer Hurrah! Joy
Negative Prayer Hmm! Sad
Prayer brings forth roses or thorns
Why?

At the chip of the thorn
He cries oh Lord at least I prayed
Yes you did; how?
With a body filled of sin or unforgiveness?

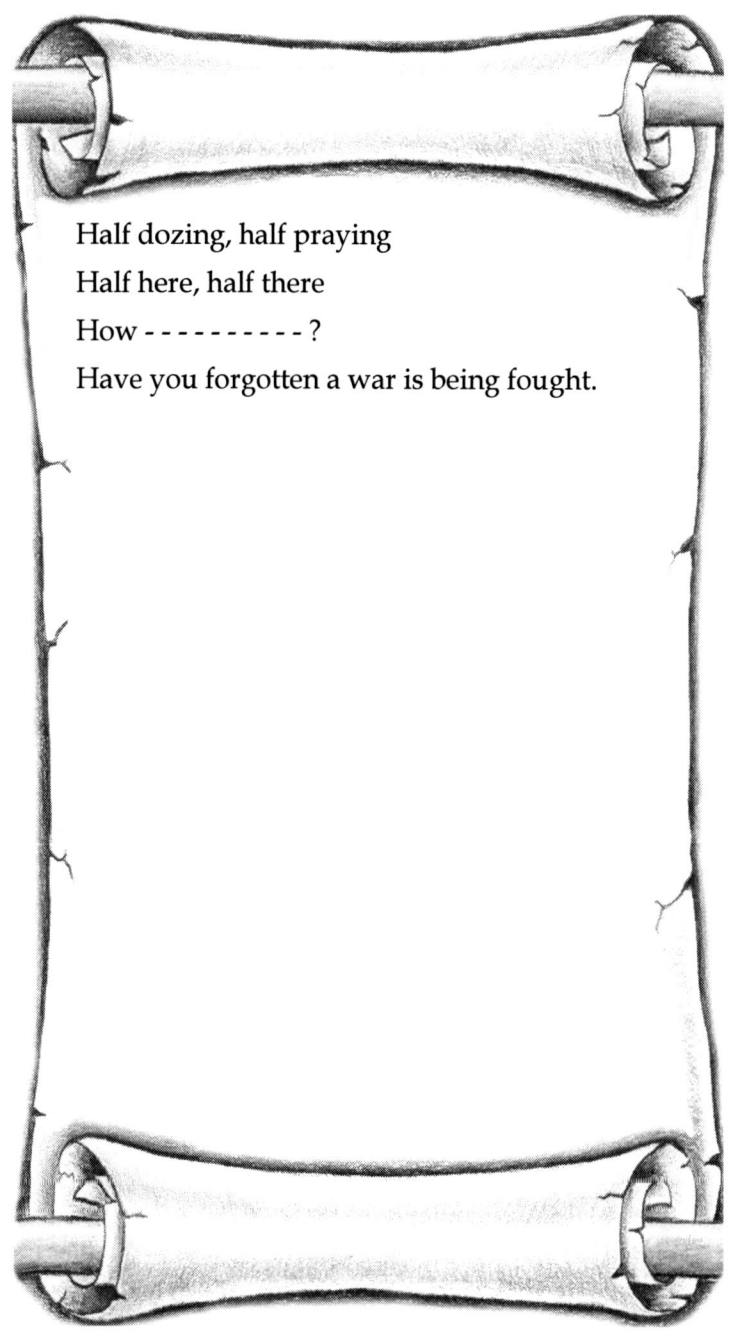

Half dozing, half praying
Half here, half there
How - - - - - - - - - - ?
Have you forgotten a war is being fought.

BELIEVE IN YOURSELF

Are you defeated in life?
You go a crawling in life
Toll in negative thoughts
Inferiority, in way, life and thoughts
Why?

    Believe in Yourself,
    Believe in '<u>Himself</u>'

Like a tortoise
Walk a way,
"I can do all things through
Christ which strengtheneth me"
A physical therapy.

Inspired by:
The power of Positive Thinking
By
Norman Vincent Paale

THE MERCY OF GOD

Man has got choices
Choice of life choice of death
Which do you choose?
Choose life for life not death for death.

God has got power
Power to give life power to take life
Is he not the potter that moulds the clay?
Then why brood fear He has the power.

Why thinkest man that he owns the power?
Is it because of your freewill?
Is it because of your technology?
Do not be deceived . . . ?

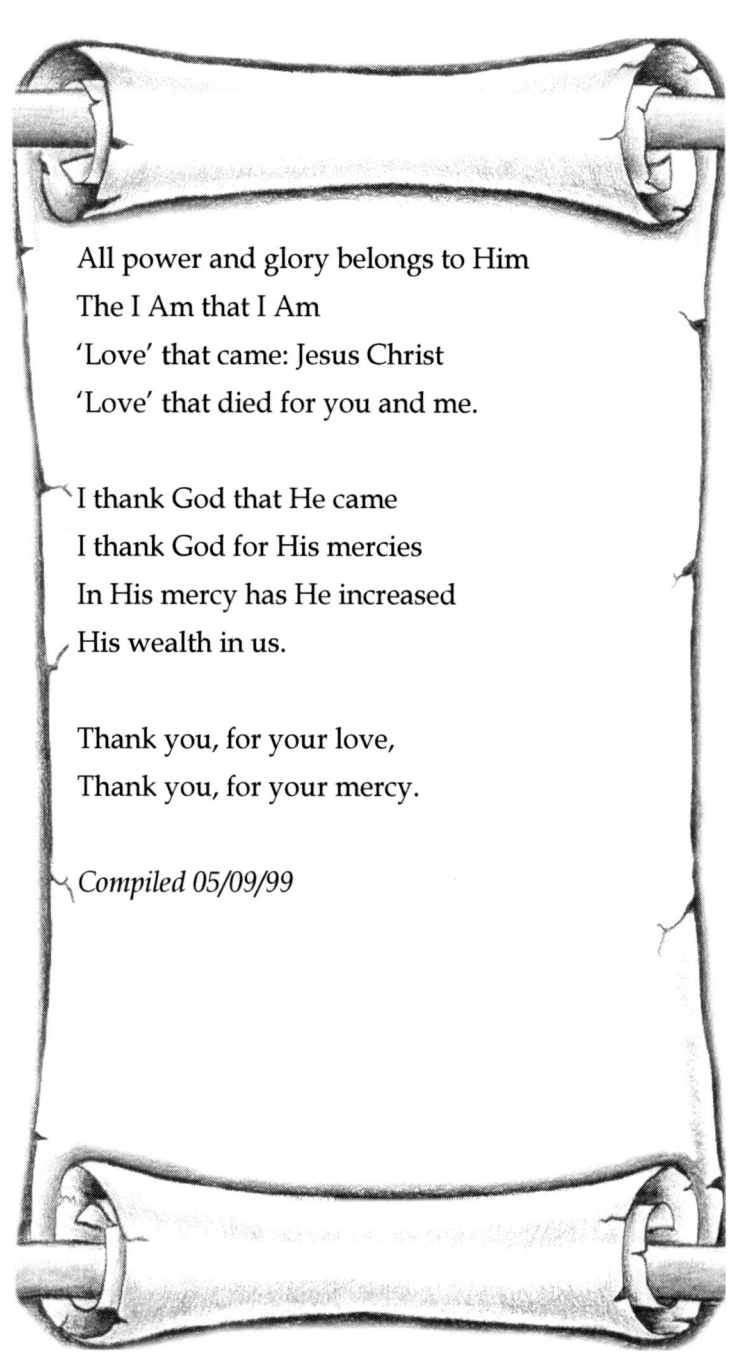

All power and glory belongs to Him
The I Am that I Am
'Love' that came: Jesus Christ
'Love' that died for you and me.

I thank God that He came
I thank God for His mercies
In His mercy has He increased
His wealth in us.

Thank you, for your love,
Thank you, for your mercy.

Compiled 05/09/99

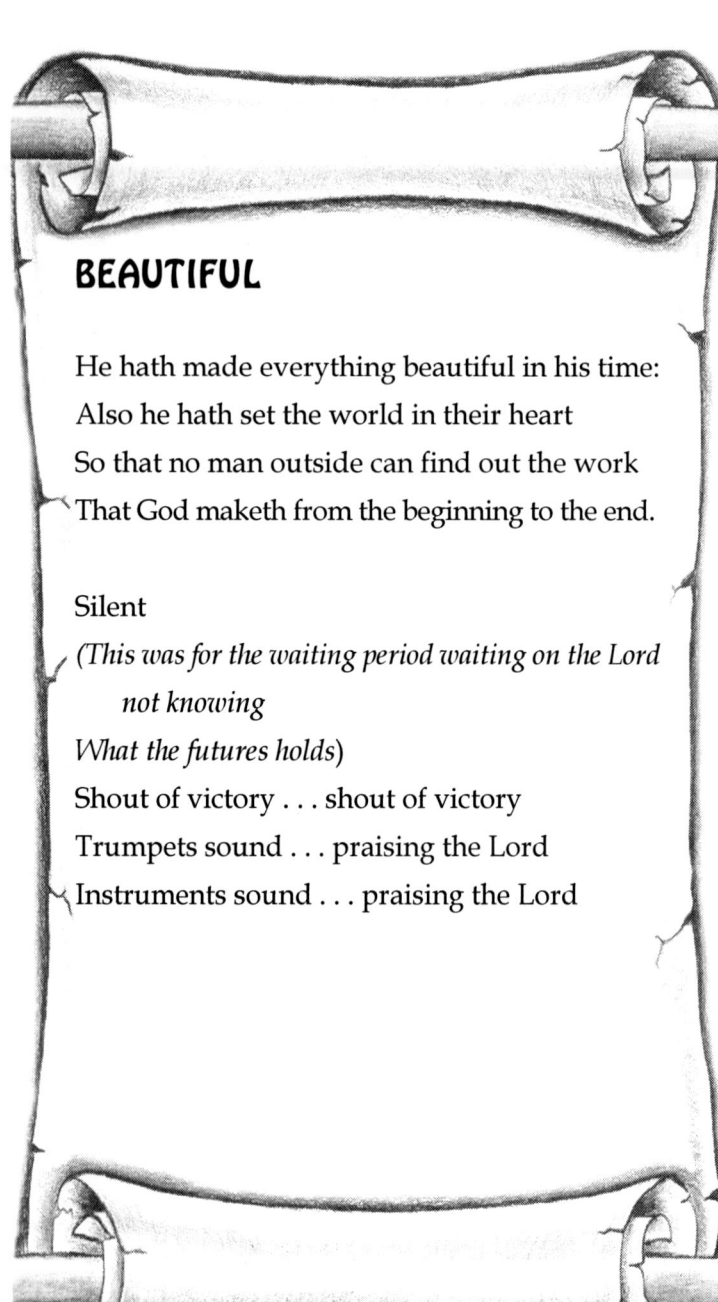

BEAUTIFUL

He hath made everything beautiful in his time:
Also he hath set the world in their heart
So that no man outside can find out the work
That God maketh from the beginning to the end.

Silent
*(This was for the waiting period waiting on the Lord
    not knowing*
What the futures holds)
Shout of victory . . . shout of victory
Trumpets sound . . . praising the Lord
Instruments sound . . . praising the Lord

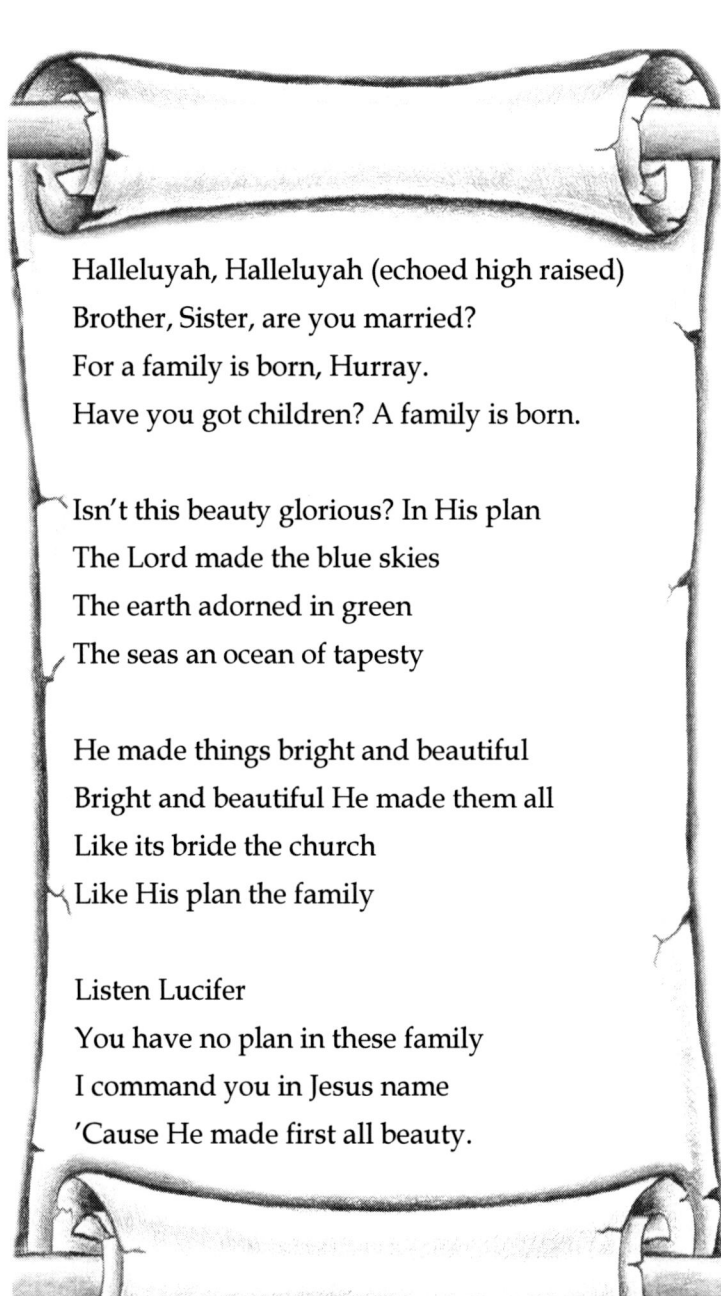

Halleluyah, Halleluyah (echoed high raised)
Brother, Sister, are you married?
For a family is born, Hurray.
Have you got children? A family is born.

Isn't this beauty glorious? In His plan
The Lord made the blue skies
The earth adorned in green
The seas an ocean of tapesty

He made things bright and beautiful
Bright and beautiful He made them all
Like its bride the church
Like His plan the family

Listen Lucifer
You have no plan in these family
I command you in Jesus name
'Cause He made first all beauty.

Listen!
Music lodged in Him is beauty
Man lodged in Him is beauty
Where is your beauty lodged?

Come:
That your beauty may be lodged in Him.

THE HOLY SPIRIT

Good morning Holy Spirit
Dearest of friends welcome
Welcome in thy 'Beautiful Regalia'
To adorn and prepare me for the journey

Good morning Holy Spirit
The one seen upon the wings of the wind
Sitted at the right hand of God
The seal of God

Good morning Holy Spirit
Third member of the Holy Trinity
The 'One' sent to lead you and I
In the journey to make it to Heaven

No doubt you and I need 'Him'
In the morning every time of the time
Have you said Good Morning to Him today?
Make it a specific time, place, moment.

THANK GOD FOR RCCG TOTTENHAM BRANCH

Thank God for our Leader
Pastor Raphael Olurotimi
Thank God for our church
Initially based in Tottenham
Thank God for the church
Thank God for His love in the church
Thank God for His care to the church

For the church has brought
Smiles, hope and life to tender hearts
Hearts of pain becomes filled with
The life of God, promises of God
Thank God for the man and woman
After the heart of God and used as a vessel to honour
For healing, deliverance, marriages, family.

A heart to a heart in Him
Is a mind of love in Him
Continue . . . .
RCCG Tottenham in this act of love.

Compiled 03/01/97
Updated 06/04/13

ZOE: LIFE OF GOD

Zoe is the life of God
Do you have a life?
Where is the life?
Is it in blood or the blood of Jesus?

You have a life today, why?
Is it to give life?
Is it to take life?
Why?

Ponder to know your purpose?
For the life of God is for a purpose
A purpose tailored to your purpose
A design just for you to the epilogue of time.

The fool says in his heart there is no God
When He creates His life in man

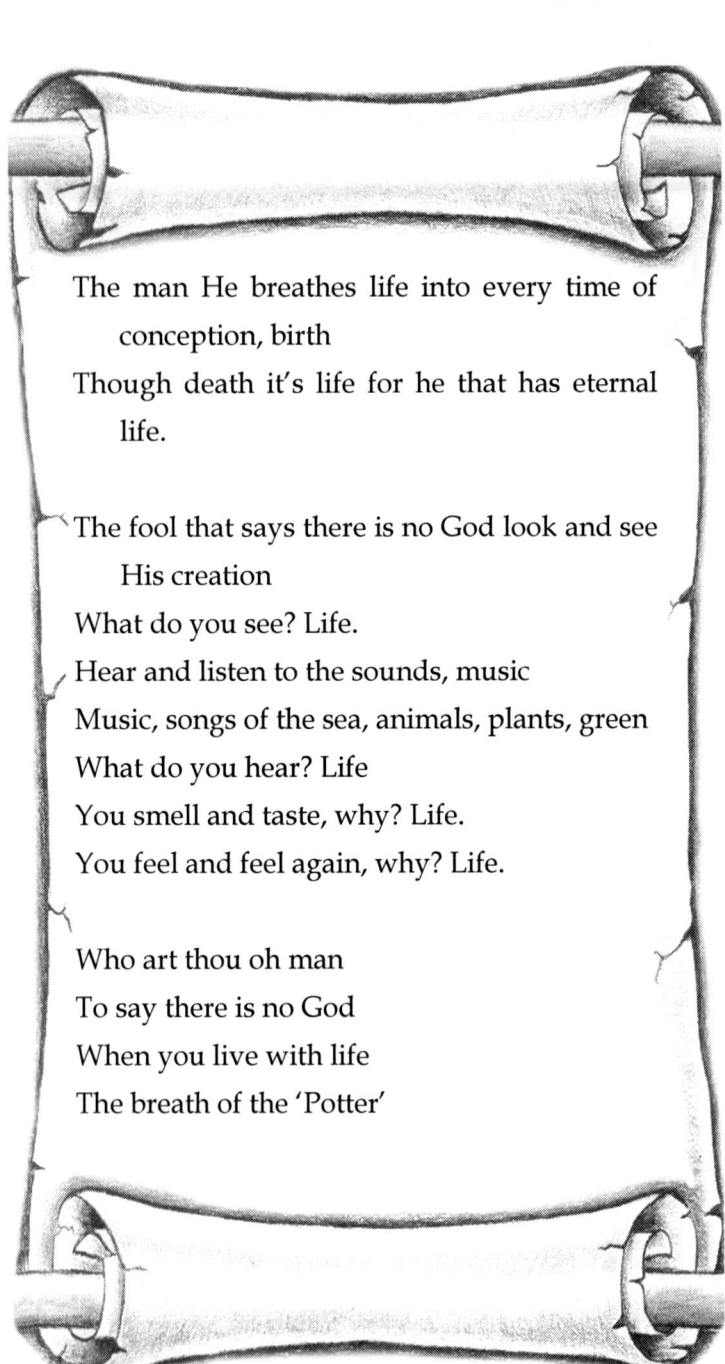

The man He breathes life into every time of conception, birth
Though death it's life for he that has eternal life.

The fool that says there is no God look and see His creation
What do you see? Life.
Hear and listen to the sounds, music
Music, songs of the sea, animals, plants, green
What do you hear? Life
You smell and taste, why? Life.
You feel and feel again, why? Life.

Who art thou oh man
To say there is no God
When you live with life
The breath of the 'Potter'

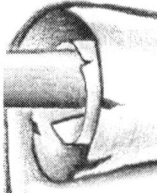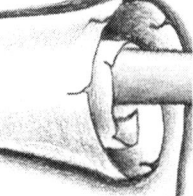

OPEN YOUR EYES

Are your eyes open or closed?
Open your eyes leave it wide open
Like that of the eagle 'cause the enemy is at hand
Seeking to destroy our children, the family, the church

Have all your bells ringing now
I have mine ringing as I know
The vulture like the roaring lion is out for your chicks
The vulture though out has lost it on the cross

Mothers fight for your children fathers fight for your children
The battle had been won on the cross so no fear
Speak out the word, your victory, your faith
Receive the authority you have in the word

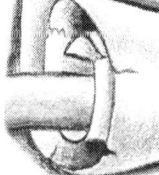

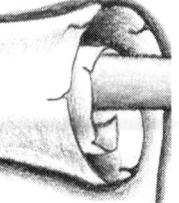

Open your eyes, mind, soul and spirit
It is high time your senses were opened
Father, Mother pray together to agree for your children
For your children is your seed, your heritage, your future

Father, Mother work together to free your children
Dishonour any iota of conflict that gives access to the enemy
Fight, separation, divorce, sin that separate the family
Fight the enemy not your wife, husband, son, daughter or yourself.

Remember,
A broom only come together to sweep away dirt

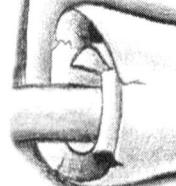

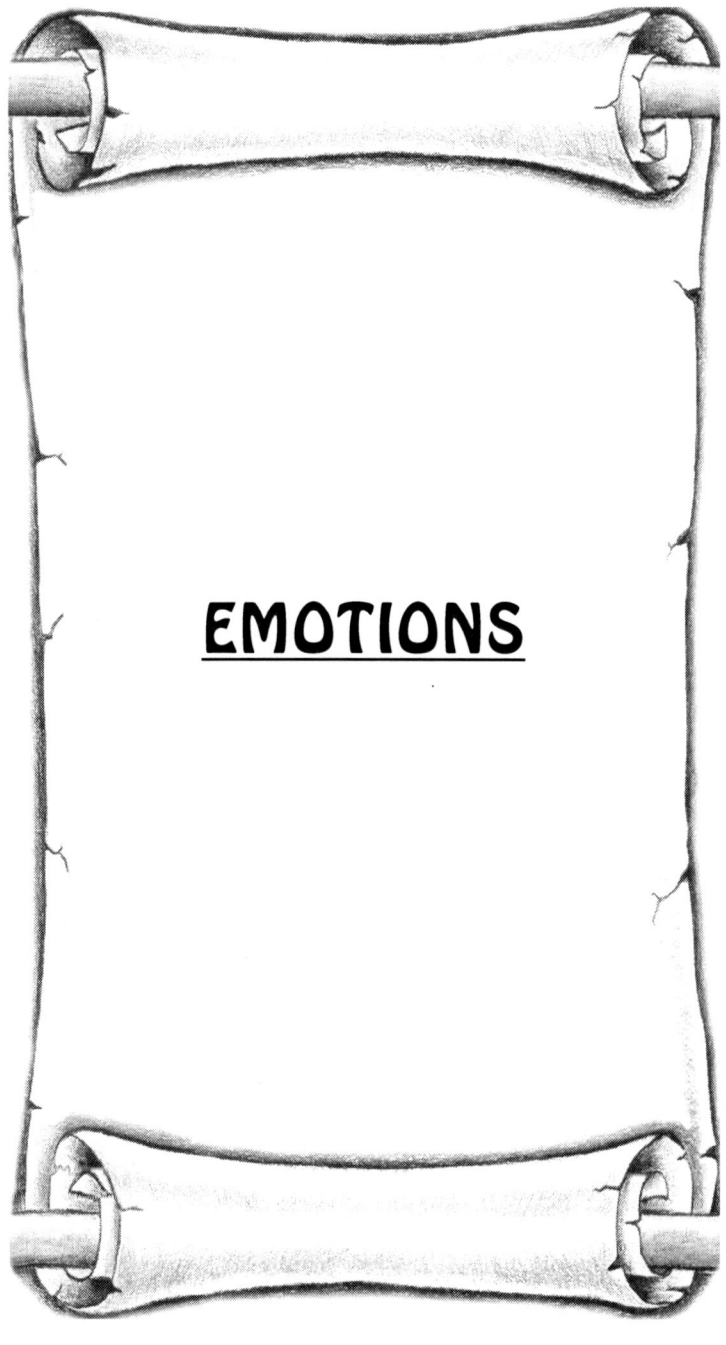

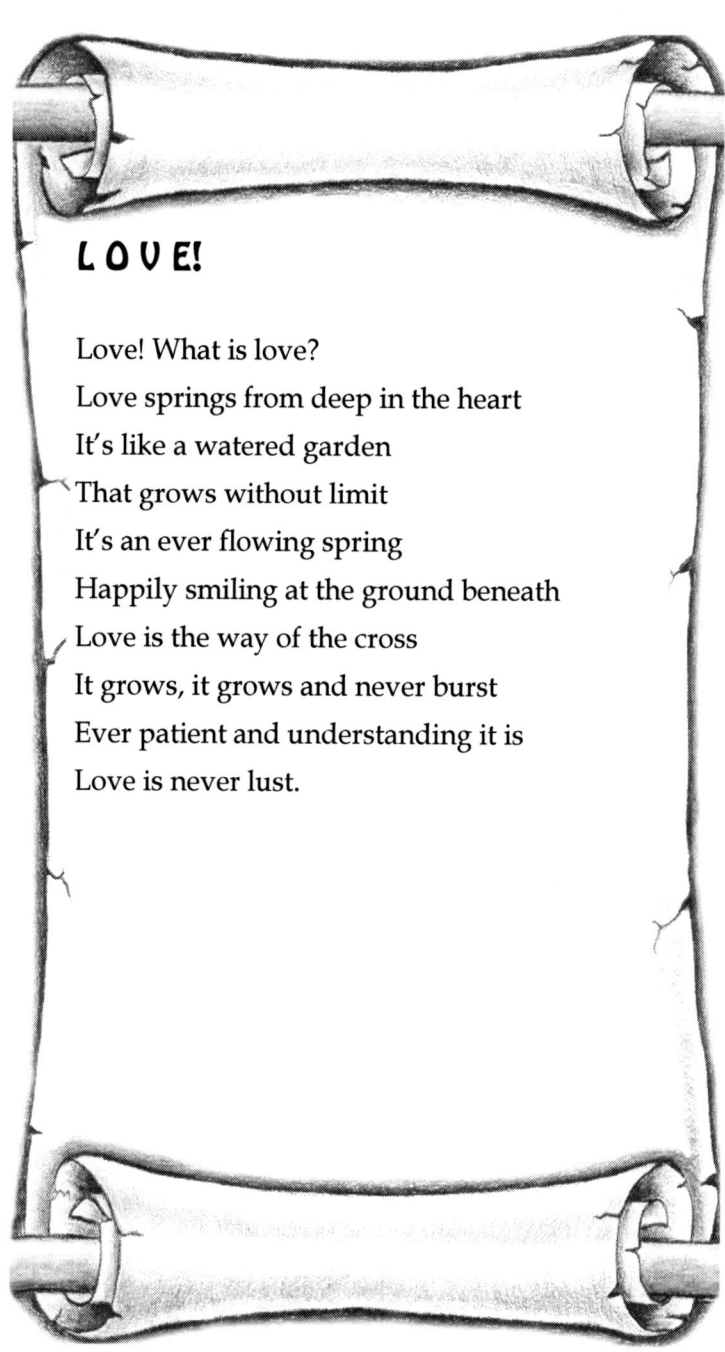

LOVE!

Love! What is love?
Love springs from deep in the heart
It's like a watered garden
That grows without limit
It's an ever flowing spring
Happily smiling at the ground beneath
Love is the way of the cross
It grows, it grows and never burst
Ever patient and understanding it is
Love is never lust.

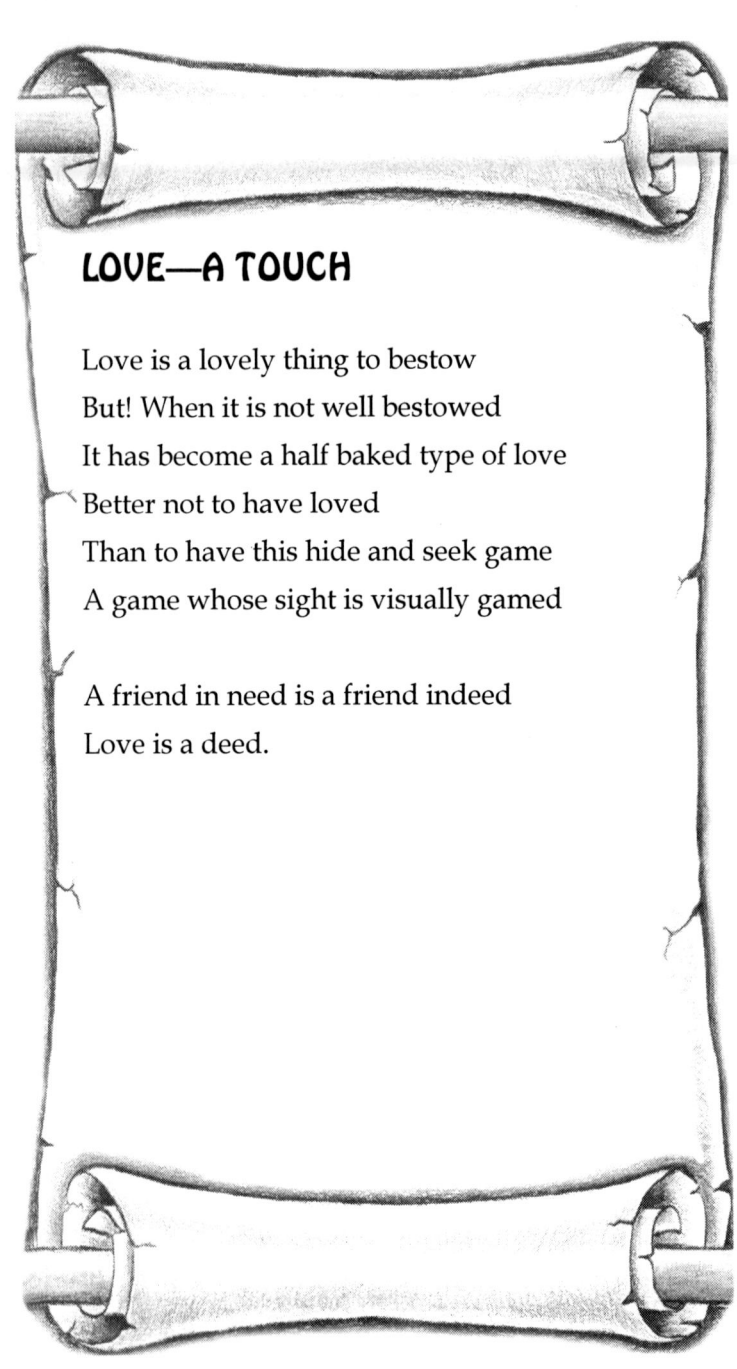

LOVE—A TOUCH

Love is a lovely thing to bestow
But! When it is not well bestowed
It has become a half baked type of love
Better not to have loved
Than to have this hide and seek game
A game whose sight is visually gamed

A friend in need is a friend indeed
Love is a deed.

HATRED

Hatred is a state of mind,
An inbuilt evil
Which spreads to the other parts
Like a drop of oil.

The act brings not joy to him
Nor does it take joy to the unlucky
It pulls down the heart, the body, the soul
Of his victim deep down below till his spirit kisses grave

The victim is full of cloudy air his sight gurged out
'Cause his sight sees no more good
No bright light is able to penetrate as it is hard to reach the heart
Even at the simplest of time as fire has engulfed the heart.

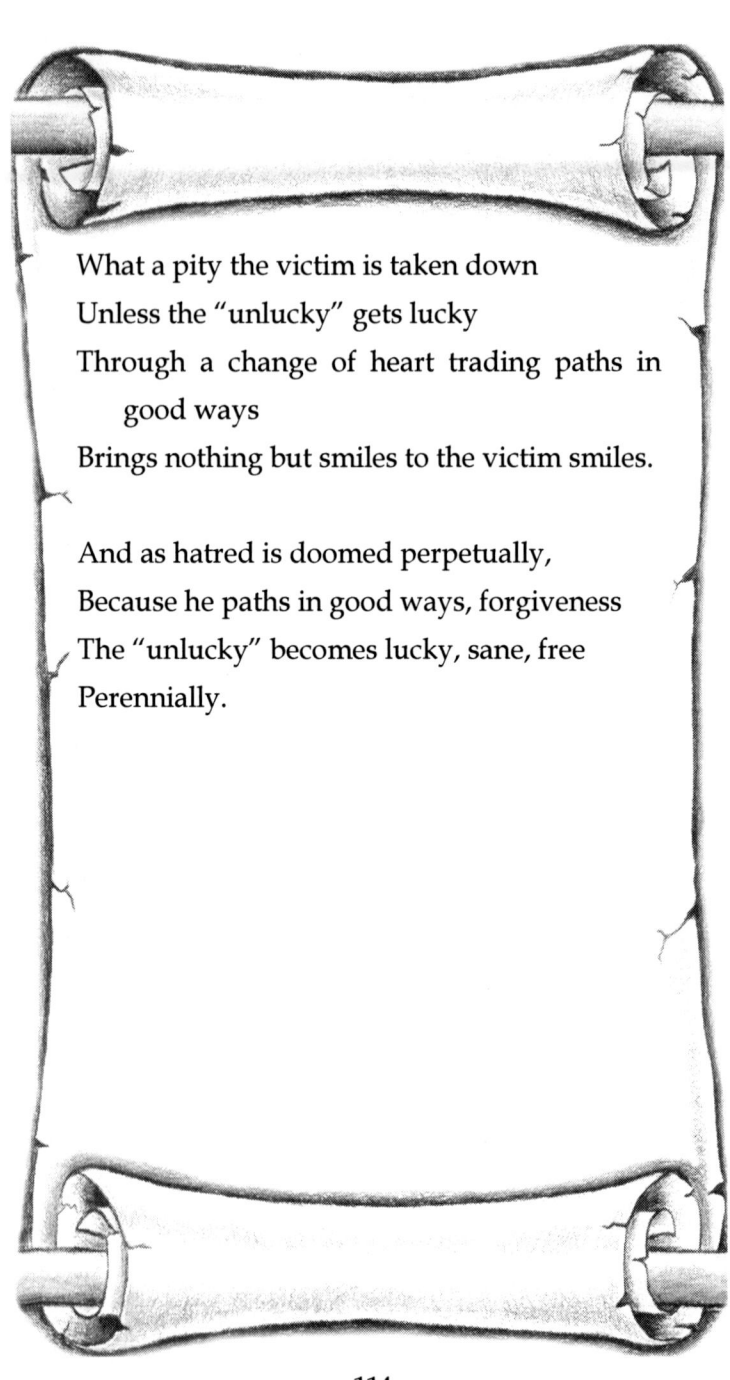

What a pity the victim is taken down
Unless the "unlucky" gets lucky
Through a change of heart trading paths in good ways
Brings nothing but smiles to the victim smiles.

And as hatred is doomed perpetually,
Because he paths in good ways, forgiveness
The "unlucky" becomes lucky, sane, free
Perennially.

FEAR

Are your scared, afraid, worried?
Are you full of fear?
Why?
Is it because of past experiences?

Is it because of current experiences?
Is it because of future experiences?
Why?
Is it because of unknown reasons?

A man stated FEAR as:
False Evidence Appearing Real
Do not allow it conquer you
Conquer it set your mind free

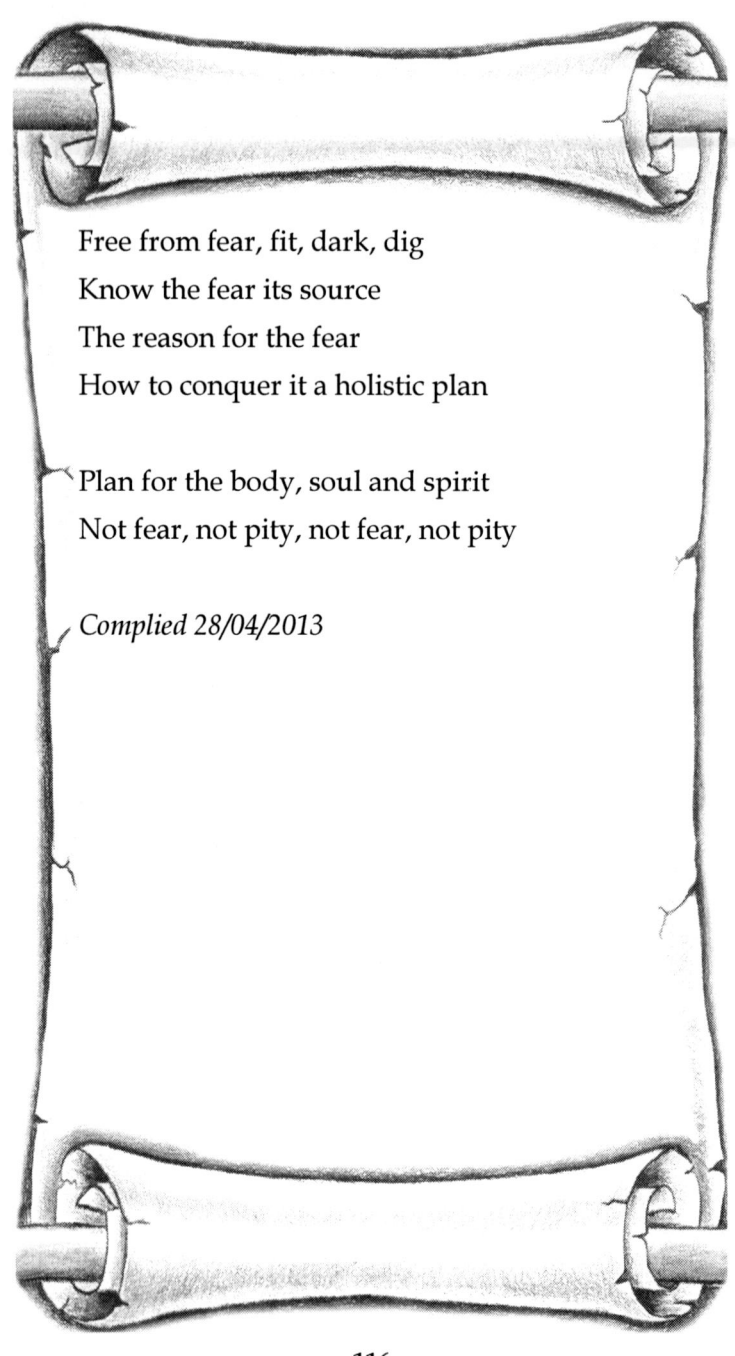

Free from fear, fit, dark, dig
Know the fear its source
The reason for the fear
How to conquer it a holistic plan

Plan for the body, soul and spirit
Not fear, not pity, not fear, not pity

Complied 28/04/2013

A NAUGHTY GIRL

In the life of a man
He thinks of what to tan
In His glory He perfects thoughts
Led by the spirit in thoughts.

Amongst men lived, lives
Always will live a maiden
Who in zeal seeketh Him
Does she listen to the Searcher?

Does she carry out His will?
Not to His best
She consciously unconsciously disobey
What a naughty girl.

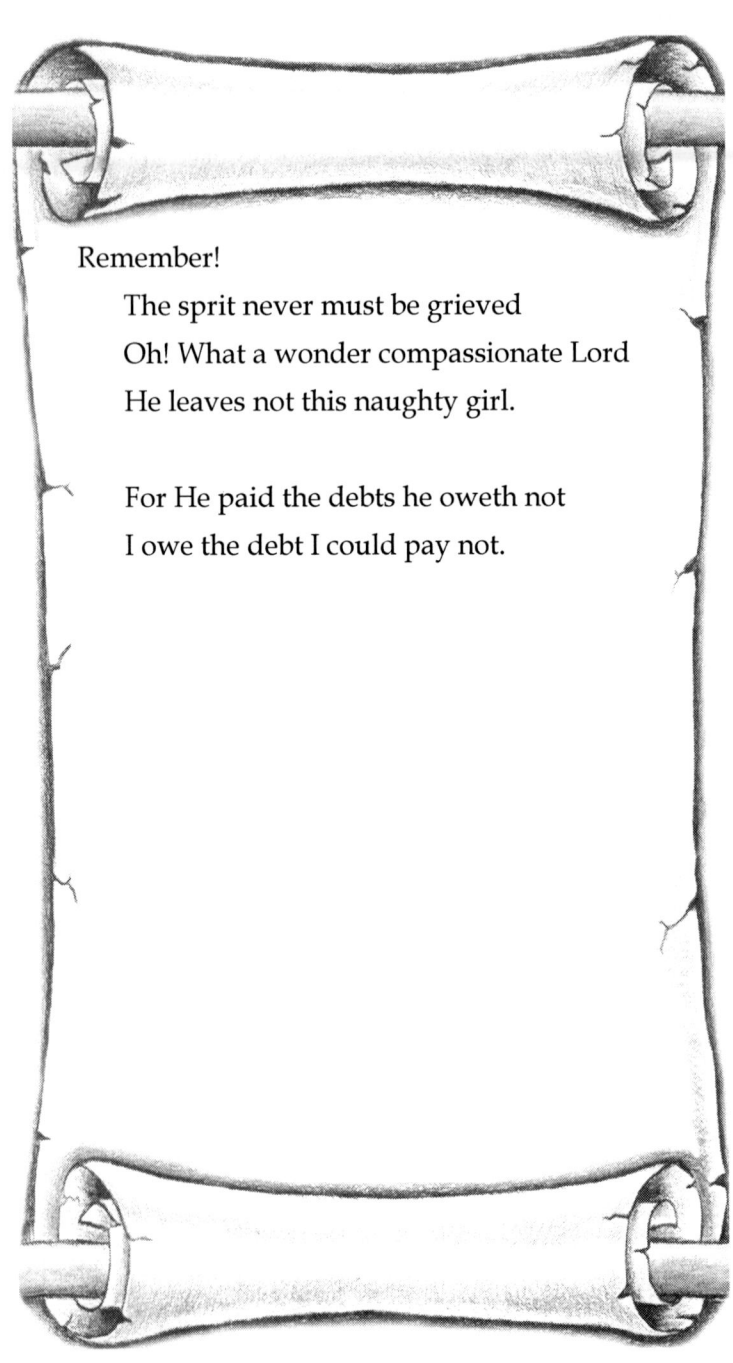

Remember!

    The sprit never must be grieved
    Oh! What a wonder compassionate Lord
    He leaves not this naughty girl.

    For He paid the debts he oweth not
    I owe the debt I could pay not.

A NIGHT TO GROW

"Satan is a liar"
A line often said time and time again
He claims to be head
When he's nothing but a tail
> I became wild
> At the touch of the cane.

We are in the 90's
Persecution! Persecution
Temptations! Temptations
> Beware brother beware sister
> Lest you get caught in lucifer's own web

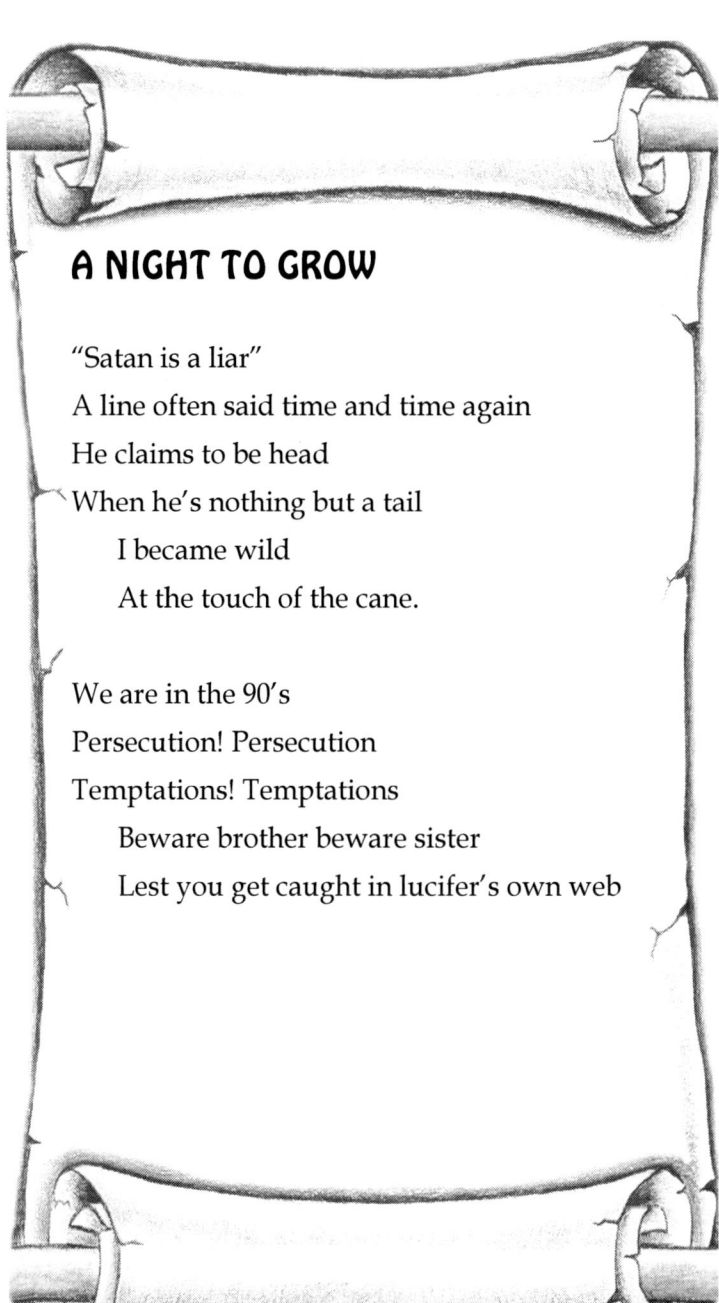

Only through prayer, our link with Christ
Let Him be gloried at all times;
Let him be shamed at all times
As we spend our days in grace and trials
    Beware brother Beware sister
    Beware.

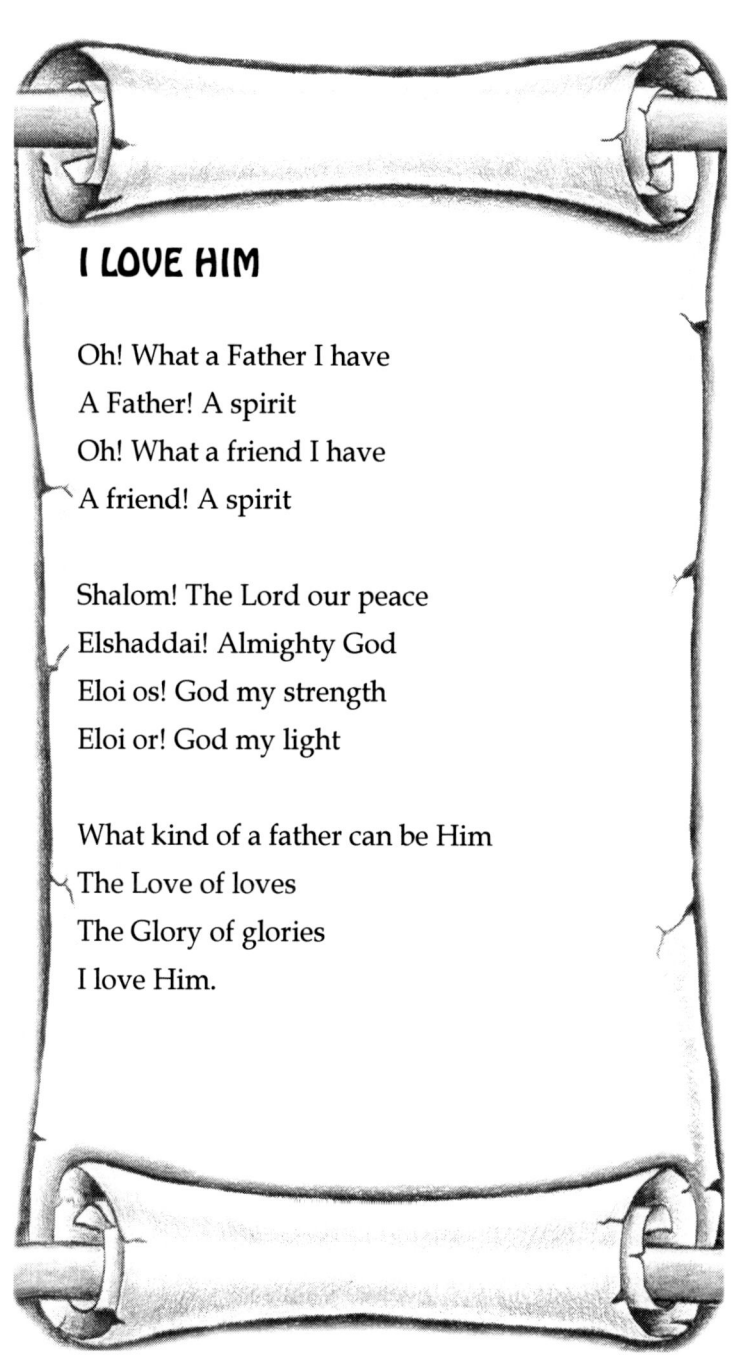

I LOVE HIM

Oh! What a Father I have
A Father! A spirit
Oh! What a friend I have
A friend! A spirit

Shalom! The Lord our peace
Elshaddai! Almighty God
Eloi os! God my strength
Eloi or! God my light

What kind of a father can be Him
The Love of loves
The Glory of glories
I love Him.

Jehovah Shamma! The Lord is present
Jehovah Hanan! The gracious Lord
I love Him

>Forgive me
>Holy Spirit

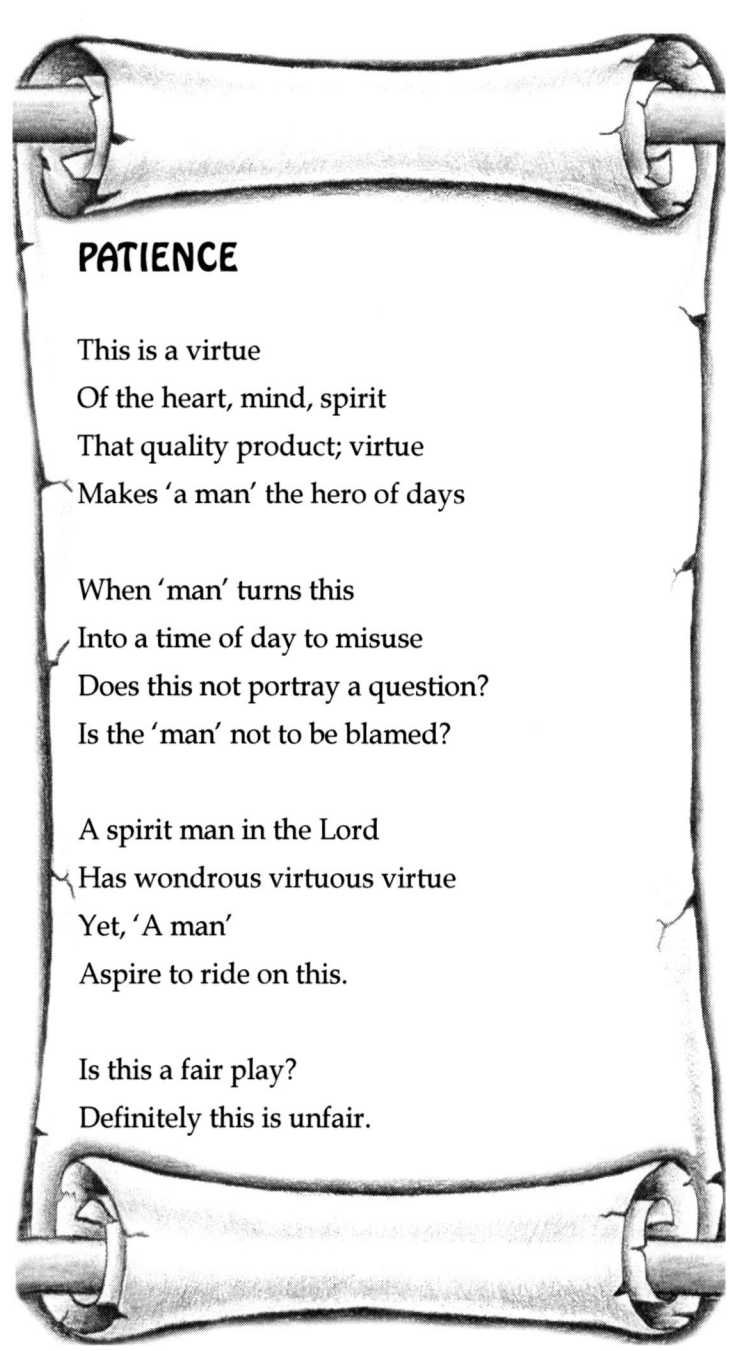

PATIENCE

This is a virtue
Of the heart, mind, spirit
That quality product; virtue
Makes 'a man' the hero of days

When 'man' turns this
Into a time of day to misuse
Does this not portray a question?
Is the 'man' not to be blamed?

A spirit man in the Lord
Has wondrous virtuous virtue
Yet, 'A man'
Aspire to ride on this.

Is this a fair play?
Definitely this is unfair.

L-O-V-E

Love is like a piece of metal
Round about you
Love is genuinely genuine
Love flows like water.

He flows out to the dead ends
He touches bare barks
He reaches with mighty victories
Love reaches in perfectness.

Lord God is love
He is excellent in love
He is wondrous in love
Love is holy.

Praise, praise, praise
Sing a shout of praise
Sing a shout of praise
To the Most High Love.

Love is love
Lord is love.

I WANT A MAN

I want a man after the heart of Jesus
A man enclosed in His love
Enclosed but in awe of Him
In awe like Father to son

I want a man that his script is of love
Love that is of God
Love that covereth multitude of sins
Love that defies divorce

So that the name of the Almighty
Our Lord Jesus Christ
May be glorified and exalted
Above all

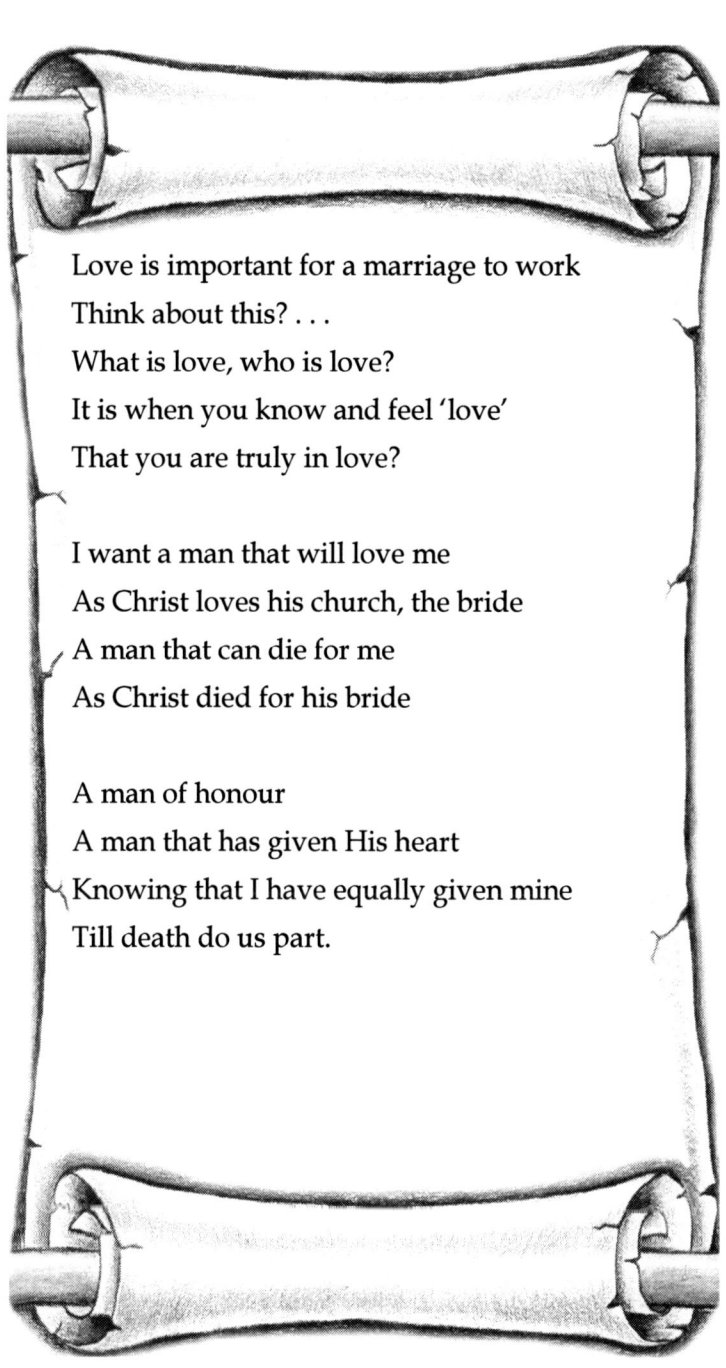

Love is important for a marriage to work
Think about this? . . .
What is love, who is love?
It is when you know and feel 'love'
That you are truly in love?

I want a man that will love me
As Christ loves his church, the bride
A man that can die for me
As Christ died for his bride

A man of honour
A man that has given His heart
Knowing that I have equally given mine
Till death do us part.

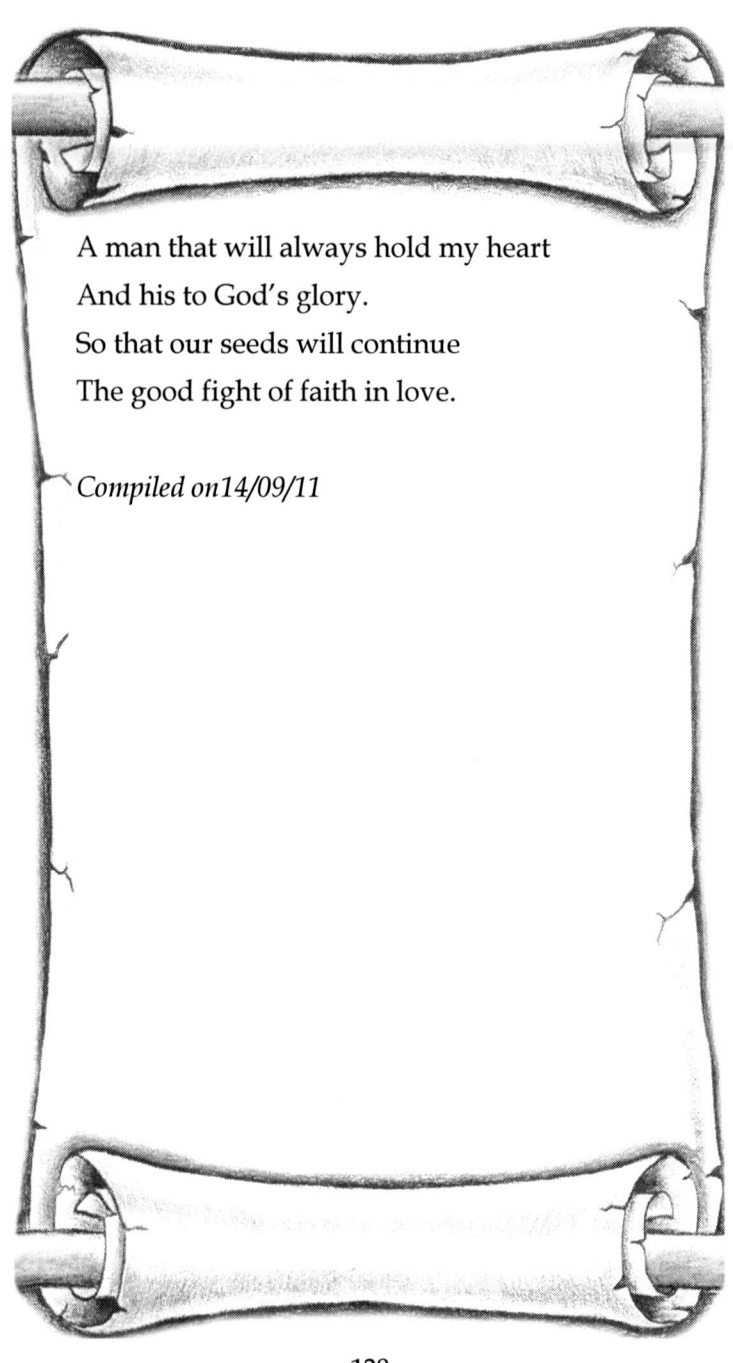

A man that will always hold my heart
And his to God's glory.
So that our seeds will continue
The good fight of faith in love.

Compiled on 14/09/11

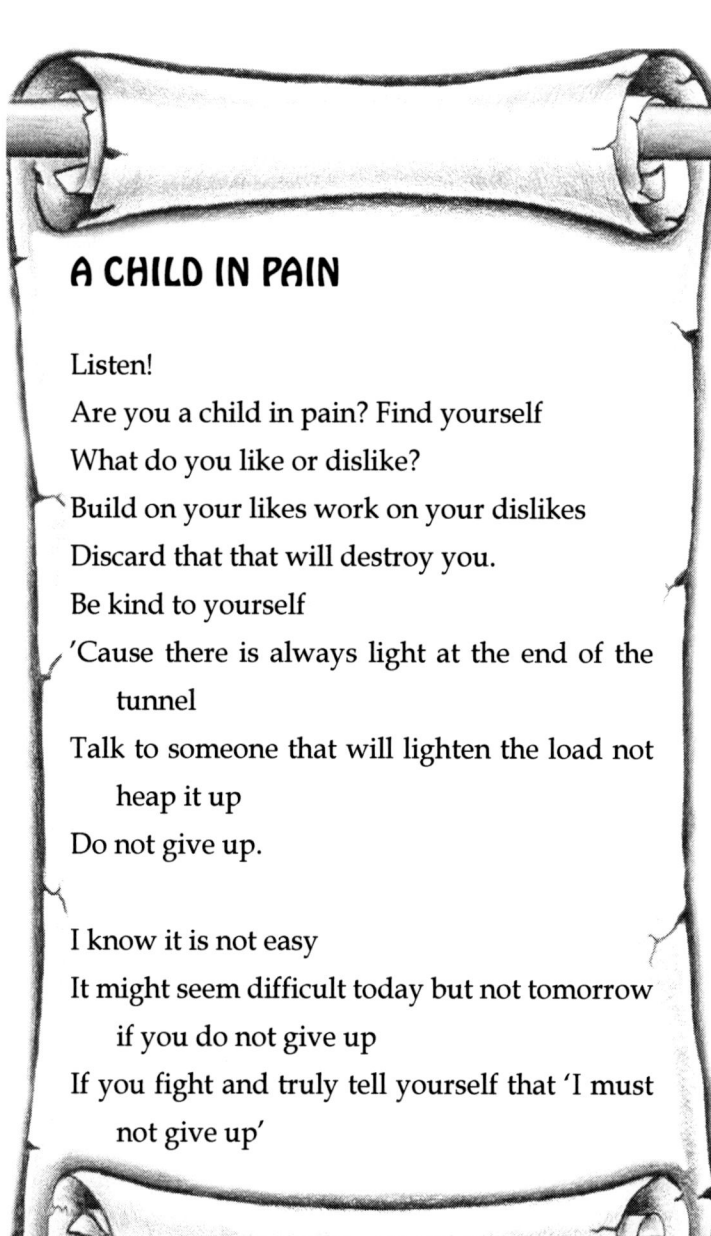

A CHILD IN PAIN

Listen!
Are you a child in pain? Find yourself
What do you like or dislike?
Build on your likes work on your dislikes
Discard that that will destroy you.
Be kind to yourself
'Cause there is always light at the end of the tunnel
Talk to someone that will lighten the load not heap it up
Do not give up.

I know it is not easy
It might seem difficult today but not tomorrow if you do not give up
If you fight and truly tell yourself that 'I must not give up'

Say it! Now. Repeat it! Now. Again and again
I will not give up but will make it as there is light at the end of my tunnel

I plead with you
Do not gradually hurt or kill yourself through
Cutting your hand, stomach or body
Thinking negatively about yourself
Believing in other peoples' opinion of you
Staving yourself to look thin because of how you feel today
Because of what another person wants you to look like for their benefit

Joining gangs or bad influence for your loved ones attention, revenge, built up pain to hatred
Joining gangs to belong, look strong from outside but full of pains inside

Drinking alcohol or taking illegal drugs

Planning any type of illicit or secret harm to yourself or other

Just because you just want to because you no longer care

Or you feel, think, say or see that someone does not love you

Or you are no longer loved and you seek that love desperately

Do not give up, have faith.

Listen; have someone told you that 'I do not care'

Listen, you do not know me and 'I care'

Stand up and do the right thing about how you feel pain

Let it all go out, out and out forever by receiving the right help.

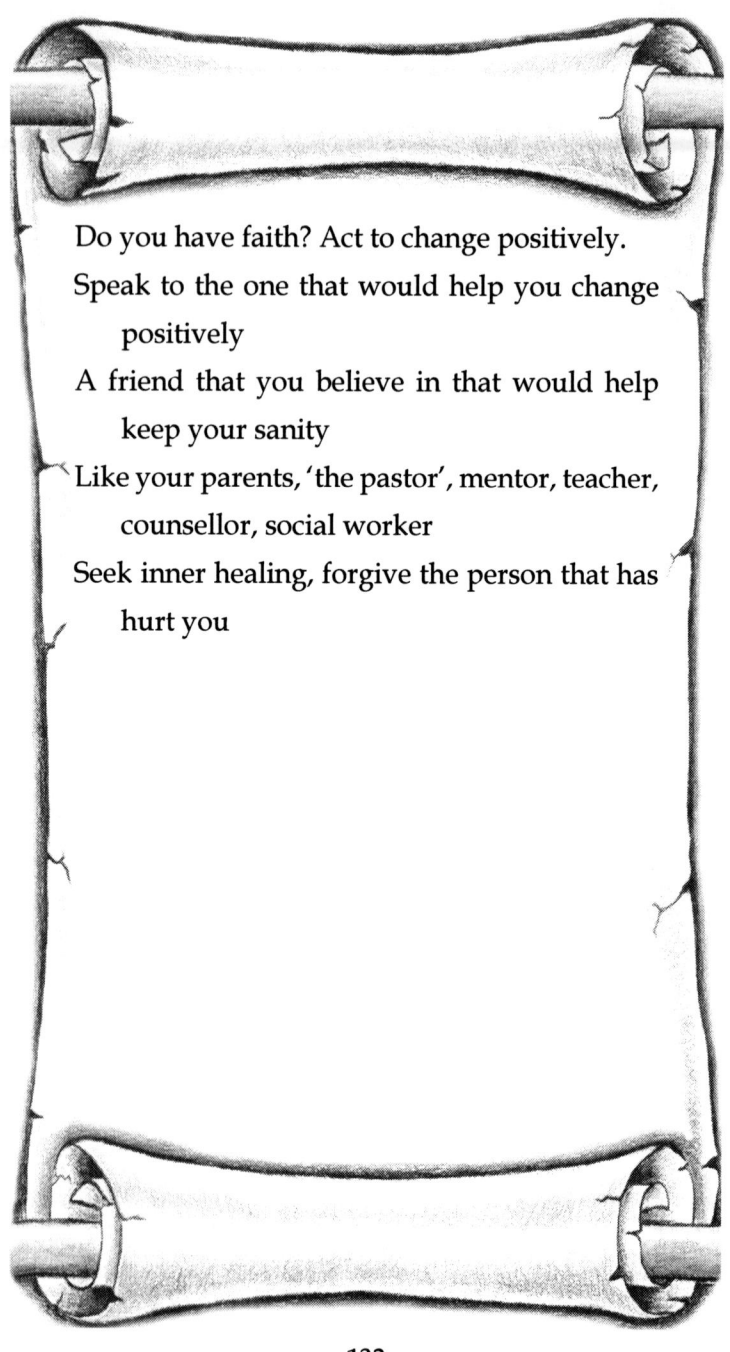

Do you have faith? Act to change positively.

Speak to the one that would help you change positively

A friend that you believe in that would help keep your sanity

Like your parents, 'the pastor', mentor, teacher, counsellor, social worker

Seek inner healing, forgive the person that has hurt you

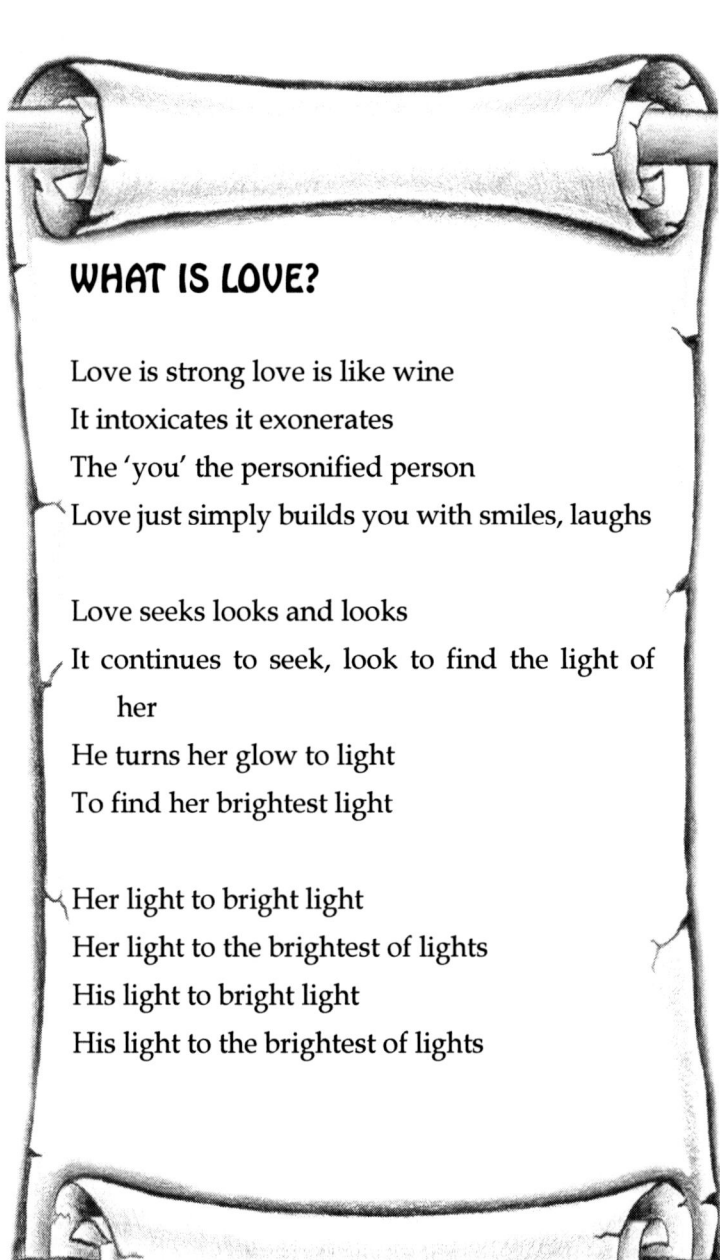

WHAT IS LOVE?

Love is strong love is like wine
It intoxicates it exonerates
The 'you' the personified person
Love just simply builds you with smiles, laughs

Love seeks looks and looks
It continues to seek, look to find the light of her
He turns her glow to light
To find her brightest light

Her light to bright light
Her light to the brightest of lights
His light to bright light
His light to the brightest of lights

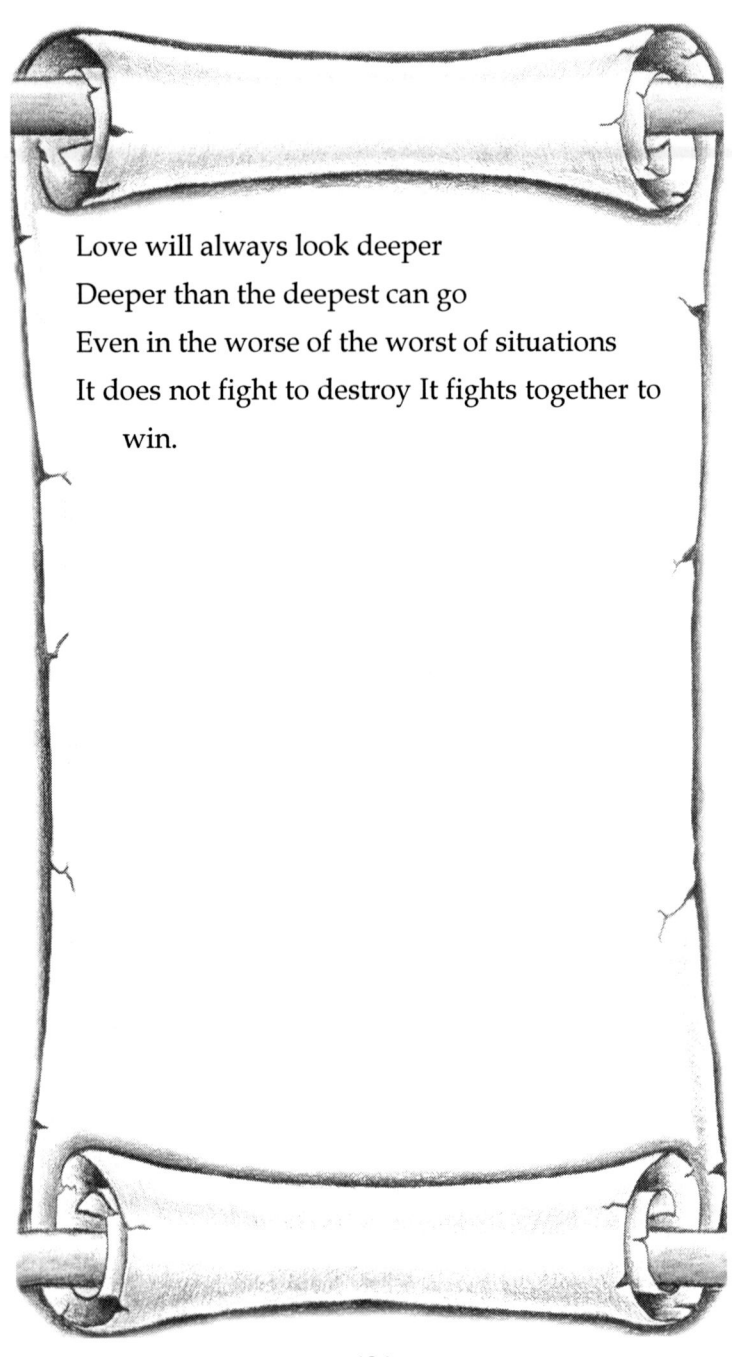

Love will always look deeper
Deeper than the deepest can go
Even in the worse of the worst of situations
It does not fight to destroy It fights together to win.

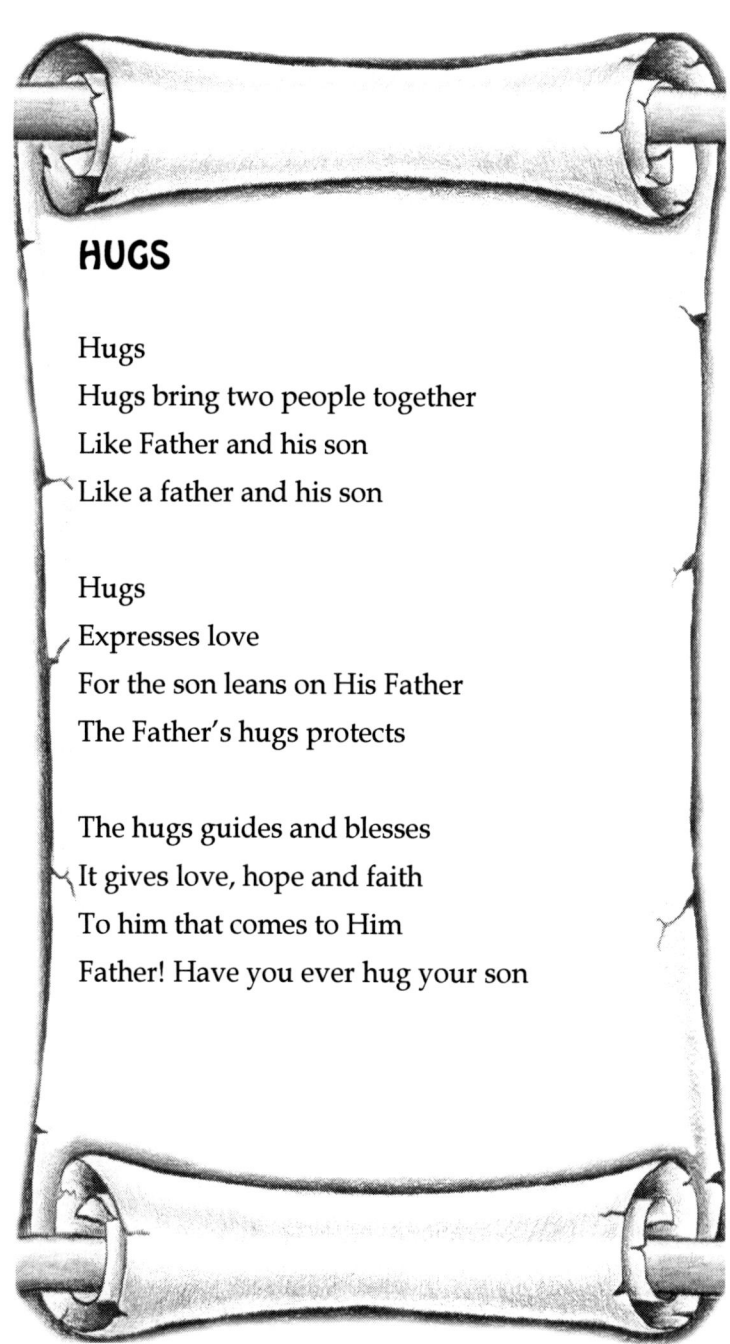

HUGS

Hugs
Hugs bring two people together
Like Father and his son
Like a father and his son

Hugs
Expresses love
For the son leans on His Father
The Father's hugs protects

The hugs guides and blesses
It gives love, hope and faith
To him that comes to Him
Father! Have you ever hug your son

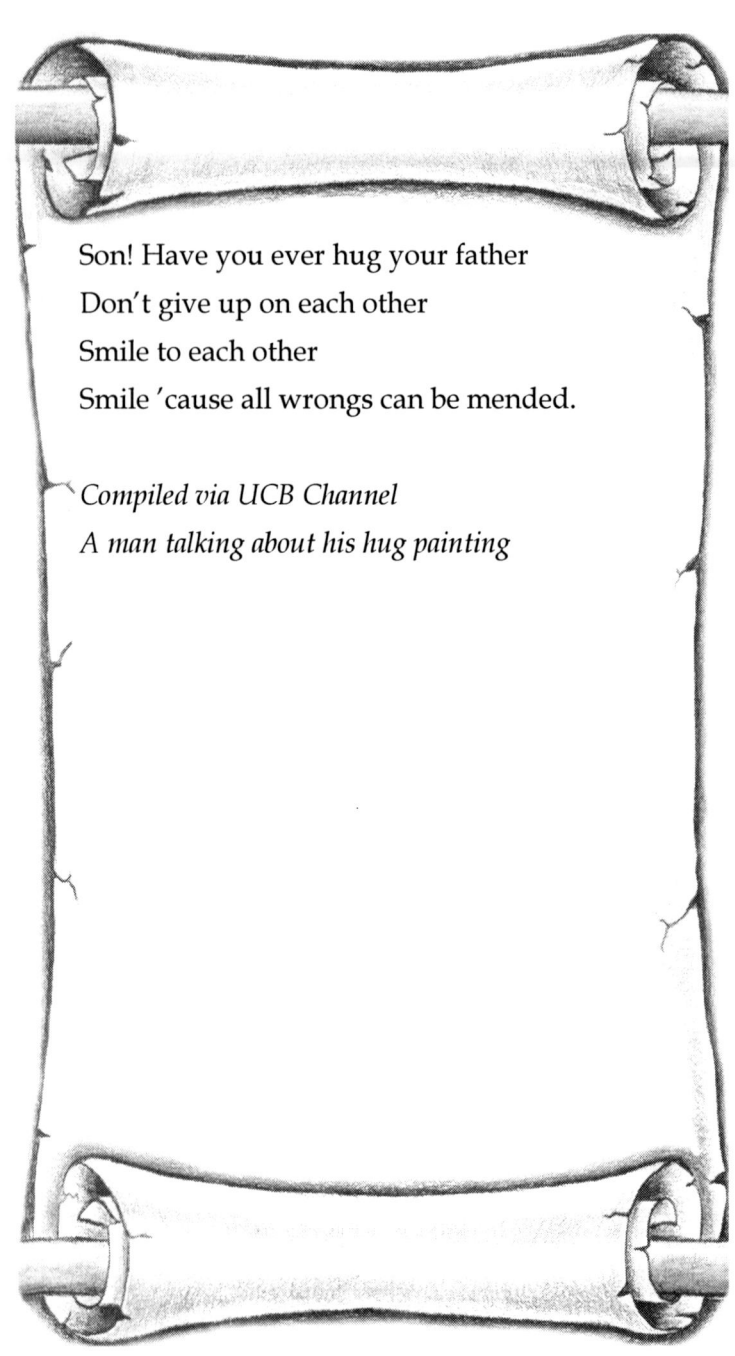

Son! Have you ever hug your father
Don't give up on each other
Smile to each other
Smile 'cause all wrongs can be mended.

Compiled via UCB Channel
A man talking about his hug painting

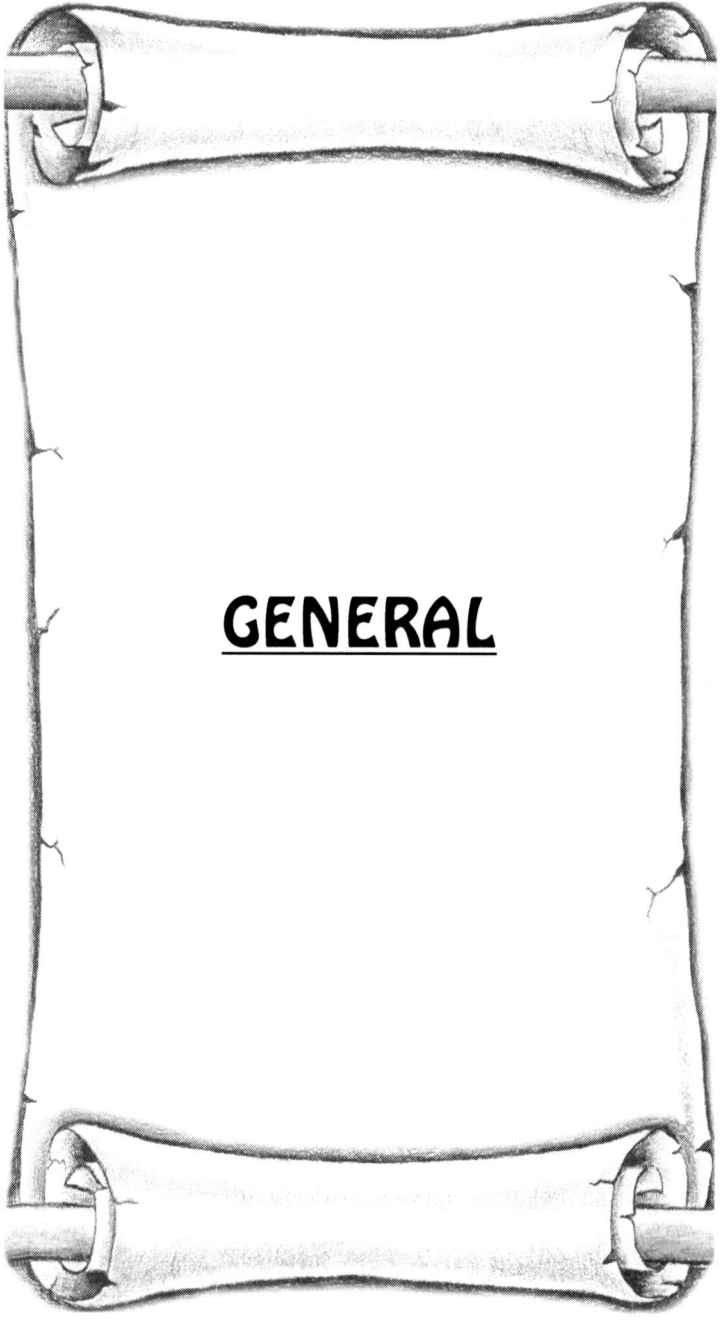

GENERAL

ROYAL WEDDING 29/04/2011

Halleluyah!   29/04/2011
Has finally come with great grandeur of royalty

A day of love, Kate and Will, married to a home not just a house
A day of faith celebrated in church, Westminster Abbey
A day of hope twined together in love and Jesus spirit
A day of life celebrated with people, trees, rolls of tree

Colours Majestic in Colours
Avenue of Trees
Sea of Poppys
Fashion statement and styles

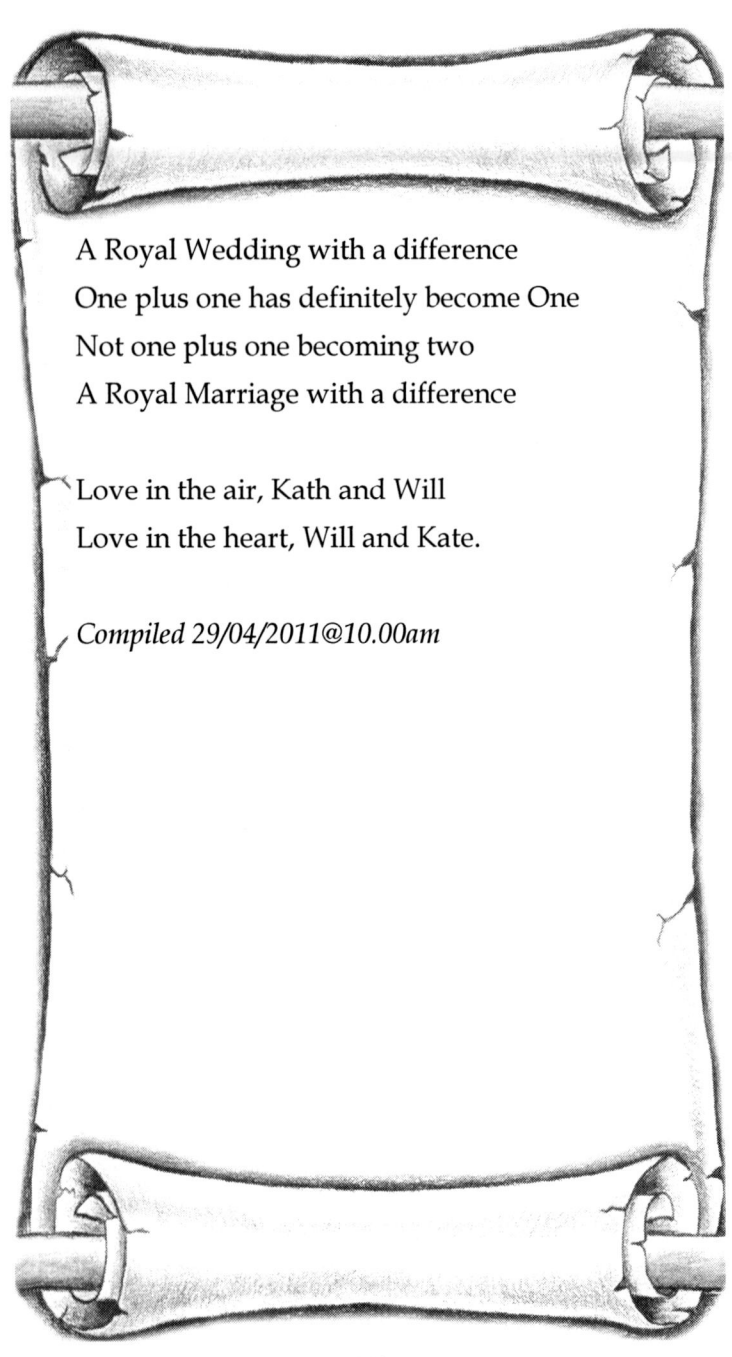

A Royal Wedding with a difference
One plus one has definitely become One
Not one plus one becoming two
A Royal Marriage with a difference

Love in the air, Kath and Will
Love in the heart, Will and Kate.

Compiled 29/04/2011@10.00am

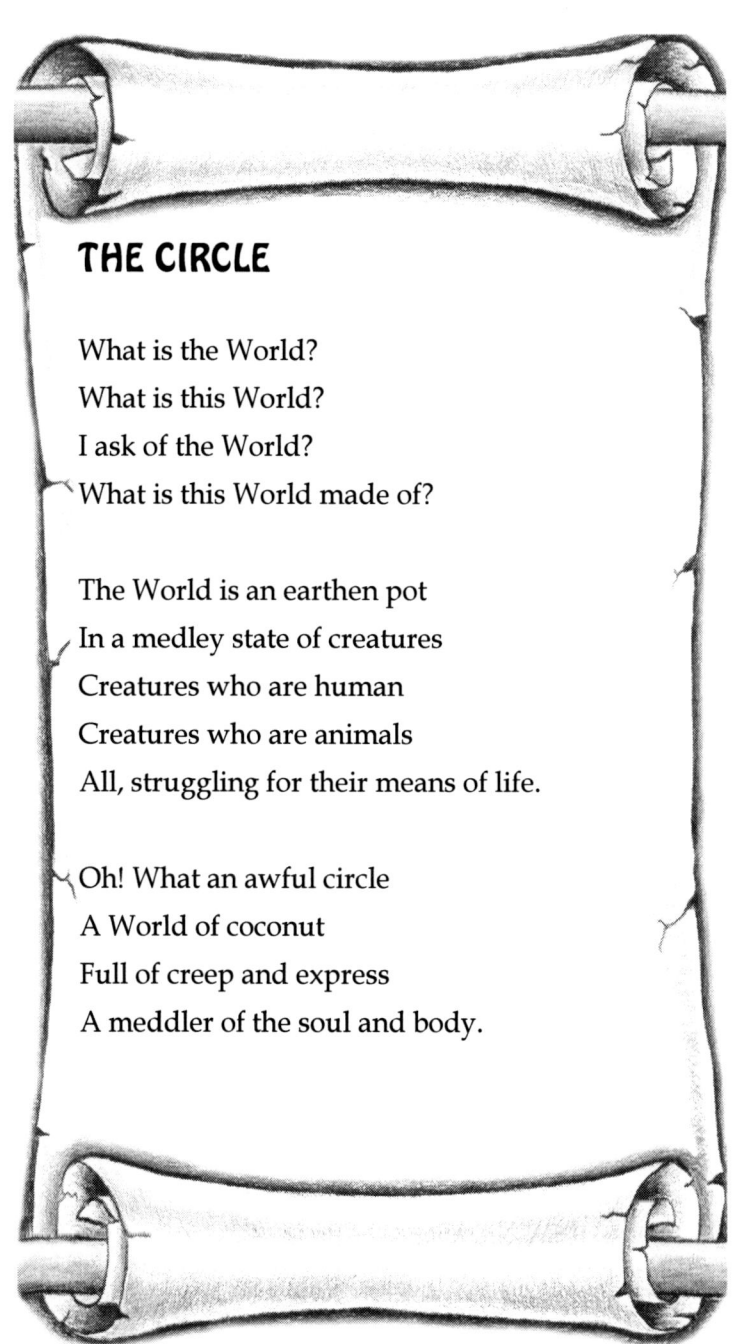

THE CIRCLE

What is the World?
What is this World?
I ask of the World?
What is this World made of?

The World is an earthen pot
In a medley state of creatures
Creatures who are human
Creatures who are animals
All, struggling for their means of life.

Oh! What an awful circle
A World of coconut
Full of creep and express
A meddler of the soul and body.

The World of beautiful horizons
Of running waters and lands
Creatively blessed by the Lord
But Man turned to that of sin.

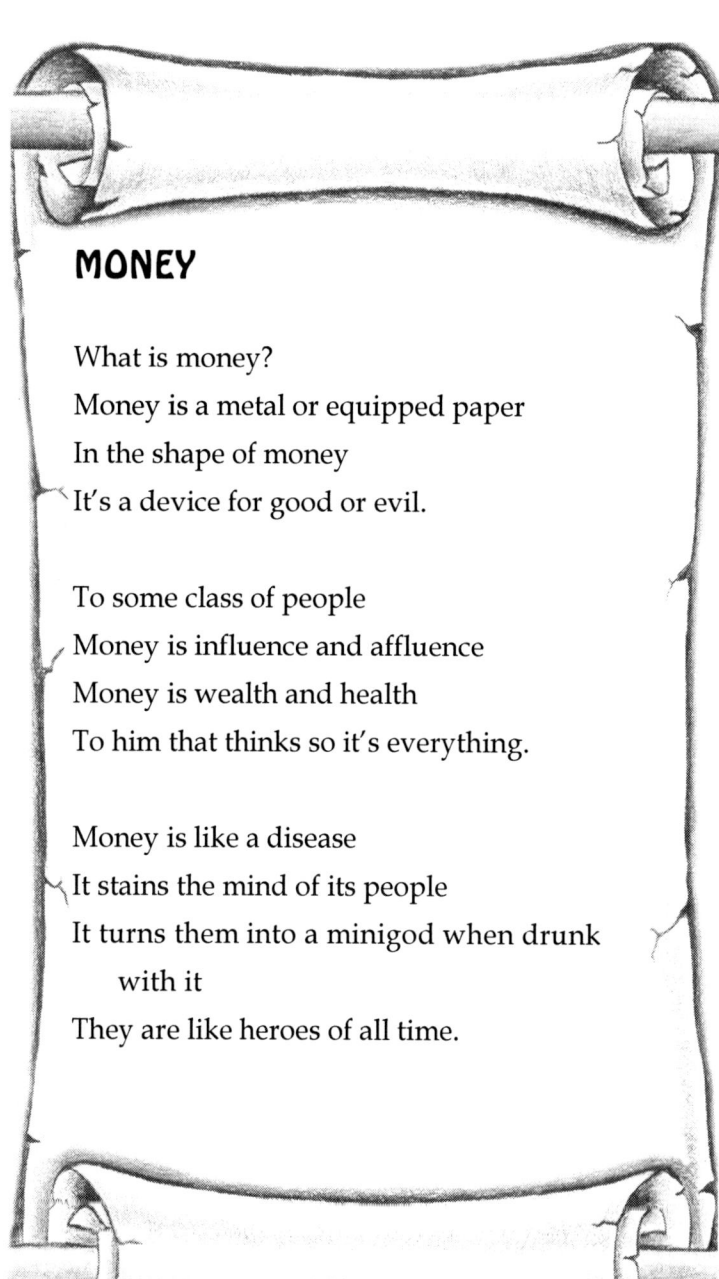

MONEY

What is money?
Money is a metal or equipped paper
In the shape of money
It's a device for good or evil.

To some class of people
Money is influence and affluence
Money is wealth and health
To him that thinks so it's everything.

Money is like a disease
It stains the mind of its people
It turns them into a minigod when drunk
    with it
They are like heroes of all time.

Money is nothing only something if serving
It cannot buy the word of God
It cannot bring lasting hope or love
Its anything you interest with for the existence of life.

SANITY

A mad man knows not sanity
A evil heart knows not sanity
A heart of unforgiveness knows not sanity
A man in the heart of the devil know not sanity

Of which are you or which are you?
Mad man because you are wicked or evil?
Mad man because you harbour unforgiveness
Mad man because of a chemical reaction or genealogy

Have a change of heart before it's too late?
'Cause the cure of your madness is to forgive
Search your heart, confess, repent, forgive and forgive again
Seek counsel, seek deliverance, seek health, seek deliverance

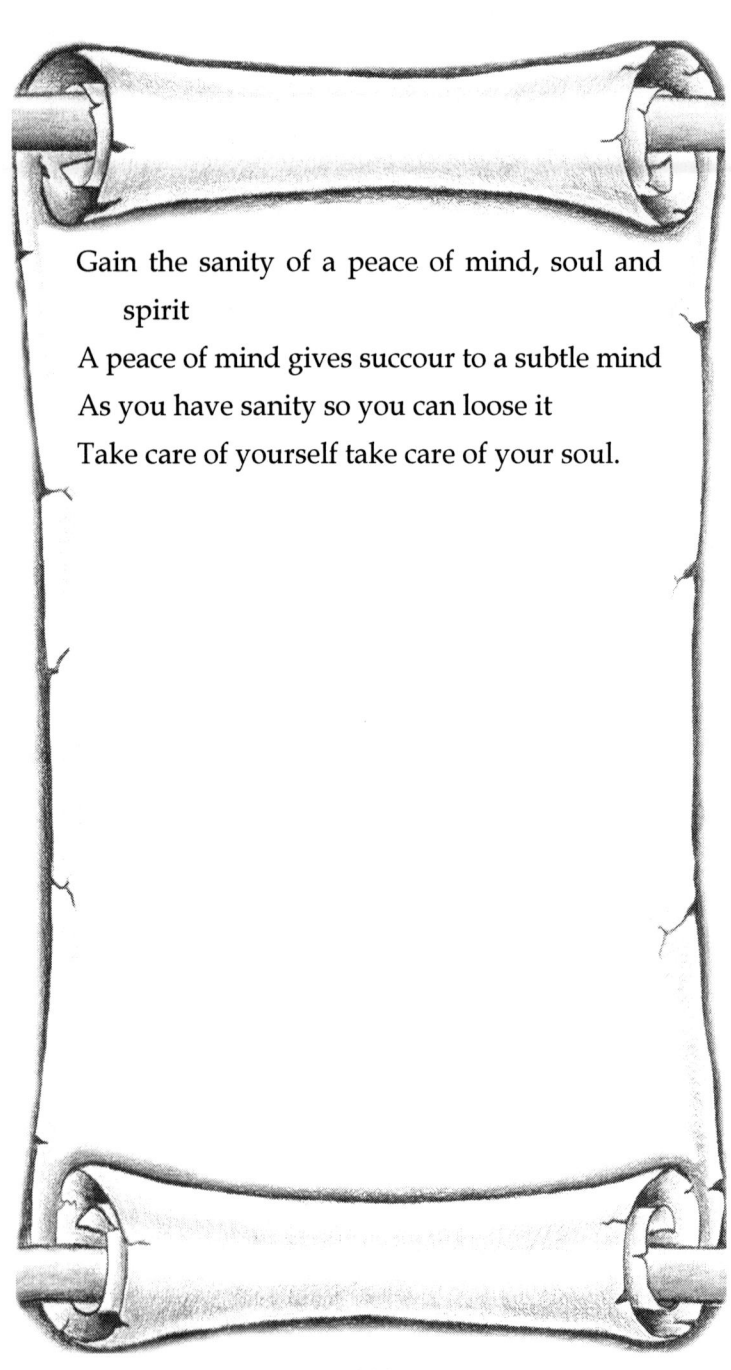

Gain the sanity of a peace of mind, soul and spirit
A peace of mind gives succour to a subtle mind
As you have sanity so you can loose it
Take care of yourself take care of your soul.

THE RAY SISTERS

The Ray sisters are rays of hope
Rays of love
Rays of beauties
For the lost sheep.

Silently' they sprang into their families
Bringing rays of joy to their loved parents
Like a pebble thrown inside water
They share their faith, they share all things.

Like flowing water
They knew one another in Ido-Ani
Where their faith grew and grew
To shine on people like the rays of the sun.

Ray sisters
I congratulate you.

THE SUN

The sun shines, glows and glitters
It burns over the earth
Over stage of people over stage of peoples
Over waring people of the world.

Sun, energy of the world
Sun a radiating image
Jesus our only intercessor the joy
The radiating Joy of our life.

The sun brightens our day
Jesus brightens our life
If we take them in success shall be ours.
Remember

The sun brightens, it brightens
Jesus saves, He saves.

TIME WAITS NOT

Tick tack tick tack
The clock moves with hands no legs
Life moves river flows
The heart beat clocks tick.

Time waits not for one
I must move I must progress
To heights higher than me
For time waits for no one

Standstill not like a statue standstill not
For currents not to part around you
As the river divides to flow around a huge rock
Leaving you behind forever.

**Some of the write-ups are inspired from:
WOMAN ALIVE by
Nelle McFather.**

THE MOUTH

The mouth! A glorious devilish thing
That leads to life Life the Saviour
That leads to death like the devouring lion
What a thing to behold.

Amenities of life – food, drinks, life, death
Have to pass through this passage
Like water passes through a channel
To produce a full wage of water.

For light brightness of body and soul
The qualities of life death passes through the passage
The mouth! A glorious thing to behold
The mouth! A devouring lion to behold.

Tame it to bring you success and life
Loose it to destroy you and death.

THE BODY

The body is a mechanism
It works like a programmed machine
A machine of 'Yes' 'No'
A machine dilated by the brain.

The nail part of the body
Which I cherish grows in nature
Naturally to beautify part of the parts
The parts that beautify the whole

The body what makes one human
A male or female humane or not
Sweeps its being to make it
A life giver the bestow of death

The body the carrier of who you are
Is but for a short while.

LOOKS

Look! A sight of seeing
A sight of seeing bright dark things
A sight of looking
A sight of thinking

Looks are pretty looks are ugly
Looks they say can kill
Looks I say can save
With a heart of a smile, a hand to reach out

Looks are hidden truly they are
Under the lipstick, perfumes, hair or body attachments
Under highs and lows hidden they are
To look real or false, to conceive or deceive

Looks are hidden
Looks truly are hidden.

FAMILY

Cryings hi hi hee hee haa haa
Proceedeth forth a child
Blameless in act or deed
To the wiles of his/her environs.

Laughter — ha ha! ha ha!
Praise, smiles, songs of halleluya
Welcomes the crying child
To an unknown that has to be known.

A family has already cropped
More croppings bringeth it forth
To the wiles of his environs
To an unknown that has to be known.

Is it not a family that maketh a whole?
Forth bringeth! A family
Bringeth forth! The world
A big large circle of families.

GOSSIP

Sha, sha, sha hai, hai, hai
Si—lent talk all na bi gossip.
'Ma yo are re' If you practise
Sha, sha, sha hai, hai, hai

Si—lent talk
You dey amongst them O
Abi you dey practise am?
Gossip fit kill O.

Note:
The first, third & fourth lines of the first stanza are sounds and words taken from the Yoruba Language. Yoruba language is one of the languages spoken in Nigeria, Africa. The second line of the first stanza and the second stanza stanza is 'Pigin English'. Pigin English is broken English.

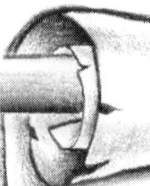
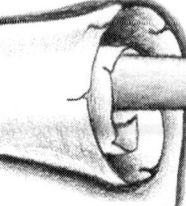

VOICES

Voices - - - - - - - Heard you of
The hi - lo - lo, hi - lo - lo, ha - lo - lo, ha - lo - lo
The shim, shim, shim, sham, sham, sham
Of the two winged creatures?

Voices - - - - - - - Heard you of
The sing, song, sing, song
The song, sing , song, sing
Of leaves and his children?

Aren't they a sight to behold?
Are they not of nature?
Isn't He the beauty and beautifier?
Is He not the morning melody?

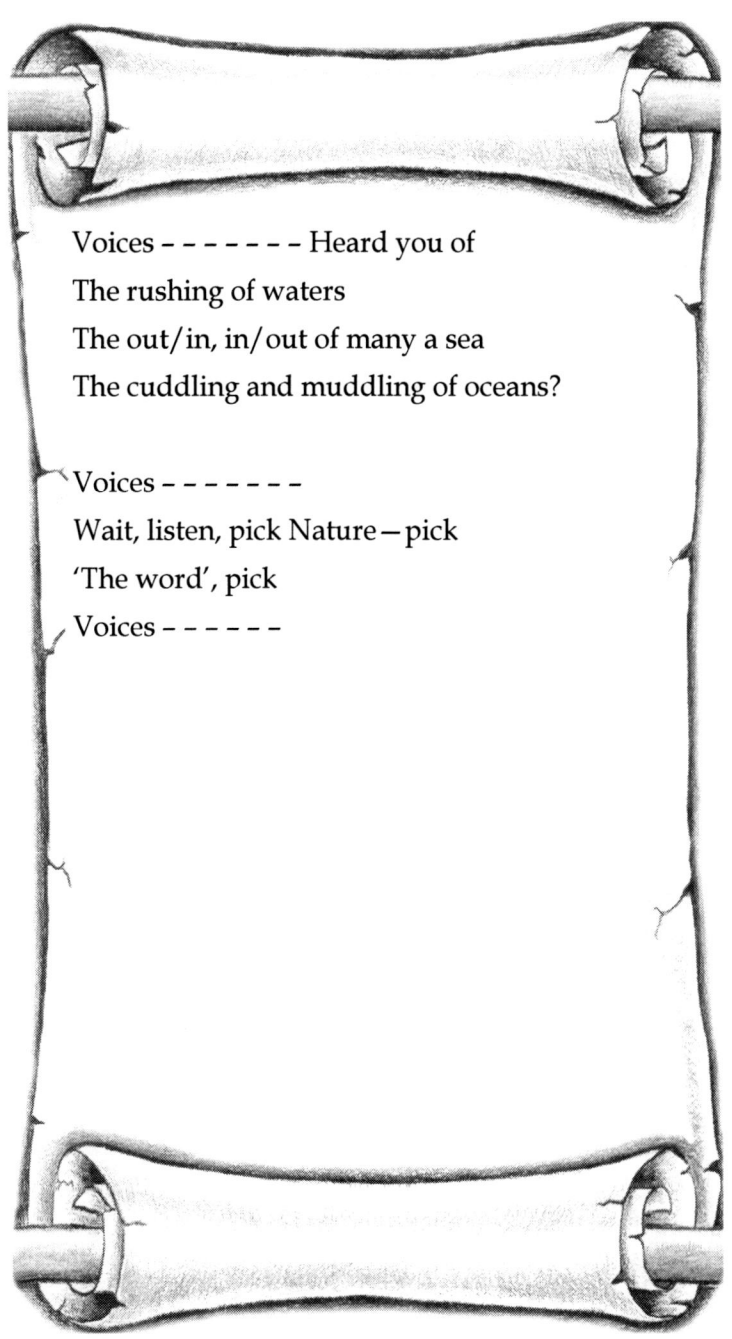

Voices – – – – – – – Heard you of
The rushing of waters
The out/in, in/out of many a sea
The cuddling and muddling of oceans?

Voices – – – – – – –
Wait, listen, pick Nature — pick
'The word', pick
Voices – – – – – –

A REVERSED COUP

Cukuroo ku – – – – – – –
Brings the early morning sun
Boom, boom, boom – – –
Greets a coup d'etat.

Nigeria,
A nation yet to be developed
Living who accept, reject or modify
A nation walking in His footsteps.

On 27th of August 1985
Major Ibrahim Badamosi Babangida
Mounted the throne of presidency
With Mrs. Maryam Babangida.

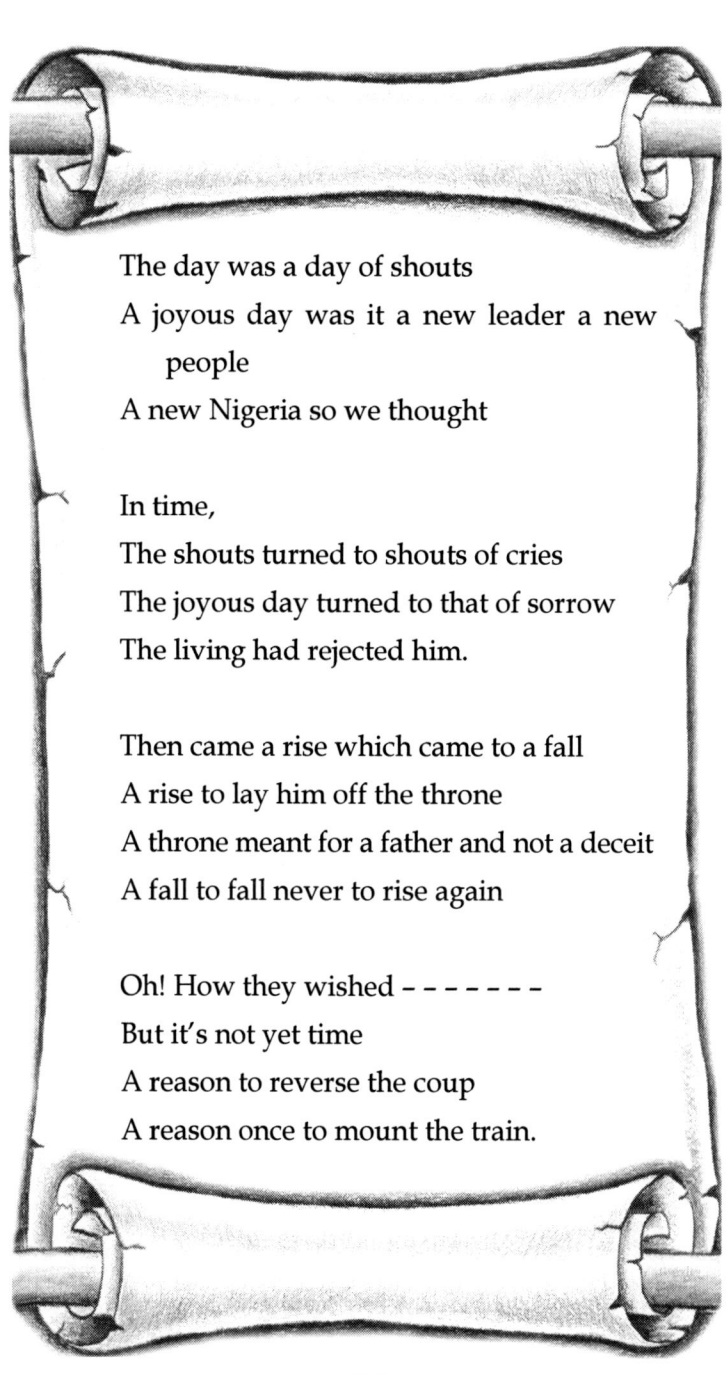

The day was a day of shouts
A joyous day was it a new leader a new people
A new Nigeria so we thought

In time,
The shouts turned to shouts of cries
The joyous day turned to that of sorrow
The living had rejected him.

Then came a rise which came to a fall
A rise to lay him off the throne
A throne meant for a father and not a deceit
A fall to fall never to rise again

Oh! How they wished - - - - - - -
But it's not yet time
A reason to reverse the coup
A reason once to mount the train.

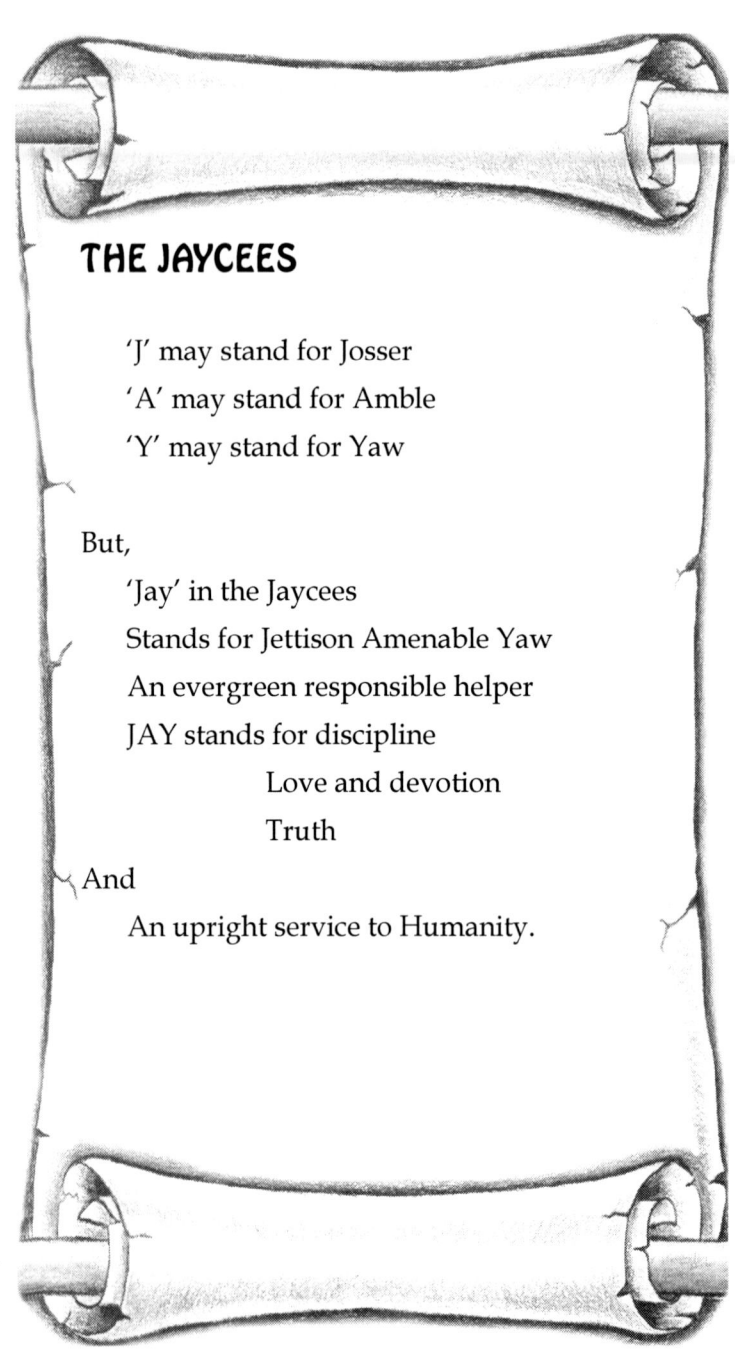

THE JAYCEES

'J' may stand for Josser
'A' may stand for Amble
'Y' may stand for Yaw

But,
'Jay' in the Jaycees
Stands for Jettison Amenable Yaw
An evergreen responsible helper
JAY stands for discipline
        Love and devotion
        Truth
And
An upright service to Humanity.

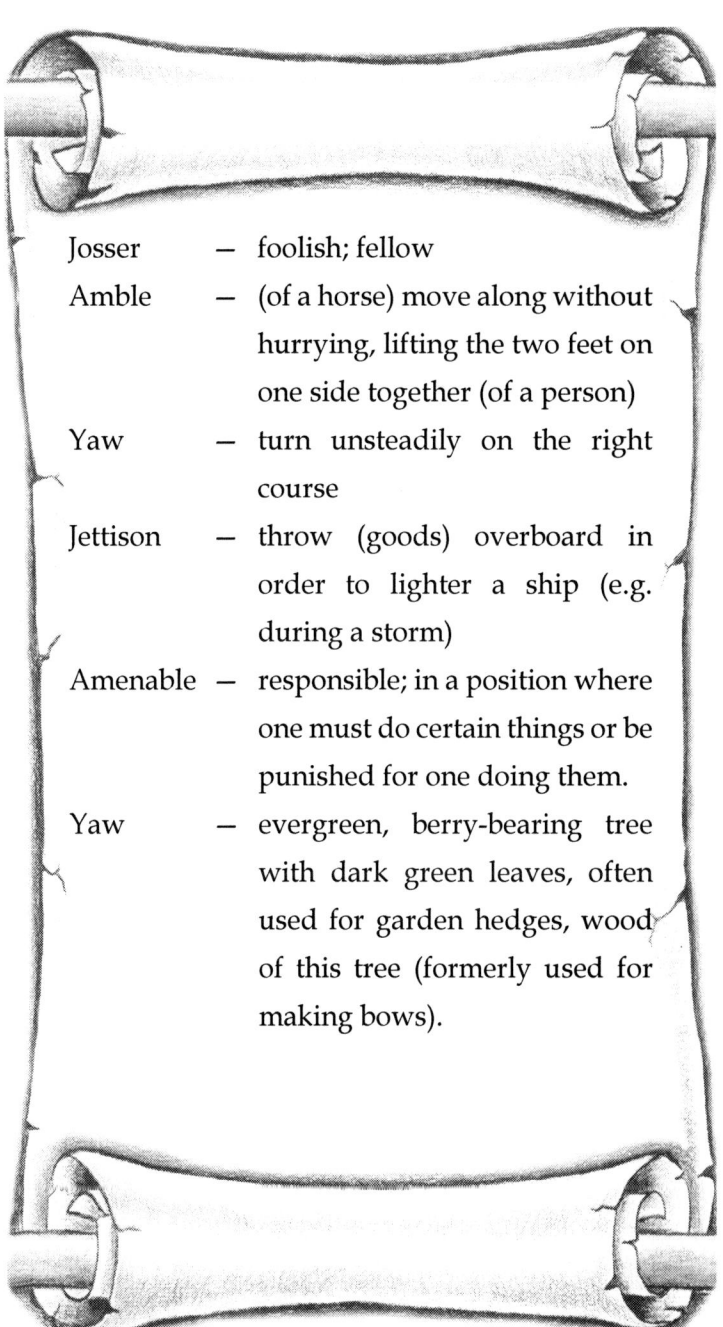

Josser	— foolish; fellow
Amble	— (of a horse) move along without hurrying, lifting the two feet on one side together (of a person)
Yaw	— turn unsteadily on the right course
Jettison	— throw (goods) overboard in order to lighter a ship (e.g. during a storm)
Amenable	— responsible; in a position where one must do certain things or be punished for one doing them.
Yaw	— evergreen, berry-bearing tree with dark green leaves, often used for garden hedges, wood of this tree (formerly used for making bows).

THREE JOLLY FRIENDS

In two you are made whole In marriage
But in three parts you remain.
There lives three jolly friends
Who are in parts not segmented

Why!
One lives in Christ
Two lives in sports with a plus
Three lives in beauty with a minus
Yet they are friends.

Hmm!
Friends whose ways are not twined
Yet they remain friends.
Hmm!

POLITICAL HASSLES

This political hazzles na wa o
Shuffle, shuffle up, down, up, down
Campaign, left, right, forward, backwards
Who go win go win
No need for soft eyes
No need for bribery and corruption
Just air out your potentials, productivity, efficiency and efficiency again
My man who go win don win
Sha! I don win patapata
For in Him I don hide.

Note: These lines are not written in proper English but broken or pigin English

SICKNESS; MAN DON SUFFER

Sickness no bi better thing
Him go hook you shampe
Like hookworm go hook ya intestine
Na your food he go first wack
No joke,
The hookworm bi waki and die
Where food concern
He go then take him water simili, simili, simili
Till he reduce man to a log of wood
He no go drive am, until you drive am
That na sickness; sin.

Note: These lines are not written in proper English but broken or pigin English

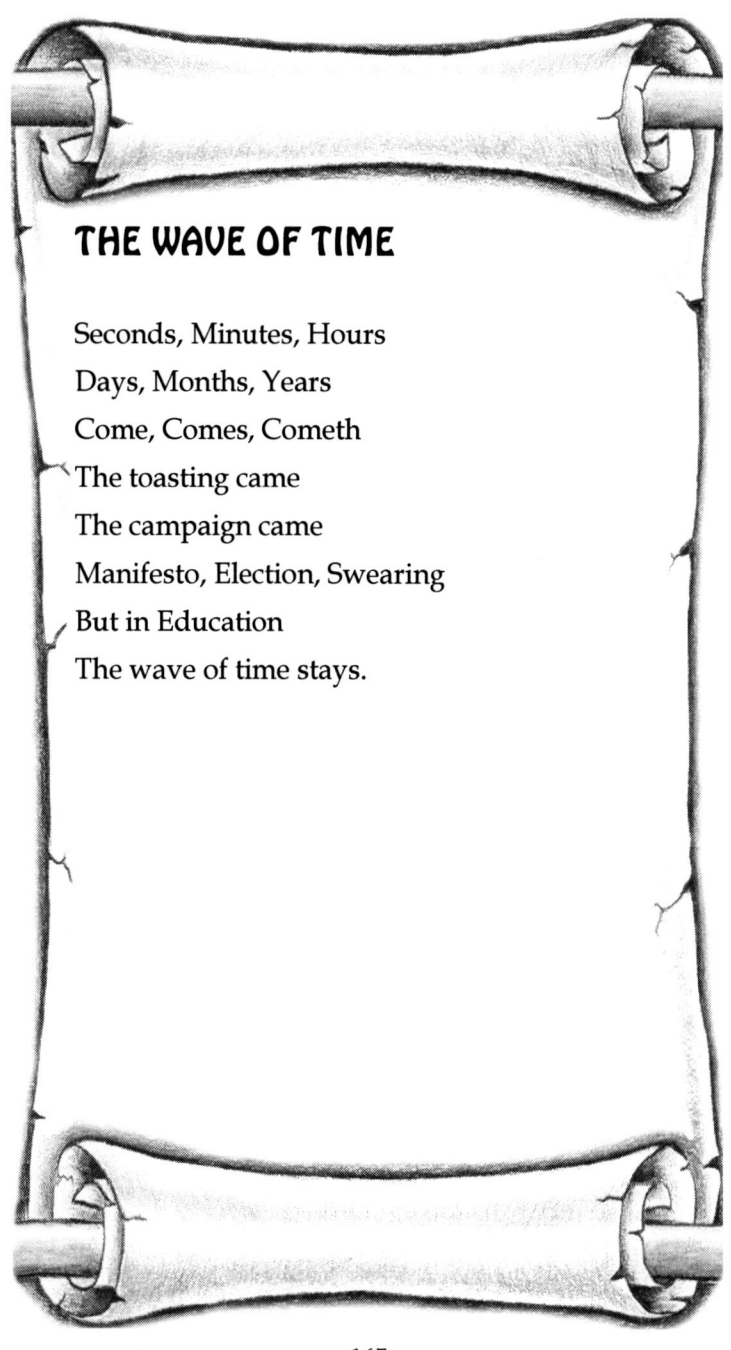

THE WAVE OF TIME

Seconds, Minutes, Hours
Days, Months, Years
Come, Comes, Cometh
The toasting came
The campaign came
Manifesto, Election, Swearing
But in Education
The wave of time stays.

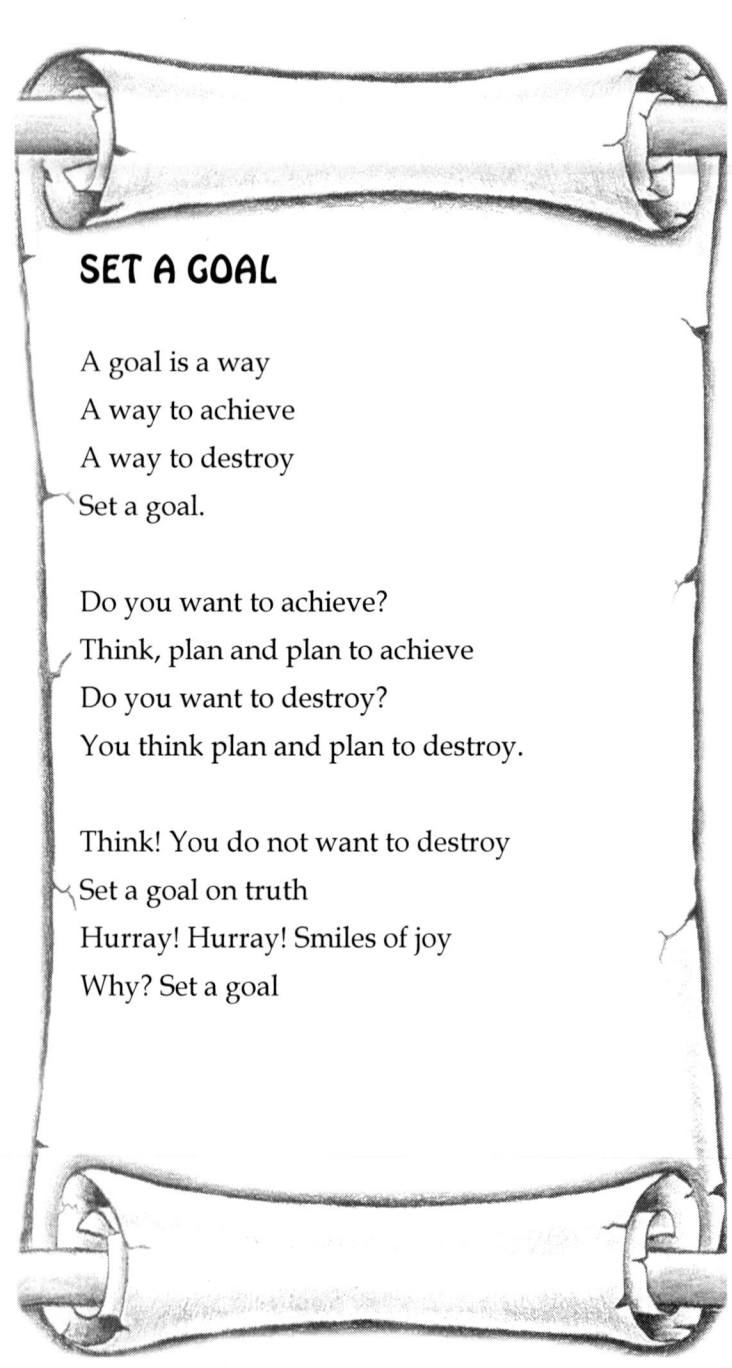

SET A GOAL

A goal is a way
A way to achieve
A way to destroy
Set a goal.

Do you want to achieve?
Think, plan and plan to achieve
Do you want to destroy?
You think plan and plan to destroy.

Think! You do not want to destroy
Set a goal on truth
Hurray! Hurray! Smiles of joy
Why? Set a goal

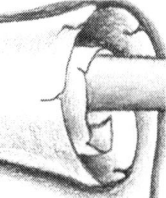

VIRTUOUS 'SHE'

Women,
>Ain't they the backbone of men?
>They are weapons that captivate men
>Gold in the wonderland of men

>As the days grow so a kid becomes a goat
>Women; a need to make 'Mother earth' to exist
>It's like the green grass that has to grow to exit
>In food, plants, animals and human beings

>The woman who represents womanhood, a 'she'
>Needs to be an example to her offspring to grow

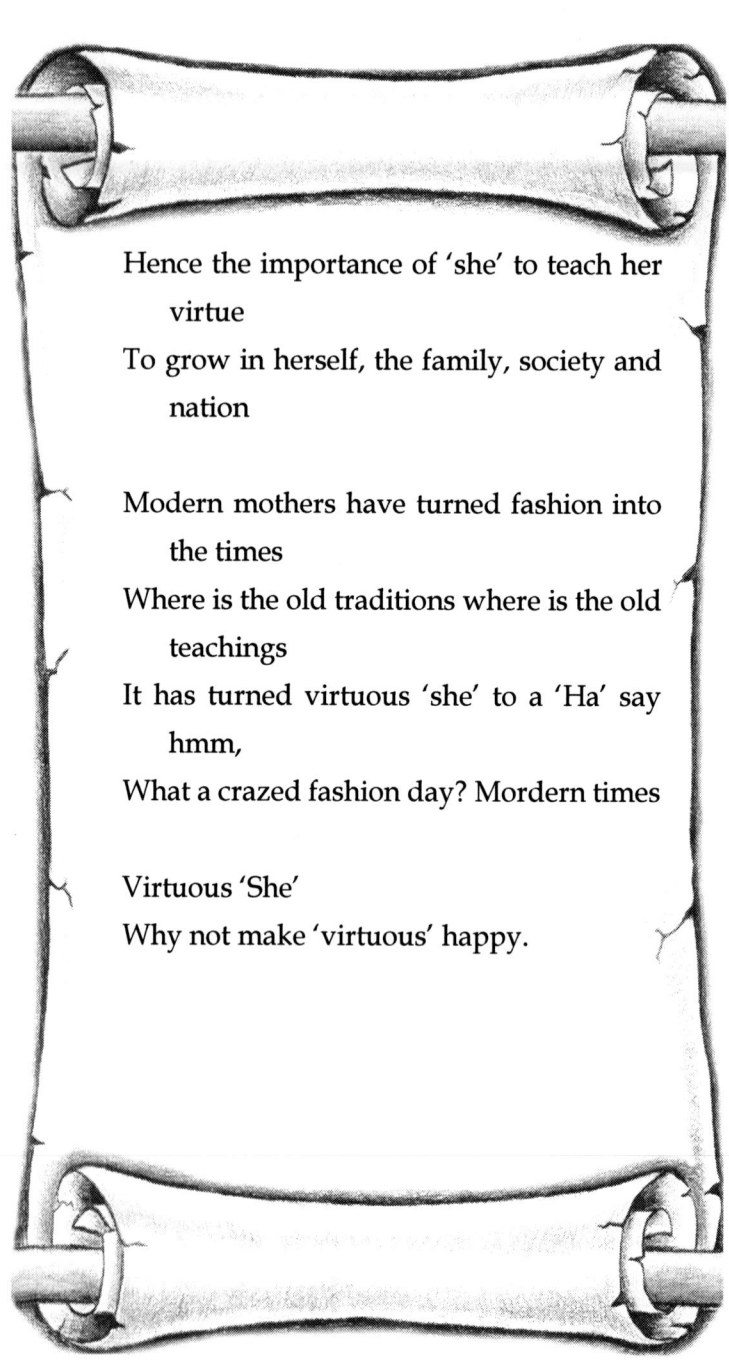

Hence the importance of 'she' to teach her virtue
To grow in herself, the family, society and nation

Modern mothers have turned fashion into the times
Where is the old traditions where is the old teachings
It has turned virtuous 'she' to a 'Ha' say hmm,
What a crazed fashion day? Mordern times

Virtuous 'She'
Why not make 'virtuous' happy.

HOSPITAL & PRISON VISITATION GROUP

Hospital and Prison Visitation Group
Is not a group for the sick or prisoner
It feeds physical, emotional and spiritual food
To the sick in hospital and the detained in prison

Out going places from hospitals to prisons
Visiting 'these' to comfort, bail the body
From cry of hot and cold emotions and feelings
Setting free from physical and spiritual bondage

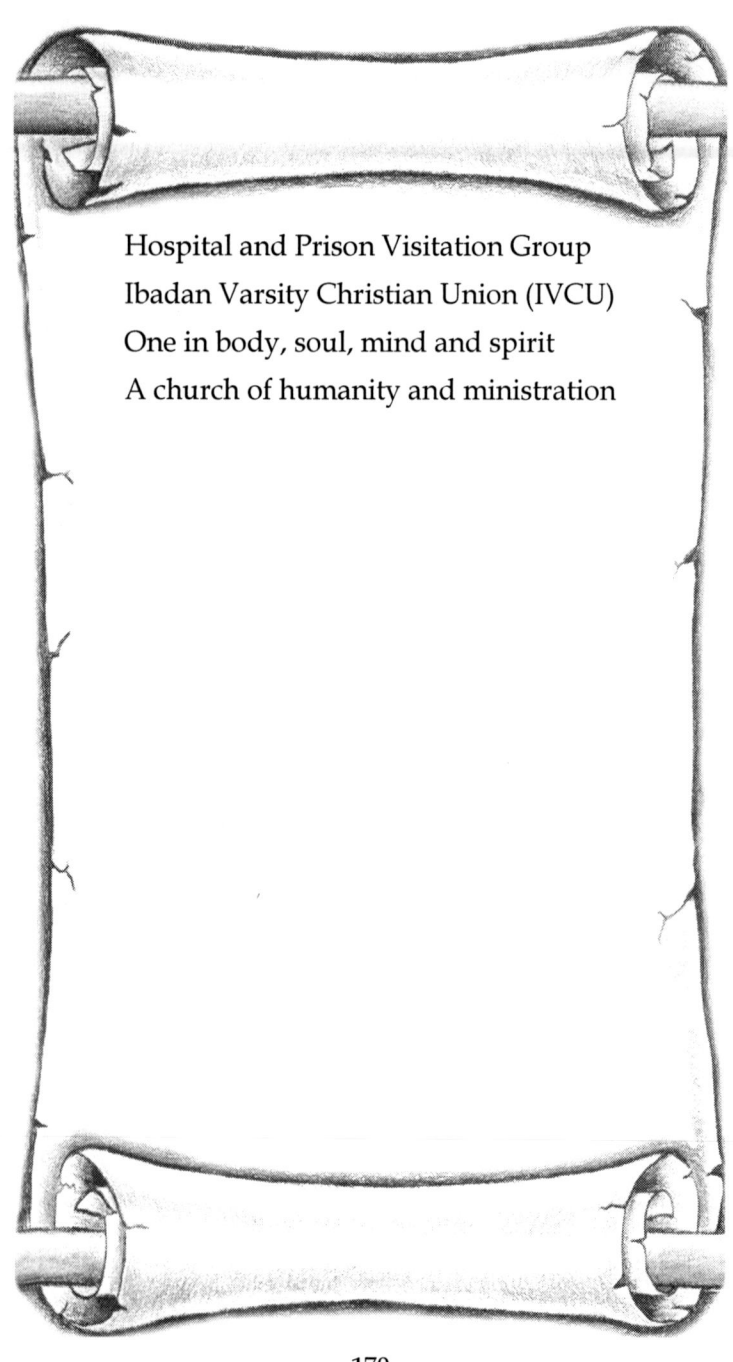

Hospital and Prison Visitation Group
Ibadan Varsity Christian Union (IVCU)
One in body, soul, mind and spirit
A church of humanity and ministration

HEIGHTS

Height! Height! Height
There are different types of heights
Height as of success, light and destiny
Or high as of failure, dark and hopeless

Which one have you chosen?
Wait! Choose wisely not foolishly
The height of heights or
The high of highs?

Have you made a decision?
'Cause heights clads success, clarity of mind, light
Highs clothes trouble, clouded mind, dark
It then clothes the trouble, the troubled mind to the highs

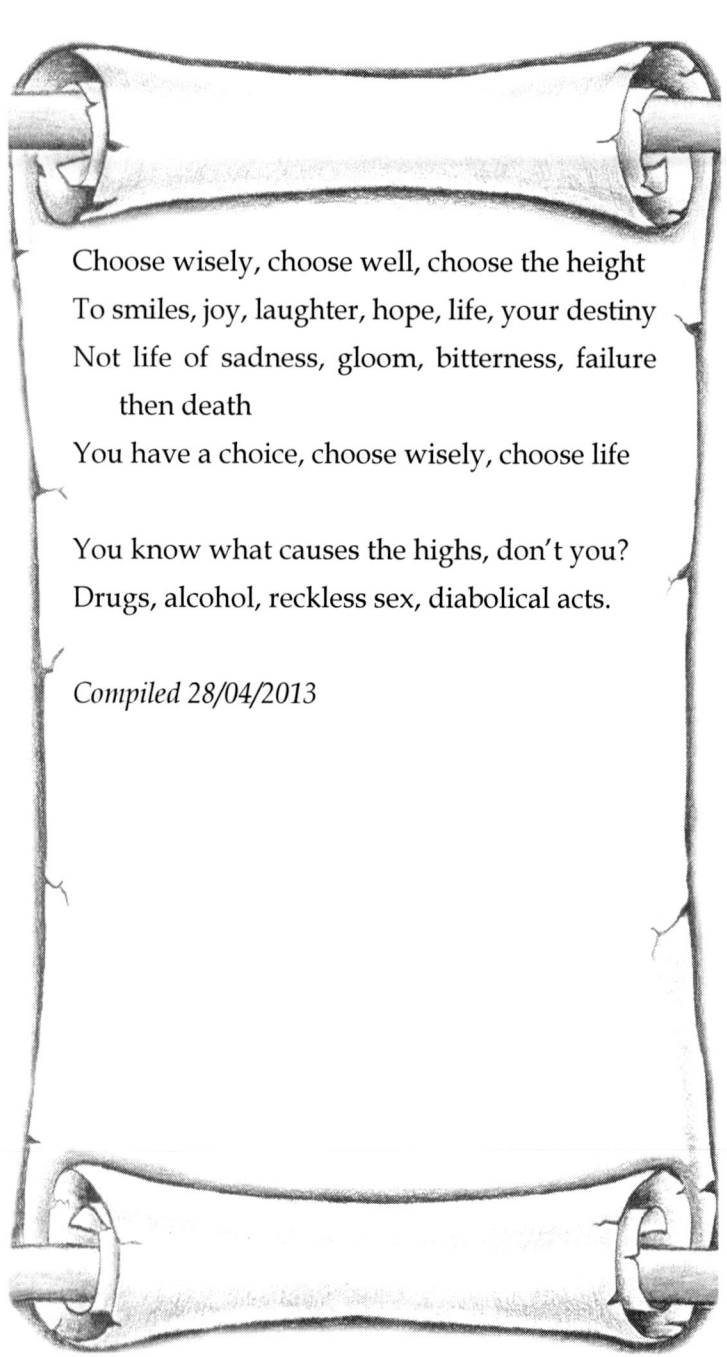

Choose wisely, choose well, choose the height
To smiles, joy, laughter, hope, life, your destiny
Not life of sadness, gloom, bitterness, failure then death
You have a choice, choose wisely, choose life

You know what causes the highs, don't you?
Drugs, alcohol, reckless sex, diabolical acts.

Compiled 28/04/2013

BARAK OBAMA: WHO IS THIS MAN?

Who is this man?
That God has decided to lift up?
He is a man of simple origin
Yet he rose beyond the pulling down of limits

He is a man of defined origin
Yet he rose beyond the limitations of destiny
To prove that there is a God
That you can make it

For prove that one day
The children of slaves and
The children of their slaves
Will not be judged by the colour of their skin.

That the children of slaves
And the children of their slaves masters
Will sit together and dine
Will think and rule nations.

For I have a dream as Martin Luther said:
That the children of slaves as cavesious
Will sit together
The time has surely come.

VOTE OBAMA

Open your eyes America
What can you see?
Vote victory
Celebrate the package of joy
Celebrate Obama
Vote him today
Vote for the victories in the package of joy
Vote Obama.

Compiled 04/11/00
On the way to work

OBAMA: EPITOME OF BEAUTY

Why has this poet called him an epitome of beauty?
Simply look at his past humble beginnings
Relate that to the poor, vulnerable, orphans
Widows, the fainted heart
Would he not have the knowledge,
Experience and spiritual hand to dig deep?
Yes, he would

Simply look at his past
Intelligence in chosen field; law, politics
Relate that to the rich and current world economy
Would he not have the knowledge,
Experience and spiritual hand to dig deep?
Yes, he would.

Simply look at his present

Epitome of Christian beauty;
Only if he remains so even in the throne
Relate that to life of
He who lings on the four corners of the universe

Simply look at the future, Change:
Would he not have the breath of life
Social skills, physical intuition and intelligence
To keep trusting for a better future change
Yes he would.

Vote not for race, black
Vote not for race, white
Vote for the man you can see perform
The man for glorious change.

Compiled
Before 1st election
Nov. 2008

ART

ART: Artisan Real Turnings
ART: Splish Splash Splish Splash
Of the brush 'wala' paintings created
The pencils and crayons have created the art

Lines, lines, round, square, triangle, shapes
Of their pencils 'wala' drawings created
Different lines, strokes, turnings, dances, splish–splash
'Wala' a creation on canvas is birth

These lines, strokes, turnings, dances, splish–splash
Are real 'cause they talk life, laugh life, live life
Open your eyes, your second eyes see beyond
The pencils, paints, brush and smell beyond

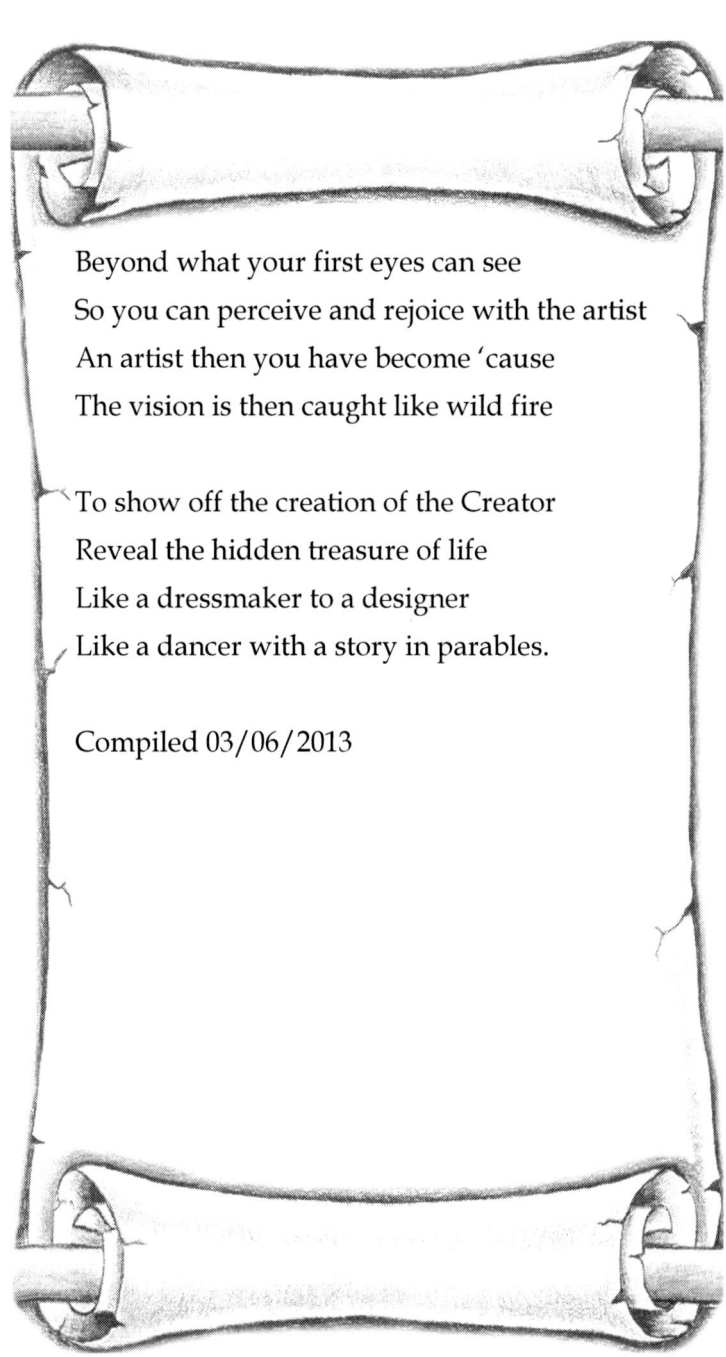

Beyond what your first eyes can see
So you can perceive and rejoice with the artist
An artist then you have become 'cause
The vision is then caught like wild fire

To show off the creation of the Creator
Reveal the hidden treasure of life
Like a dressmaker to a designer
Like a dancer with a story in parables.

Compiled 03/06/2013

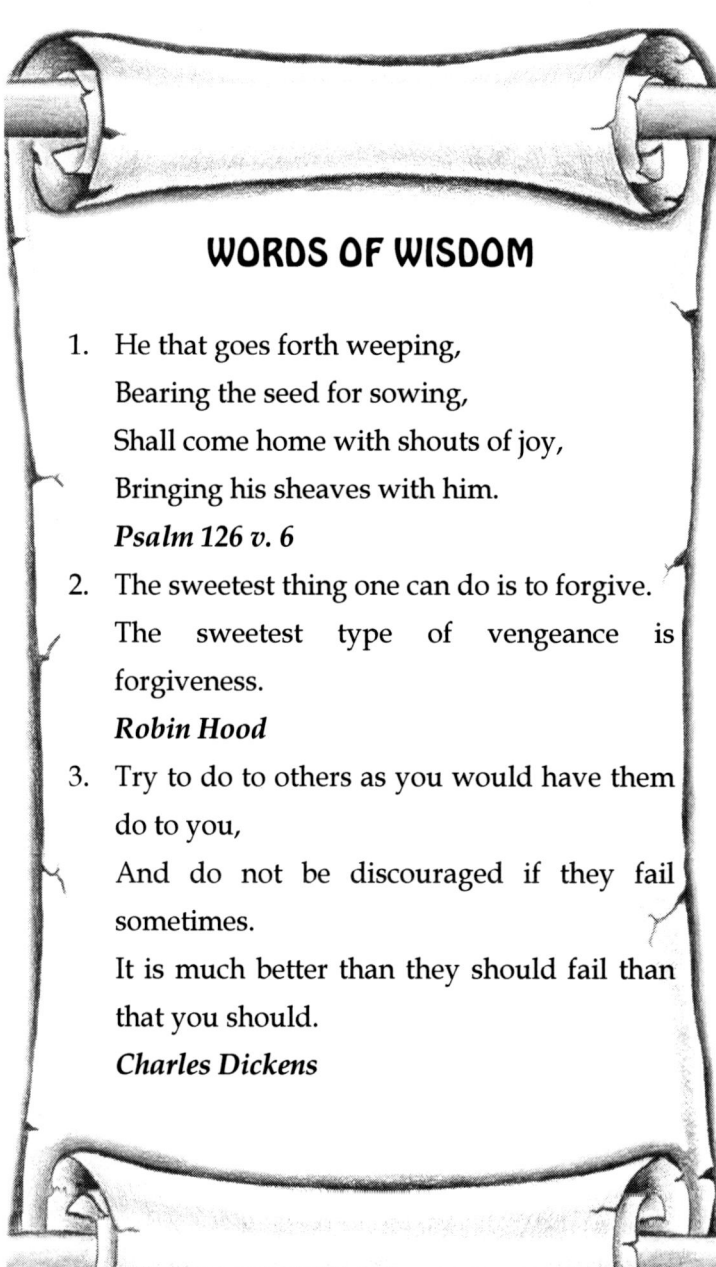

WORDS OF WISDOM

1. He that goes forth weeping,
   Bearing the seed for sowing,
   Shall come home with shouts of joy,
   Bringing his sheaves with him.
   Psalm 126 v. 6

2. The sweetest thing one can do is to forgive. The sweetest type of vengeance is forgiveness.
   Robin Hood

3. Try to do to others as you would have them do to you,
   And do not be discouraged if they fail sometimes.
   It is much better than they should fail than that you should.
   Charles Dickens

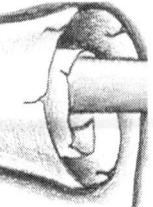

4. The greatest thing one can dream of is love
   The greatest type of hatred is love.
   Sola Adejuwon

5. One who stands a little nearer in faith and true sincerity whose heart and hand grow ever dearer in their unknowing ministry.
   Heifi Knecht

6. The righteous shall prevail
   The evil doer shall also prevail.
   Sola Adejuwon

7. A friend is a person who knows all about you
   And still likes you.
   Elbert Hubbard

8. The world is filled with characters, fighters
   And the likes
   People act on stage
   Warriors fight at battle
   For only one purpose

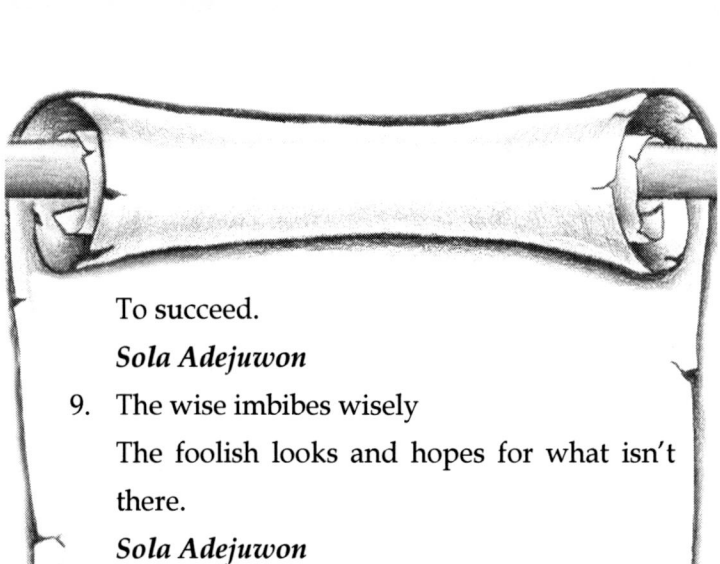

To succeed.

Sola Adejuwon

9. The wise imbibes wisely

   The foolish looks and hopes for what isn't there.

   Sola Adejuwon

10. Never do something because you just have to do it

    Do it wholeheartedly.

    Sola Adejuwon

11. Better is a dinner of herbs where love is

    Than a fatted ox and hatred with it.

    'The Word'

    Pro. 15 v. 17.

12. He who loves purity of heart, and whose speech

    Is gracious, will have the king as his friend,

    The Bible

    Pro. 22 v. 11

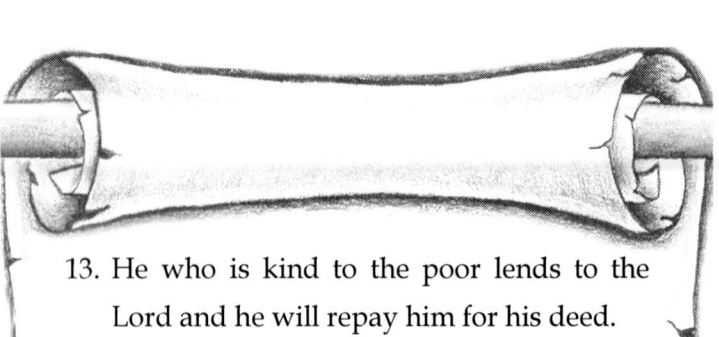

13. He who is kind to the poor lends to the Lord and he will repay him for his deed.
'The Book'
Pro. 19 v. 17.

14. Love is a good thing
Better still is love that never fails
Best of all is love that never fails in God.
Sola Adejuwon

15. To Err is human but to forgive is divine
The evil that men do live after them but the Good is often interred,
Life is too short to worry about problems.
Author Unknown.

16. Seeing a new thing does not mean you throw
Away the old one.
The old usually is better than the new.
Sola Adejuwon

17. Friendship is the only cement that will ever
    Hold the world together.
    Author Unknown
    From
    Everyone Needs a Friend Like You—
18. Whatever is in anyway beautiful hath its
    Source of beauty in itself.
    Marcus Aurelius
19. There is no problem on earth
    That the heavens can't solve.
    John Moore
20. People are beautiful and ugly in their own way
    No matter who beautiful, you are ugly
    No matter how ugly, you are beautiful
    Only a faithful child of God is perfected.
    Sola Adejuwon

21. The thought of the Lord is very deep
    Deeper than the oceans
    Deeper than that of the best men.
    Sola Babatunde
22. It's how you think towards something that it becomes.
    13/10/94
23. A mother!
    What a mother
    A suckling mother
    She cuddles her suckling
    Her hear ever warm
    Thou she hurts her heart
    She remaining ever warm
    A mother
    Sola Babatunde
    13/11/94

24. You don't have knowledge of what you are not.

    You don't have knowledge of what you don't do.

    Sola Babatunde
    12/10/94

25. Work for Jesus, work for yourself
    Preach for Jesus, preach your life
    Think Jesus, think yourself
    Love Jesus, love life love yourself and His creation.

    Sola Babatunde
    12/10/94

26. You live life to the fullest
    When you fulfil your destiny
    On an ongoing basis until His plan for your life is accomplished.

    Shola Babatunde
    27/04/2013

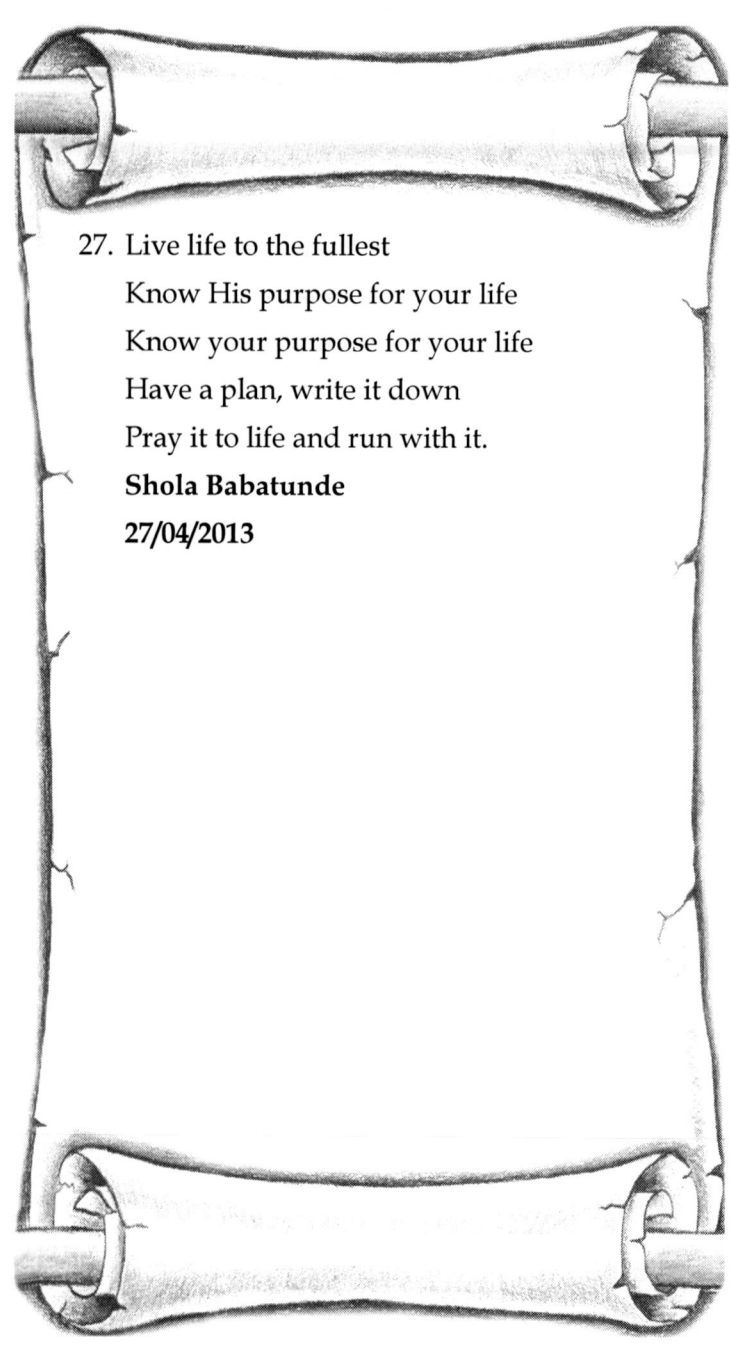

27. Live life to the fullest
    Know His purpose for your life
    Know your purpose for your life
    Have a plan, write it down
    Pray it to life and run with it.
    Shola Babatunde
    27/04/2013

Lightning Source UK Ltd.
Milton Keynes UK
UKOW050403060713

213335UK00001B/9/P

GO
CREATURELY

Patricia Leighton

Go Creaturely
Patricia Leighton

Published by Aspect Design, 2025
Printed and bound by Aspect Design
89 Newtown Road, Malvern, Worcs. WR14 1PD
United Kingdom
Tel: 01684 561567
E-mail: allan@aspect-design.net
Website: www.aspect-design.net

All Rights Reserved.

Copyright © 2025 Patricia Leighton.

Patricia Leighton has asserted her moral right
to be identified as the author of this work.

The right of Patricia Leighton to be identified as the author
of this work has been asserted in accordance with
Section 77 of the Copyright, Designs and Patents Act 1988.

This book is sold subject to the condition that it shall not, by way of trade
or otherwise, be lent, resold, hired out or otherwise circulated without the
publisher's prior consent in any form of binding or cover other than that
in which it is published and without a similar condition including this
condition being imposed on the subsequent purchaser.

Cover image bazilfoto via iStock
Design Copyright © Aspect Design 2025

ISBN 978-1-916919-38-9

Contents

Dream Wolves. 1
Swift Escape. 2
Wearing Feathers 4
Butterfly Love 5
Quiet Reflections from Jacobs' Hide. 6
Suburban Nocturnes 8
Owl Call to the Dying 10
On the Tiles 11
Animal Instincts in a Time of Lockdown 12
Leaping the Odds. 14
Viewpoints 16
Lover of Hares 18
A Mite on the Wing of a Buzzard 20
Flying on Pheromones. 22
September's Spiders 23
The Closest Things to Titania's Fairies 24
Lakeside Cameo. 25
A Lone Cormorant 26
Wren Song. 27
Gifted 28
For Love of a Hen 30
Sophie. 32
Benison 33

Sortie. 34

A Pastorale of Restrained Freedoms 35

Old Man of High Wood. 36

We Are Not all Capercaillies. 38

Casual Deaths. 40

Warriors. 41

Losing Direction 42

Greece and Goats. 44

The Power of King Cobra 46

The She-Wolf Speaks. 47

In a Fantasy World 48

Fly with Pegasus. 50

Acknowledgements 53

Dream Wolves

Dream
    half-seen shadows sifting through woods
    slicking between trees   across clearings

ghost paws padding an effortless lope
    leaping streams   lapping at cool headwaters

    dark shapes fanning out over plains
    quickening at prey scent   a pack moving as one

Dream
    white-outs   tell-tale tracks in snow
    the shelter and stink of caves

rest time   muscles and fur at ease
muzzles beneath curled tails   breathing soft

thrown heads   howls   ancient instincts
    rough tongues kissing the amber resin of time

Dream
the gold of glittering eyes   moving
slowly   to hold yours

Swift Escape

Screeches of ecstasy tinkle my eardrums
and I look up   see this summer's swifts
dissecting cloudless skies

Abandoning trowel   hoe   the burden of
insistent weeds for the faded garden chair
I lean back and watch

these acrobating
    black arrows
        cartwheeling
            the sky
the sureness
    lightness
        freedom
            of their flight

their swoops
    flips
        sound-breaking falls
            rocket-fuelled ascents

and I am mesmerized

They'll soon be off

over the ship-laden Channel   gothic cathedrals
vineyards   lavender fields of France   the mountains
orange groves   umbrella-decked beaches of Spain
the sun-tipped waves of the Mediterranean

to Africa they call   invite me to join them

Why not?
I've never been to Africa   flown on the wing
nothing to keep me here

For a nano-second I consider bird nets
being blown off course   survival statistics

but these birds are experts and if worse comes to worst
well – what an elemental way to go.

I'm in! I cry
give me a gang screech when it's time –

I'll be waiting
    no baggage
        no strings attached.

Wearing Feathers

Once I flew with starlings.
They loaned me a jewelled
 cloak of iridescent colours
dropped nectar into my eyes
until they were brighter, keener
than I had ever known, pulled
out my soft lips to beakiness
delicately pecked them into sharpness
spittle-sealed them to a high gloss.

They taught me the art of probing with
my sharp beak for worms and grubs
the trickster's prank of mimicking
whistles, car alarms, phone rings
the call songs of other birds.
They let me tag on, clumsy tail gunner
to jaw-dropping murmurations.
Come evening, roosting like black monks
they let me snuggle in group warmth.

One winter morning, sated on berries
they congregated in sunlit branches.
Sotto voce exchanged snatches of songs
a tuning up, conversations which seemed
to hold meaning for them. Try as I might
I couldn't crack the code.
The feathers fell off.

Butterfly Love

Five centimetres of pure folded beauty
this peacock butterfly eases herself from
her sanctuary as spring's warmth seeps
into the year, opens her wings and flies.

Red-browns glowing with life, purple and
white wing eyes flickering, she rests on
a nettle leaf, soaks in the day and is off;
ready for lekking males, the mating game.

With flashes of eyes, a hiss of beating wings
she warns off predators and for a few
brief weeks lays treasure hordes of tiny
grape-green eggs among the nettle beds.

They'll hatch, take their chances, lose or win.
Love was ever a learning curve, a longing for
warmth again, that opening of wings – but love
pinned down, a perfect macro image captured?

Not the real thing. What comes first is
the stillness of looking, really looking,
that flutter when something or someone
enters your soul.

A keeper or not, you never forget.

Quiet Reflections from Jacobs' Hide

Late November and the hide's window opens
to a wide calm of water that barely moves,
the sky a sheet of blotting paper greys
against which shoreline trees and shrubs
look almost sorry for themselves.

There is a quiet stillness, barely a bird note
as I move it all into focus.

A convoy of coots sails silently west to east,
gulls rise briefly, add flashes of white to the sky,
settle again; a line of cormorants, beaks held high,
stand to attention on a strip of island, a grey heron
bent as a retired colonel brings up the rear.

Below me, a dog-leg runnel of water from the main
pool circles a browning swathe of reedbeds.

Great and blue tits catch the corner of my eye, flit
from hedgerow and reeds, raid the bird feeder nearby.
A lone mallard paddles down the runnel, a moorhen slips
from the reeds to join it – they forage together briefly
then wander off, one behind one, to wider waters.

Look – a cohort of lapwings has flown in, performs
an air ballet of black and white, stirs memories . . .

that first time I saw a bittern creep from reeds on
the far shore, a kingfisher's dive from reed to water,
the flash of silver as it emerged, rats filching dropped
feeder seeds – the one time a tyro-me met old Jacobs,
learnt that patient looking and listening was the key.

One window is open on the far hide as I close up
. . . a shaded face behind it.

suburban nocturnes

soft air cools this autumn night and light clouds pass lazily
across a pale full moon below which creatures
come and go...

moths nose among borders and shrubs for nectar
are lured by the false sat nav of a street lamp
dance and flutter in confusion...

reynard slinks into and through its beam pads
softly and swiftly off to the local take-away its
promise of tongue-licking bins...

hodge squeezes its spines through gaps   tours
a length of gardens   guzzles slugs   sips at ponds
leaves its autograph in mud...

beetles and bugs nibble at damp greens   snails
slowly meander between eating spots   etch
I-*have-been-here* trails wherever they go...

a barn owl floats between a gap in rooftops   ghost wings
it silently towards the park   tawny sends a far off
twooo into the night...

marauding pipistrelles click thin wing skins   prick up ears
dart and twist after weaker wings   snap up food stores
as hibernation looms...

brock reclaims old territory   claws up turf   wolfs down
worms/slugs/frogs   feasts on seeds/berries/fallen fruit
chews slyly on newly planted bulbs . . .

a prowling cat wanders the shadows   knows it all
halts eyes glinting patiently watches   waits
chooses its prey pounces and kills . . .

a dark shape solidifies on an estate road Mohammed's cab
its radio muffled   quietly cruising towards the bypass
his next pick-up . . .

behind the enclosed darkness of locked doors and curtains
unconscious dreams stream   loop   until dawn releases
an uncertain scrap of memory . . .

Owl Call to the Dying

curtains closed   doors bolted   lights out
the house is surrendered to night

all but this bedroom   its window undressed
half-open to hopes and doubts

come-and-go moonlight sifts through clouds
odours of leaves and lawn seep in

drift into corners   wrap the prone sleeper
stir memories dreams

the reaper owl sweeps from the dark
wide-eyes the window   lands nearby

sentinel-still it *too-woos* its clear call
all is in its right time

a breath eases towards its end
stillness and peace float beyond walls*

---

* There is an old superstition that to hear an owl calling at a window signifies a death in the house.

On the Tiles

Lady Slut   groomed and spruced   I'm off over walls fences
slick through suburban niceties to bright lights   shadowed nooks
those jazz den throbs.

Soho saunter perfected   hit home turf   linger beneath neon
flash gilt eyes   tongue a few seductive licks of my fur
tail-flick green for go.

Player of many parts I know how to please   meek/raunchy/playful
I can do them all   rarely get paid   but I've a few soft touches
on my client list.

Flat 6 is treats-happy after a few strokes   a plaintive *yow* and
the late night deli man is all mine   and I've regular daytime slots
with some uptight surburbanites.

Let's face it though   I prefer the wilder side – can be rough tough
but – know what I mean? Of course I breed   boy do I breed
always a price to pay for freedom.

I know the score   age claws us all in the end   one day I'll settle for
warmth regular meals   no squalling kits   I'll do the curl-up-sweets
the soothing purrs but still

one glimpse of cloud-drifts riding the moon   the slit of an open window
lure of night air   one distant yowl   and the urge will be there
I'll stray.

Animal Instincts
in a Time of Lockdown

It slunk through the churchyard,
padded on silent night paws
into the town, the High Street washed
with a paucity of off-peak lighting.

Part moving darkness, part glimpsed sleekness,
it slipped between benches, doorways, bollards,
sought familiar litter bins, sensed
something was wrong.

Rose on its haunches, stretched to topple
one over with deft paws. All but empty
sifted lean pickings, staleness the only smell.
Made for richer feeding grounds.

Eerily tidy, the yard of the Golden Plaice yielded
only blow away paper scraps; no nibbles of fish in
tail-end batter, half-bitten chunks of pie; a dry nothing
where once saliva flowed to the tang of rich scents.

Scouting precinct 'backs', no cornucopias flowed
from council bins, no on-its-side half empty bottle
leaked liquor to lick, no take-away pickings or
spewed-up curry sludges tempted its tongue.

Here nothing on two legs staggered across its path.
No pack lurched from the back of The Cross,
no lone figure, head down, walked ghost-like
across to the one-way link out of town.

Puzzled, it paused at Clegg's Entry, padded in.
The curled bodies, the mingled scents of man
and dog missing, gone cold, it froze with unease.
Not tempted to linger, it shivered, quickened its pace.

Glided swiftly through streets, alleyways, gullies,
back between gravestones, through hedges, gardens,
course set for the warmth of den
the safe stench of home.

Leaping the Odds

I feel it   we feel   it this magnetic pull which signals
it is time to leave   that we have destinies to fulfil

flesh strong with feasting in familiar seas of plenty
I join the moving shoal   its glory of silver scales

flicker-swim mile-upon-mile-upon-mile   tasting salt
until tide pulls change   wideness narrows   and I lip

the almost forgotten water of my beginnings   water
which flows against me   impedes   strains fins

the fiercer it comes   the harder I fight
    rise up
    to torrents
    cascading
    down
        swish tail
            side shuffle
bend and arc muscle
      leap
          body slap
          its strength
     leap again
          leap again

    climb
    blind
    to what's
    ahead

I sense change   swim tiredly into calmness   pebbles
glinting beneath me   water-washed glimpses of green

memory oozes   I follow latent scents until   yes   this is the spot
I wriggle   stir gravel   scrape my redd and lay eggs

he sperms and I cold-eye their futures   with all my
bright silver transmuted to bronze   I come close

cover them whisper of freedom   wide seas   the urge to
return   that they are *salars*   leapers   water thumpers

my strength spent I do not tell them of all that leaping demands
its failures   my one in nine chance of tasting salt again

Viewpoints

my eyes scan
the vastness of moorland slopes
I breath in
earthiness   heather   wild gorse
tilt my head up
to a sunlit infinity of clear sky
drink in
the perfection of the day

fail to see
a hare nosing green   intent on nibbling
an eagle
scanning wide   silently gyring down
the subtle closing
of gap between sky and ground
until the eagle
positions wings   swoops earthwards

and the hare
senses shadow   bounds at full speed   weaves
the eagle's eyes
are precision honed   its frame on auto drive
it strikes
the hare talons grip tighter
and together they rise
wings powering   fur frozen in fear

back-of-the-neck gripped
the dying hare sees nothing of ground or sky
only curved bone
yellow leg scale   feathered under-belly
the eagle is focused
on the nest it is aiming for   rests nearby
tears at flesh
gulps down its victor's share   flies on

Lover of Hares

(For Gillian Clarke, poet)

'*We never kill hares in our part of the country,*' she says,
the words raw with feeling against those who do.

She doesn't say why not but tells
of her love of a full-sized limestone
hare carved for her by a friend,
the aliveness of hare in the sculpting
shared with the fossilised stone.

On a strong chain round her neck
a silver hare leaps its limbs to the full
into the wild scent of her white hair
which flows loosely, two clips
keeping her face clear.

Her tongue runs quickly,
eyes glint, catch secret moons,
words shaping themselves
from the long deep to jump,
dance in sheer delight.

In the aloneness of necessary journeys,
she makes herself small scrapes
of familiar things and curls up,
safe but still surface-close
to the quick reach of beyond.

Love chains, clips, friendships;
these light ties anchor her
to the now and lately-has-been.
For the rest she is sky, turf, stone,
stream and a thousand sounds.

Hare woman,
elemental leaper of time.

A Mite on the Wing of a Buzzard

Far further than I could journey alone
I am lifted over fields spread to the limit
of its almighty eyes. We bank along wooded
hillsides, swoop between clouds, over rooftops,
patrol broad tarmac highways. Some days
we ride a dance-floor's worth of sky with
others of its kind: turning, twisting, the music
of the air punctuated with ecstatic cries.

On the coldest of nights I am warm,
can burrow into the deepest recesses
of a soft wing pit. I am never without
sustenance – and sometimes there is
stillness, the perfect peace of idleness
perched on post or pole where what is
below seems somehow more within
the compass of my comprehension.

But I have also felt the swoop of raw murder,
shuddered with the tearing of talons; I have
heard shrieks, screams, the silence of pure terror
and I know (somewhere deep in the confines
of my small mind) that however well I navigate
the feathered terrain of this seeming sanctuary
there will come one nip, one casual scratch
(inconsequential in the vast plane of its existence)

and I will be obliterated, a minute blood sacrifice to this brown god.

Flying on Pheromones

happy we are   lazy   browsy
schlunch-sclunch   munch-munch   munch-munch
hopping among green shoots

content we are   with our me-only
wanderings   casual matings   increases   until
numbers   needs   temperatures soar

and call-to-arms odours of
phew-phwor-mmm thicken the air and we morph
merge to winged armies

abandon parched earth
stir   rise   fly   clwick-clwick-thwack   clwick-clwick-thwack
swarm in our millions

ride on the air   gouge
our own highways   long   broad   dark
on our way

to blacken your skies
deafen your ears with our battle cries
strip your greens clean
beware

we are Locust

September's Spiders

Summer fattened, they mimic the shapes
of autumn's leaves and twigs, these cocky
Brunels which spin mammoth threads from
posts, bushes, across garden paths.

Their intricate weavings coat borders, film
over jaded flower heads, the brown and
gold of curling leaves, blonde jungles of
turning grasses – so many you need eyes

everywhere not to walk straight into one,
see a thread break and the quick body
swing easily along its lifeline to start again;
lay traps, scheme, strike, gorge more in

the last of the sun's warmth before frosts
coat the tableau and we throw out words
such as *wonders, miracles,* like dice into
the unknowns of the turning year.

But it's work, not magic, that is underway,
seizing what's there to live safely cocooned
below winter's parapet or die grey as a shroud
which lands at zero whichever way it falls.

The Closest Things to Titania's Fairies

...are summer's demoiselles flittering over
the balsam and meadowsweet lacing
the brook's banks, perching their delicate
frames along tangles of reed blades.

They dazzle the eye with flickering dances
of gleaming emeralds and blues, a metallic
translucency of wings, their brief
courtship ecstasies above ground.

They are rivalled only by pebble
glitter, glints of sunlight on tumbling
water, the pale flicks of grazing
sticklebacks, a kingfisher's quick flash.

But these are creatures born of an underworld
of silt mud and roots, fickle-faced and devious
as any fairy – see the crouch of a thorax
the small demonic head, bulbous black eyes.

Lakeside Cameo

haloed in promise
a single warbler's egg
gleams in the cup of a nest
suspended between reed stems

thick with blossom a swathe
of hawthorn arches over it
a lacewing etched
on its tipmost leaf

in shifts of light and shade
a jewelled demoiselle
clings sentinel-still
to a green blade above it

a grass snakes weaves
through water and reeds
slicks it tongue upwards
begins to climb

a lone cormorant

… serene in its dark majesty   is rock-perched
at the edge of a lozenge of pebbled scree

the day is sharp with winter sun   clear sky   a bowling
breeze which sweeps the lake's reflected blue
with flights of flint-grey shadows

it stretches a slim neck skywards   opens a heraldry
of black wings into the breeze   long minutes pass
it shifts   preens its pale breastplate

eases sleekness into the water   glides softly
long and low   plays beak and head beneath
the surface   indulges in casual forays

with easy lopes   flaps itself onto a perching rail
turns serious lookout   erect   still   patient
only its eyes move to scan the dancing ripples

a twitch   and it's off   missile-straight it skims
over the lake   smoothes to a perfect landing
arches its head and dives

it surfaces   hooked beak high   flips a wriggling fish
into its gullet   swallows the prize down   sails on
sure in the gloss of its ascendancy

Wren Song

The first moment I heard the wren
saw it there in the holly bush
– so there was no mistake –
I was shaken to my bowels
by the sheer volume of its song.

Small and brown, it perched
tail cockaded, gargling its throat into
the morning air with such intensity
that size seemed nothing to it.
It rivalled blackbirds in
assertiveness, its declaration
of an absolute right to be there.

And I thought how it would be
if all the small, brown, seemingly
non-descript lives
in all the world rose
and suddenly in one moment
– the exact same moment –
poured out their songs.

It would be enough surely
to shake even the Creator
out of his complacency
to consider
how he had let things slip.

Gifted

late spring   sunlight on the wide wetlands lake
the hide's windows open to a cooling breeze

above the raucous cries of nesting gulls
the sky calls of swooping terns

a clear song close at hand
pure   sweet   arresting

I turned and saw it   a small bird
perched high on a tall willow branch

no binoculars were needed
I could have reached out and touched it

for what seemed an eternity I listened to its notes
watched its pulsing epiglottis stretched to the max

I was mesmerised   mentally noted
its chestnut browns and greys

the way this stocky little bird
cheekily cockaded its tail as it sang

only looked it up when I got home
a Cetti's warbler

I've glimpsed one only a few times since
hidden among thick bushes and trackside trees

mostly I hear its insistent carolling
listen!... what's my name?... Cetti-Cetti-Cetti... that's it!

For Love of a Hen

What is it about this hen
that fingers itch
to hold and stroke
her plumpness? Simply,
she is so good to watch.

Look how silkily
she moves between
sun and shade, brown
feathers multi-patterned
as a forest floor.

Up goes her soft rump,
comb and red wattles
flop and her head drops
to peck, peck-peck
at a parcel of dirt.

Upright once more
she scans to front –
from left – to right
like an automaton
then moves off

lifting her long feet
precisely, delicately
as an old spinster,
her vanity all
shoes and hat

ignoring the rotunda
of flesh between.

Sophie

soft of name soft of soul
fur cloud
of white and grey
gentle of paw and claw
practised climber
ace explorer

mischief maker
love seeker
tapper of laptop keys
twiner of legs and necks
reader of smiles
reader of tears

long-time purrer
grade one lap curler
years ago
I buried you deep
beneath the veg patch
where I swear

the beans grow greener taste sweeter

Benison

bees in my head
        fed
from childhood fingers of
        honey-coated bread
throat soothing lemony balm
        the calm
of still   hot summer days
        the buzzing eyes-closed haze
of far off busy lives
        the sinking of mind
                towards hive
a filter of gold
        the acceptance of dark

Sortie

    moving silently in soft snow
        through the quiet of dawn
    its snout twitching   slippers of
        white on each raised paw

    the fox sleeks across fields
        cloisters its pelt against
    the bark of a sycamore tree
        stills itself   considers

A Pastorale of Restrained Freedoms

A pasture emerging from winter   this man
testing the soil with knowing feet   rubbing
grass through fingers   surveying the sky

An old cowshed   its musty fug stirred by restless
hooves   slavering mouths thrust through iron
railings   snotty noses sensing an air of change

The shed unchained   clatter of hooves across yard
an ushering of thickset bodies through a swung-open
five barred gate   release to a rich freshness of green

Space to breathe easy   roam   chew   cogitate
cast soft eyes over thick impenetrable hedgerows
back to the now closed gate

The other one's amble back home   casting off the day's
muck and weariness   sustenance piled on a plate   a last
quick wash and brush up   then keys in the ignition

Off to the pub to swallow what's left of grime down
into the gut with ale   talk of market prices   subsidies
the vagaries of weather ambering what's to come.

Old Man of High Wood

Small   fenced off   too up and down
for the farmer's plough   timber's profit
just landmark now

One small track   north to south
is all that remains of the tread
of men's feet

the rest long forgotten   a tangle
of wild impassable undergrowth
thorns and roots

I am its guardian   chronicler   bard
shift through its layers of shadows
leave no mark

I am soil made man   gnarled as bark
tendrilled   twisted   voiceless
always here

Some nights I drift to its heights   gaze down
over meadows   homesteads   bathed by
clear skies

I haunt the track's edges   merge into trees by
the boundary's barbed gate   look for lights
ascending

but no one comes

no one comes

We Are Not all Capercaillies

'Let me escape a commonplace death,
let darkness adorn me in willow and ice . . .
Take aim. It's all over. Fire as I fly.'

(Boris Pasternak, 1928)

The bird with one leg
was finding it decidedly tough.
Hop-flop, hop-flop it went
as its commando forays
on morning-dew grass
became an uneven contest
with recalcitrant worms.

Flights became shorter
(the uncertainties un-nerved it),
landings were accompanied
by any number of desperate prayers.

Lost its grip on sex
faced fickle mates
eggless, parentless days
no nest.

---

* Singing its mating song in flight, the capercaillie is said to be so lost in ecstasy that it is an easy target for hunters.

Scientists might have redeemed it,
played with an adept prosthesis,
calculated flight patterns, weight, velocity.
Interesting stuff – but – the mileage
would have been insignificant.

One soft warm day it rose
with a wobble, flew,
felt the wind in its wings,
wrapped its soul in sky;
closed its small eyes ... drifted
    ... remembered ... until
it fell in brown bracken

and no-one knew it was there.
It lay
quietly breathing
then expired.

casual deaths

roads punctuated with death   torn
wings   smashed bones   crushed guts
sometimes still recognisable by fur
snout   tail   the curve of an ear

scavengers hone their senses
seize opportune time slots
grab morsels of survival
dice with death's wheels

springtime is worst   the mink-grey corpse
lacking the bulk to be a full-grown badger
the pink ears of a rabbit   translucent
as a baby's first growth of nails

the fox cub   breath cannoned from
its rib cage before it has smelled
its first summer   rolled
in the richness of autumn

Warriors

The wasps do not go gentle – no way.
From the stupor of a late summer
they are suddenly all a-buzz, zipping

like a barrage of retractable spearheads
in and out of the thick coverage
of untended laurel and ivy.

Deep within the dense foliage, all season
they have built, hidden from view, paper
fortresses crammed with their futures.

They are angry, sense a Masada ending
when they will fight the first frosts to the death
with every orange/black bristle and beating of wings.

Like an idiot I stray too close with the hoe
and the sting is sharp, cuts through thick
jeans to thigh flesh beneath.

Excruciating! Stripping off I see the hard white
core, the spreading red. The target throbs
with their valediction. Remember us.

Losing Direction

Cool and white as a ghost
the compass moon is large
in the sky   rides high
washes the earth with
a pale imitation of day
until rolling clouds
hide it from sight.

At an open window
a lamp's false moon
glows and a speckled
moth flies in   circles it
closer and closer
towards the hot pole
of its death.

A hand flicks the switch
stunned   the moth falls   edges
its way to the windowsill –
night breezes sooth
push clouds apart
and the moon reappears.

Gently the moth
launches itself over
a silvered garden
flies moonward
on course.

At the window a lone figure
watches   speculates.

Greece and Goats

. . . coupled close as crusty bread and feta,
a signature marriage captured in holiday shots.

That first disbelieving laugh at angular bodies
spread in comedic balances among the branches
of leaf-laden olives.

In the white heat of day, a rambler's glimpse of
mottled bodies huddled in a grove's shade
lazing time away

or at a goatherd's banging of stick on bucket
cascading from a hillside so swiftly and lightly
they seem almost to fly.

Hardy, cantankerous, wily and independent
as cats, they are so much more than just
meat and milk.

Outsourced to small islands pocked with the ruins
of abandoned settlements, they are at ease with
a feral life, non-fussy chancers

taking whatever is tongueable, startling
walkers lulled by the sun's heat on wild
thyme and marjoram.

Ghost-devil faces thrust from between scrub and thick thorns; persistently inquisitive, instinctively instilling feelings of wariness.

The Power of King Cobra

An unbasketed king cobra has
woven its way through my life
since before I knew it was there.

It reigns supreme, prefers its own space,
inhabits prime land where it roams and feeds;
rarely attacks if left to swallow its needs in peace.

It lovingly cares for its nest of eggs, keeps
them cool from the sun, dry from the rain;
rears to attack, strike, at the slightest threat.

Its sight is sharp, its flesh tuned to vibrations
however light but – if I raise my voice there
is no response, not a flicker to say I'm heard.

I should have recognised it from the start,
this powerful, elusive snake of a creature
    which
        p reys on the small
        o perates with stealth
        l ies quietly alert
        i mpervious to blame
        t akes no prisoners
        i njects venom
        c asually
        s pits in my eye.

The She-Wolf Speaks

Why did I do it, foster these brats of pups
left mewling and crying on a Tiber bank?
They're no part of the pack, not even
of the same kind, but something's there.
I'd milk to spare and it's what mothers do.

Now I'm having second thoughts.
Lusty and grasping the pair of them.
How they cling on, ravage my teats
will drink me dry at this rate –
and look how they're filling out.

Real scrappers, too, not the play fights
wolf pups need to survive in the pack.
It's more than that, something I can't
put my paw on which raises my fur.
I'll pick my time. Step back.

No moon tonight. I'll drop them
close to their kind; they'll be found.
Look at them, though! Fighting still.
Which of them's stronger? Who knows?
I can tell even now it will end in a kill.

In a Fantasy World

a topsy turvy tip of climate change

polar bears claw and snuffle seas of sand
pale tan coats gleam   a glitter of grains
sparkles in throbbing sun

    penguins huddle in seaside circles
    fan faces and feet   cool
    their fretting young

seals break menisci of warm seas
turn belly up to sunbathe
dive deep

    river trout glide   weave between
    bollards   post boxes   bus stops
    nibble in ponded flower tubs

rabbits scuba dive up from burrows
dog-paddle the branches of weeping
willows stretch necks to nibble

    lowland cattle roam mountain tops
    thicken their hides into furrowed wrinkles
    gorge on lichen and moss

giraffes grow snow-shoe hooves
elegantly glide white steppes
bend long necks to excavate snow

    a sidewinder snake sashays
       dunes of ice   flicks its length over
       below zero cold   hunts what moves

poison dart frogs shimmer crystal and quartz
skins   tongue with refrigerated acids
piggy-back their tadpoles to icy pools

      comatose   man wanders where and
      when he can   draws up algorithms
      of how best to come out on top

Fly with Pegasus*

Why would a horse need wings
when its hooves can already
fly across turf

when the air it flies through
sings to eardrums   whispers
and lifts its mane

when muscle and bone
soar it over a five-bar gate
across a high hedge?

Because

all living things which
take flight must eventually
come back to earth.

I stroke this tiny silver
Pegasus brooch   slant
it this way and that

conjure jewelled glass
wings to glitter   catch
reflect light.

---

* Pegasus represents speed and strength, the ability to rise, attain creative and imaginative flight, and is often used as a symbol of poetic inspiration.

Perhaps it flies as we do
not with muscle   bone
or mythical wings

but through flights of the mind
which carry us far and wide
into worlds of imagination

unfettered   unburdened
unhindered   free to be
the us only we really know.

Acknowledgements

Thanks are due to the editors of the following magazines and anthologies in which some of these poems first appeared: *Artemis Poetry*, *Dreamcatcher*, *Indigo Dreams*, *Iota*, *Other Poetry*, Offa's Press (*Away with the Birds* anthology), Vole competition 2025 (*Can Spring be Far Behind?* anthology), Border Poets (*Nettle Trick* and *Wolf Hoard* anthologies).

Also with special thanks to all staff and volunteer members of the Wildlife Trusts who do so much to protect and preserve our wildlife.